Cry in the Night

Other Books by Colleen Coble Include

THE ROCK HARBOR SERIES
Without a Trace
Beyond a Doubt
Into the Deep

THE ALOHA REEF SERIES
Distant Echoes
Black Sands
Dangerous Depths

Alaska Twilight

Fire Dancer

Midnight Sea

Abomination

Anathema

Lonestar Sanctuary

Cry in the Night

A ROCK HARBOR MYSTERY

COLLEEN COBLE

THOMAS NELSON
Since 1798

NASHVILLE   DALLAS   MEXICO CITY   RIO DE JANEIRO   BEIJING

Published in Nashville, Tennessee. Thomas Nelson is a registered trademark of Thomas Nelson, Inc.

Thomas Nelson, Inc., books may be purchased in bulk for educational, business, fund-raising, or sales promotional use. For information, please e-mail SpecialMarkets@ThomasNelson.com.

Publisher's Note: This novel is a work of fiction. Names, characters, places, and incidents are either products of the author's imagination or used fictitiously. All characters are fictional, and any similarity to people living or dead is purely coincidental.

Library of Congress Cataloging-in-Publication Data

Coble, Colleen.
    A cry in the night / Colleen Coble.
      p. cm.—(A Rock Harbor mystery ; 4)
    ISBN 978-1-59554-248-9 (pbk.)
      1. Foundlings—Fiction 2. Upper Peninsula (Mich.)—Fiction. I. Title.
PS3553.O2285C79 2009
813'.54—dc22
                                                      2008038799

Printed in the United States of America

08 09 10 11 12 RRD 5 4 3 2 1

For my "other" daughter,
Donna Coble.
You were so worth waiting for!

THE BABY IN THE CARRIER SLEPT PEACEFULLY, TINY FISTS thrust against her chubby cheeks blissfully unaware of her danger. Pia Westola clicked off the phone and sat back in her chair, gazing at the baby, sick with the awareness of this new, undesirable turn her life had taken. What had started out as a job she could believe in—even if it did sometimes drift into the law's gray areas—had just become clearly criminal. She would never have agreed to take this infant if what Florence had just told her was true.

One glance at the clock told her her boss would be here soon. Pia just had to keep the little one out of his reach. Adrenaline pulsed through her at the thought. Her decision made, she slipped on her coat, adjusted the insulating cover over the baby carrier that fit on her like a backpack, then grabbed the bottles and diapers and stuffed them in with the baby. If she could hide out long enough, maybe she could get the baby to safety.

Before she reached the garage door, she heard a car out front. Peeking through the curtains, she saw him get out. His car blocked Pia's getaway. Biting back panic, she realized she'd have to escape through the kitchen door.

She exited quickly with the baby and stood on the porch. She knew she had to hurry, but which direction? He'd see her on the road. Her only hope was through the thigh-high drifts across her backyard and into the woods. Her cross-country skis were propped against the side of the house. She shouldered into the baby backpack, slung the diaper bag over that, and then snapped on her skis.

She set out across the frozen landscape. Her muscles were warm by the time she reached the edge of the woods, and her breath fogged the frigid air. But she'd reached the path other skiers had used, and the going would be easier.

Her back aching from the weight of the carrier, she spared a glance behind her. Her spirits flagged when she caught a glimpse of him. He was on skis too. She'd forgotten he always carried them in his car. He wasn't burdened with the baby either. She was never going to make the sanctuary she'd hoped for. He hadn't seen her yet though. She hoped he'd lose her tracks on the more highly trafficked trail.

Tension coiled along Pia's spine as she whirled and looked for a place to hide the baby. There—a fallen pile of logs had enough space under it to hide the infant. She slipped out of the backpack, and a crumpled piece of paper fell from her pocket. She wedged the carrier under the logs. She layered several insulated blankets around the tiny girl. At least the child was sheltered.

Picking up a branch, she erased the evidence of her tracks to the logs. She stared down the hill at the approaching figure, then retraced her steps. She met him at a bend in the trail. She'd never known him to be a violent man—maybe she could reason with him.

His narrowed gaze nearly cut her down. "Where's the baby?"

She tipped up her chin. "I'm not going to be part of this."

He grabbed her arm and twisted it. "Where is she?"

Reeling from the shock, Pia's shoulder shrieked with pain. Still, she held his gaze defiantly. "Where you'll never find her."

"I saw you carrying her!" He slapped her, then slapped her

again. Both hands moved to her shoulders and he shook her. "Where is she?"

Pia's cheeks burned. Her head flopped with the violence of the shaking. Then he shoved her, and she was falling, falling toward a broken tree limb that jutted from the ground like a giant spear.

2

DAVY CAME BARRELING DOWNSTAIRS WITH HIS RED HAIR sticking up. Bree Matthews swiped at it as he passed. "Hey, big guy, you want cereal or an egg and toast this morning?"

"Cereal," he said. He went to the table and pulled the cereal bowl toward him, then dumped Cheerios into it.

She glanced out at the sun glinting off the thick snowdrifts, then saw the clock on the stove. "Miss Florence is expecting you in twenty minutes."

"It's the start of the winter holiday, Mom. I like Miss Florence, but I'd rather go fishing with you. Can't I skip tutoring today?"

She frowned at his reluctance. She'd never known him to be less than eager to go to Florence's. "We'll go fishing this afternoon."

When had he started to call her Mom instead of Mommy? She should have noted the transition. Now she mourned it. He would be a young man the next time she blinked. Nearly eight years old. Where had the time gone? He rarely needed her help now. Not with breakfast or getting ready for school. His bed would have been made. He was the neatest kid she'd ever seen.

Just as Rob had been.

It fascinated her to consider how much of Davy's qualities she could credit to heredity and how much to environment. Even though he looked like her, he walked like Rob and he had Rob's cowlick at his forehead. He was a neatnik and he loved trains, just like his dad. His favorite color was green, and nearly every shirt he owned was a variation of that shade, as were Rob's, the ones she'd given to the Salvation Army after his death.

She snapped out of her trance when Kade walked with a heavy tread into the kitchen. He brushed a kiss across her forehead. "Morning, hon," he said before continuing on to the table. "I wish it were Saturday instead of Monday. I'd like to go fishing with you two."

"Breakfast?" she asked. "I'm in the mood to cook."

He smiled. "I'll have eggs and toast if you don't mind. I've got a busy day at work."

"I don't mind," she said, her spirits deflating. She'd hoped he would remember her doctor appointment without being reminded. He'd change his plans and go with her if she asked, but he'd been so distracted lately she hated to add to whatever burden he wasn't sharing with her.

He ruffled Davy's hair. "Looking forward to your winter holiday?"

"You bet!"

Bree turned to the stove and whipped him up an omelet—his favorite kind, with spinach, mushrooms, ham, and cheese. The coffee aroma filled the kitchen, and then the pot beeped. Bree poured him a cup and handed it to him. He grunted a thank-you from behind his newspaper.

She would not cry. She turned back to the stove and flipped the omelet over. These days she felt on the verge of tears most of the time. Probably the fertility drugs. Sliding the omelet onto a plate, she placed it in front of Kade.

He looked up. "Thanks, babe." He caught her hand and kissed her palm.

The love in his gaze soothed her. Were they ever going to have their own baby? They'd both been devastated when she miscarried three months ago. Glancing at the calendar again, she started to ask him about going with her today, then shut her mouth. No, it wasn't a big enough deal.

When Kade pulled her close before he left for work, she almost changed her mind. If the news was bad today, she might need his strength. It took all her determination to nuzzle her face in his neck and keep back the words.

Once Kade was out of the house, she grabbed her keys. "I'll run you to Miss Florence's." She snapped her fingers, and her search dog, Samson, got up and came to her. His dark eyes were eager, and he ran to the door.

Driving to the cottage at the edge of the vast tract of forest where Florence Hawkins lived, Bree glanced at her son several times. "You okay, buddy? You're quiet this morning."

"I dreamed about Daddy last night," he said. "He told me to watch for him, that he was coming."

Bree hid her wince, but her fingers tightened on the steering wheel as she navigated the icy curves in the road. "You know that's not possible, Davy."

He scowled. "Don't call me Davy," he said. "I'm not a baby."

He'd always be her baby. "Your daddy is in heaven. He'd come for you if he could, but he can't."

Her boy's mouth turned mutinous. "Maybe he could come see me as a ghost. I wouldn't be afraid. I heard a cry outside the window last night and got up to look. I thought it might be him."

Bree stopped the Jeep in the driveway behind Florence's bright yellow convertible. "Maybe you were dreaming. You know there are no ghosts. Your daddy didn't want to go to heaven when he did, but you have to accept he's gone, son."

She'd thought these discussions were long past. Rob had been gone for almost four years. She and Kade had been married for two, and Kade had been such a good father to Davy. His visits to the psychologist had tapered off to a couple per year, and they'd all thought her boy had made the adjustment. Now she wasn't so sure.

There was no more time to talk now. Florence met them at the door. In her fifties with dyed red hair, she was a kid magnet. She'd been a teacher for years, and she tutored children in town. Davy's grade in math had come up to an A since Bree hired her.

Davy glanced up at his tutor. "Miss Florence, did you find the baby?"

Florence's smile faltered.

Bree frowned. "Baby?" she asked Florence.

The older woman waved her hand. "I think he means the doll I keep for the little girls. I couldn't find it last week." She turned to face the street. "Oh, here comes Timmy," she said.

Davy turned on the stoop. "Yay!" he yelled as Naomi O'Reilly, Bree's best friend, pulled up in her minivan. The van stopped and Timmy climbed out. The boy lugged his backpack and joined Davy on the stoop.

Naomi stuck her head out of the window, and her long braid slipped along her shoulder. "Hey, can Dave come for a playdate this afternoon?"

Davy's smile beamed. Even Naomi remembered he hated to be called Davy. "Sure, after we go fishing, right Dave?" Bree said. She glanced at her son as he ran back to Florence.

"Right!"

Florence touched the knitted cap on Davy's head. "You ready for your lessons, boys?"

"You bet!" the two boys said in chorus. They scampered into the house and toward the kitchen.

"Work hard and we'll go fishing this afternoon!" Bree called after him. Samson pressed against her leg, and she plunged her cold fingers into his warm fur.

"They're doing so well," Florence said. "You can be very proud of your boy." She closed the door.

Bree jogged to the idling van to talk to Naomi. She smiled at Naomi's toddler in the backseat. Matthew's gummy smile made her own widen.

"Is something wrong?" Naomi asked.

"Just a weird day. I've been thinking about Rob, and Davy was talking about him this morning. It made me sad for a minute."

Matthew wailed. Naomi flipped her braid behind her and pulled her head back into the car. She turned to the backseat and gave him a toy before facing Bree again. "You've got nothing to regret, Bree. You were a good wife to Rob, but he's gone. You've got Kade now, and a better man has never walked the face of the earth. Other than my Donovan, of course," she said, smiling.

"Of course." Bree returned her friend's smile, feeling the weight fall from her shoulders. "We landed our Westleys."

"'Wuv, twue wuv,'" Naomi said, mimicking the Impressive Clergyman in *The Princess Bride*, their favorite movie.

They both burst into giggles. "I'll be praying for you!" Naomi shouted before running up her window and pulling away in the van.

A smile still pulled at Bree's lips when the car disappeared around the curve. The stiff wind blew snow into the tracks left by Naomi's vehicle. Life seemed to be doing the same to Bree, the winds of change obscuring the path she'd seen so clearly a few years ago.

As she left Rock Harbor, she saw people parked along the frozen shoreline. They stared and pointed out across the frozen water. What had captured everyone's attention? Then she saw it.

An ice volcano. Sometimes high surf slamming against the face of the ice shelf created a cone formation resembling a volcano. The ice built up, and the surge of waves erupted through the cone like lava through a volcano tube. It was always a sight to see, so she drove slowly and did her own amount of staring until she left Rock Harbor's city limits behind.

Driving to Houghton, where her doctor's office was located, she felt the knot in her belly tighten with every mile. She'd handled worse than this by herself. Turning on her CD player, she cranked up her favorite Elvis album, *Elvis in Concert*, and fast-forwarded to "Can't Help Falling in Love." In her mind that was Kade's song, and the lyrics strengthened her.

The music blared loud enough to drown out the fears. She left Samson in the Jeep when she parked. All eyes turned to look when she walked into the ob-gyn office. Most of the women were pregnant, and Bree saw their eyes drop to her belly. She swallowed her hurt and smiled as she checked in at the window, then sank into a black leather chair nearby. If nothing else, it was good to be out of the cold. She slipped off her coat and laid it across her knees.

She'd barely had time to warm up when the nurse called her name. Her pulse ratcheted up a notch as she followed the nurse down a long hallway lined with pictures of smiling mothers holding newborns. She kept her gaze firmly latched on to the nurse's back. It hurt too much to see those photos. The nurse led her to an examination room, then took her blood pressure and pulse before leaving Bree behind the closed door to await the doctor.

Bree had waited here too many times, just like this with her heart in her mouth. Maybe she would give it up. This path was so difficult.

The door opened, and Dr. Zook walked in. About fifty, the female doctor had been Bree's ob-gyn ever since Bree moved to the area. The stylish pumps, khaki slacks, and red-and-khaki striped blouse she wore fit her slim frame impeccably. Her pageboy blonde hair swung in a perfect curtain to her chin. Bree always felt dowdy in her doctor's presence.

"Good morning, Bree," the doctor said. She carried a manila

file. Perching on a stool, she flipped it open and studied the top sheet of paper. "How are you feeling?"

"Fine. No problems. I started my period last week." She couldn't keep the disappointment from her voice. "I've been on Clomid two months. This will be the last month you said I should take it."

Dr. Zook closed the file, crossed one crisp pant leg over the other, then laced her fingers together on her knees and smiled at Bree. "I have the test results back. There's no obvious reason why you aren't conceiving."

That sounded like good news. "What do you suggest?"

"We could try another few months of Clomid, but you might want to jump directly to in vitro."

Bree suspected in vitro was way too expensive for them. "I got pregnant before."

"And miscarried at seven weeks," Dr. Zook said. "The problem may be genetic. With in vitro, we could maximize your chances and have fifteen or so fertilized eggs to test for problems."

Bree shook her head. "I'd want to implant every fertilized egg. It's for God to decide the outcome." Dr. Zook's face remained impassive, but Bree knew the doctor didn't agree with her stand. "How much does it cost?"

"About five thousand dollars a month. I'd guess we might have success the first month."

Bree winced. "I'll need to talk to my husband." How on earth could they afford something like that? Tears hovered dangerously close when the doctor left Bree alone. Maybe she and Kade would never have a child together.

He claimed to love Davy like he was Kade's own flesh and blood, and Bree knew it was true. But she saw his stares at small children and the way he fielded questions from kids who came through park headquarters. If ever a man was cut out to be a father, it was Kade Matthews.

She gathered up her purse and slipped on her coat in a daze. Clutching her purse, she walked back down the hall and through the waiting room. A newborn baby mewled in her mother's arms as Bree neared the exit. She had to look, and her heart melted at the sight of a rosebud mouth and smooth, perfect skin. The Native American baby had the biggest thatch of black hair that Bree had ever seen.

"She's precious," she said.

The mother smiled and thanked Bree, who quickly escaped into the harsh wind that scoured the tears from her face.

Kade glanced out his office window into the back lot. There were no baby animals in the rescue area that he was so proud of, but come spring, the pens would be full.

Judith Kettrick stuck her head in the door. "You hear the report?" The ranger-brown of her uniform accentuated her sallow complexion.

Kade turned from the window. "What report?" He hoped she hadn't gotten her pink slip. The place was becoming a ghost town since the budget cuts.

"A woman on the reservation reported her baby was taken by a windigo."

Kade raised an eyebrow. "Windigo? Why would she say that?" Windigos were the Ojibwa Indians' version of a vampire. The evil spirit was said to have an insatiable hunger.

"She heard a scream. I'm wondering if she heard a cougar. Thought you might be interested in checking it out."

"A cougar, huh? Interesting. Did they find the baby?" He suppressed a shudder at the thought that a big cat might have taken an infant.

"Nope."

"Where did it happen?"

"In the community building. She was there with a bunch of other women, and they heard a scream outside. There were several babies in carriers along the inside wall. The women went to the door to look. When they came back in, she went to check on the baby, but he was gone."

"A cougar couldn't have taken the baby then. Not from inside the building." At least that was a relief.

"Which is why she's blaming a windigo. She claimed they heard weird screams and saw huge humanoid tracks."

"Bigfoot," Kade said, and then wished he hadn't. It was too flippant for the seriousness of a missing baby.

Her brown eyes widened. "You think bigfoot would take a baby?"

"It was a joke, Kettrick. Not a very good one though. When was this? You tell Landorf?"

"Yes. He wants you to go check it out. This was about ten days ago. Not sure why we're just now hearing about it."

"Who's the mother?"

"Diann Meadowlark. The res police have filed a missing person's report with the different sheriff's departments around." She lowered her voice. "Way I heard it, this is the second report of a missing baby."

"You're kidding! Why hasn't this hit the media?"

She shrugged. "You know how the Natives like to handle their own problems. They might not have reported it until now. I heard both babies were part Caucasian."

"I'll see what I can find out. But you know, they may not talk to me."

"I do. Let me know if you find out anything." Kettrick left the doorway.

Kade turned to his computer. This grant application he was

trying to complete was a nightmare. Landorf wanted it done though, so he had no choice.

As if summoned by Kade's thoughts, Head Ranger Gary Landorf stepped into the office. Landorf was a slight man in his early fifties. His quick movements and keen dark eyes had always reminded Kade of a ferret. He ran the park with an iron fist that seemed out of keeping with his small stature.

"How's that application coming?" Landorf asked.

"Working on it."

"How's the wife?"

"Good. I'm a lucky man."

"It was her lucky day when she met you. That last husband of hers was a piece of work." Landorf shook his head.

Kade glanced up and watched him fiddle with the bird band on his finger. It was the band from the first eagle Landorf had ever tagged, and he'd worn it for three years, ever since he found the twenty-five-year-old eagle dead. Landorf's love of eagles was one of the things the two men had in common.

"I've only heard people speak highly of Rob," Kade said.

Landorf shrugged and shut the door. "Listen, Kade, just between you and me, that grant has the power to save some jobs around here. I want you to pad some of the lion sightings and ask for more money. Maybe get out in the woods and fake some tracks." He held up his hand when Kade shook his head. "Hear me out. It's for a good cause. If we can show more wildlife activity, we can justify money to pay for manpower. Do you want to see your friends have to move away?"

"No," Kade admitted.

"Neither do I. And it doesn't hurt anyone. It's just government money. There was no call for them to let our people go. This is a way around it."

Landorf made sense, and Kade had no good reason to contradict

him. It *was* a boneheaded decision by the park service to slash jobs
here. They were doing important work. Getting enough grant
money to hire more people would rectify the error. Still, his nod
was reluctant as Landorf told him to have the application ready by
the middle of next week.

⸙

Quinn Matilla was in no mood to listen to whining. He sat on
the mahogany coffee table to remove his shoes, dropped them
onto the plush hotel carpeting, then leaned forward. He glanced
out the window at the quiet Sault Sainte Marie street. "The baby
has to be somewhere. Find her," he barked into the phone.

"I've looked everywhere," Rosen said in his high voice.

Quinn glanced at his watch. The newscast should tell them
tonight if their orders were being followed. "You check with her
friends? Maybe she asked someone to watch the baby."

Rosen sniffed. "She told me I'd never find it. I saw her with a
backpack, but when I caught up to her, it was missing. I looked
all over."

Quinn wanted to smash something. What a nightmare. "Are
you telling me that baby could be out in the woods? *Find her!*
We've got no leverage if she dies." He picked up the remote control and threw it across the room. "I didn't want to get involved
in this in the first place."

Probably the wrong thing to say. Their partnership had been
fraying since a storm sank a boatful of drugs in Lake Superior. It
hadn't been his fault, but their first argument over this latest deal
only made things worse.

"We might have to assume we'll have no baby to give back."

Quinn balled his fists. "What'd you do with the body?"

"I left her there. It looks like she just fell and hit the branch."
He swore. "I didn't mean to kill her."

Quinn let his contempt show in his voice. "You're an idiot, Rosen."

"I'm not the only one who messed up. Some kid saw you bury the other one in the snow last Saturday. The autistic dude saw too. The boss thought you should know so you could handle the situation."

Quinn straightened. He'd caught a glimpse of figures in the woods on his way back to the car but was sure they'd seen nothing. "How's he know what they saw?" He shouldn't be surprised though. The man had eyes in the back of his head.

"His old lady told him. Florence was with them."

Quinn hadn't made out much beyond the kid's IU jacket and hat and the other guy's size. "The adult is autistic? Would he even say anything?"

Rosen shrugged. "Maybe. Maybe not. Can't take the chance though."

If Florence hadn't gotten cold feet, he wouldn't be in this situation. The past few years he'd managed to stay out of Rock Harbor, and now here he was, being forced back twice in three days. "I'll handle it." He hung up the phone.

He'd done a lot of things in his life, but kid killing wasn't one of them. First he'd find out what the kid saw. And the autistic guy. Maybe nothing would have to be done.

Glancing at his watch, he realized Jenna would be back any minute. As if on cue, he heard the front door open, and Jenna Pelton stepped into the suite.

She stamped her feet in those stupid fluffy boots. "I found the best deal on Donald J Pliner shoes." Carrying four bags, she padded across the thick carpet. "And I bought a darling Prada bag for five hundred dollars. What a sale they had!" She sent a sultry smile his way. "I got a darling pink teddy too. Wait until you see it."

She sank onto the sofa and curled up into the throw but said nothing. Her blue eyes studied his face. Her blonde beauty turned heads wherever he took her, but she was higher maintenance than he liked.

The boredom slid from her face as she studied his expression. "What's wrong?"

"What isn't?" He sighed, dropped a kiss on top of her head, then sat next to her.

She kicked off her high-heeled boots. "You're not the only one with troubles. My brother called babbling about some baby being put in the snow."

"Brother? I forgot you had a brother."

She nodded. "Victor. He's autistic. High-functioning though, and he keeps down a job, so he's never been any trouble to me. He lives in Rock Harbor."

Quinn's gut twisted. He'd known all that once but forgot. Could there be two autistic men in Rock Harbor? "He prone to tell stories?" She moved over to snuggle against him. Her perfume made him dizzy, but he stayed motionless as he tried to sort out how much of a risk Victor might be.

She ran her hand over his face. "He's very imaginative. I calmed him down."

"Maybe you should go see him. I have to make a trip up there anyway. Right away."

She pouted. "I had other plans for this afternoon." Her fingers began to unbutton his shirt.

He caught at her hand. "Later. I need to pack. You too, if you're coming with me." He got up, nearly dumping her on the floor.

3

SAMSON BARKED AND BOUNDED AHEAD THROUGH THE snow with Bree and Davy trailing behind. Davy didn't have much to say about the lesson he'd had with Florence and Timmy, nor about whether he was excited to fish today. Bree settled into his silence, wondering if his mind was on last night's dream.

The trail through the woods was packed and easy to navigate. Little Wolf Lake was a popular ice-fishing destination but today it was deserted.

Paulie, a cardinal that had "adopted" them, circled and swooped above their heads. Samson ducked and whined when the bird dive-bombed him. Bree could almost hear Paulie laugh as he flew away. He perched on a branch nearby and watched them.

The wind pierced Bree's down jacket but not her depression. Stopping to see her dad in the nursing home hadn't helped either. He was totally gone now, buried in dementia. He never knew her or responded anymore. Her sister, Cassie, had left town to go back to her job last week, knowing their father might slip away before the next visit.

Sometimes Bree thought it would be for the best if he could escape the body that trapped him.

Her son showed no sign of noticing the cold. She held his mittened hand as they trudged along the path. Just ahead, the forest opened onto a frozen glade. Ice shanties dotted the lake, and Davy and she could have their pick. They were alone today, a perfect time to talk, sitting side by side, fishing with their poles.

She set down the box of tackle and retied a loose bootlace. "Where do you want to fish?"

He pointed out the closest shanty, a blue and white plastic one. "Can I cut the hole in the ice?" Davy asked.

She couldn't resist his pleading green eyes. "All right, if you're careful." They stepped inside the shanty, and the structure blocked the bite of the wind. The weak sunlight bounced off the ice and lit everything with a gentle glow. They wouldn't have long. It got dark early this time of year.

She sat on the bench and began to unpack their gear. Davy knelt beside her, and she handed him the ice auger. He put it on the ice and began to turn the handle. She doubted he'd have the strength to get the bit through the ice, but he kept at it. She watched his smooth movements. Kade had taught him well, and his thin frame was beginning to lose its baby fat. Soon he'd have muscles like Kade too.

What was she thinking? He'd never have Kade's burly frame. Davy's body was built for Rob's long, slim muscles. She shook her head and smiled at her self-deception.

"It's through!" His face shone with achievement.

She used the ice chisel to widen the hole, and soon she and Davy had their lines in the water. Samson crowded under her legs and helped keep her warm. With her arm around her son, Bree realized the day that had started out badly had turned perfect.

He leaned his head against her. The sock hat he wore would soon be too small for him. It was both a pain and a pleasure to see how fast he was growing. He wouldn't be her little boy much longer. Adolescence would be here before she could blink, then his teenage years. Time was so fluid and slipped through her fingers with every day.

She pressed a kiss on his brow. "You've been quiet, honey. Anything you want to talk about?"

His skin paled at her question, bringing the freckles on his nose into more prominent display. "I saw a windigo the other day, Mom. I didn't want to tell you."

She tried to make light of his sudden preoccupation with the legendary monster. "A windigo? Did it have big teeth?" He wasn't so grown-up if he still saw boogeymen.

He shook his head. "It wasn't that kind of windigo. It's the kind that possesses a person."

Most Rock Harbor adults were familiar with Ojibwa legend and Bree was no exception. In Ojibwa lore, the windigo monster stood as tall as a tree. It had jagged teeth in a lipless mouth and devoured people. She'd never talked to Davy about the legend, though some parents frightened their children into obedience with the story of the monster, much like a bigfoot. In some stories the windigo possessed a man instead, causing the hapless fellow to become a cannibal. Bree figured Davy had heard talk at school.

She hugged him to her. "You know there's no such thing, right?"

His green eyes studied her face. "But I saw it." Relief struggled with doubt in his face.

"Where, honey?"

"At the pond with Miss Florence and Victor, when she took us fishing last Saturday."

"What did you see?" she asked, her voice neutral.

"The windigo."

They were going in circles. "I mean, what made you think it was a windigo?"

"Because it looked kind of like Daddy." He rubbed his eyes. "It looked right at me too. I was afraid and ran away."

Alarm prickled along her spine. Maybe last night's dream

and today's sighting was a new manifestation of Davy's longing for his real father. She should discuss this with Davy's child psychologist.

"He was mad."

She put confidence into her smile. "Well, there you go. It couldn't have been Daddy. He was never mad at you."

He cupped his hand to the side of his mouth and stared out the opening of the shack before he whispered, "I saw what it did."

"What did it do?"

He pressed his lips nearly against her ear. "It put a baby in the snow. I think it was hiding the baby from Miss Florence."

Bree frowned and tried to ignore her unease. She recalled his asking Florence if she found the baby. "Maybe a guy was getting rid of an old doll," she said. "Sometimes people are bigger than we expect. And distances can distort size. Dad's explained that to you before, right?"

He nodded and chewed on his lip. "This was close though, Mom."

"Dave, there's really no such monster."

"Maybe it was a ghost," he whispered.

"There are no ghosts either," she assured him. "I think you're missing Daddy and look for him in everyone you see."

"I saw a windigo with the baby," he insisted.

Could there be an element of truth in what Davy was talking about? Her lame theory about disposing of a doll didn't hold up either. Why dig a hole in the snow for a doll? "What did this person look like?"

Davy pulled away to check his fishing pole. He jiggled his line in the water. "I told you—it was a windigo. They change every time you see them. This one sort of looked like my daddy, then it changed and had big teeth."

She wanted to pull out her hair. "What was he wearing?"

"A black parka and jeans. Boots."

Rob hated black. The stray thought burst out of nowhere.

"Maybe it was a vampire," Davy said, his grin breaking out. "They have teeth and wear black. And it had blood dripping from its fangs."

"Now you're really pushing it, buster." She poked him. "I'm not that gullible. You pulling a fast one on your old mom?"

His smile faded. "I really did see it, Mom. Maybe it didn't have big teeth, but I'm sure it was a windigo. I was scared. So was Victor, and we ran away."

"Was Miss Florence scared?"

"I don't think so. She went to talk to him. She was really brave."

Bree hugged him. She'd clear this up with Florence. "I want you to forget all about this, okay? There's no such thing as windigos. Or vampires or ghosts. Who's been telling you such stories?"

"One of the older kids at school showed me a book of monsters," he said. He bared his teeth and growled. Samson raised his head as though to make sure things were okay, then flopped it back onto the ice.

She had to laugh. "You make a good monster." Those kinds of things were going to happen at school, and she couldn't protect him forever, but she wanted to throttle the kid who had done it. "There are no real monsters. You know that, right?"

Only human ones, who preyed on the defenseless. She wanted to protect him from that kind of knowledge too.

"It sure looked real," Davy said, his voice hesitant.

"Why did you think it looked like your daddy?"

"I don't know. I just kind of thought of Daddy when I saw him."

For a time after Rob died, Davy was drawn to any man with a superficial resemblance to his father. Bree had hoped he'd outgrown that tendency for good.

"You'll see your daddy again someday," she reminded him. "He's happy in heaven. He's looking down on you and he's glad you're such a good boy."

"I know." He hugged her back, then pulled away. "I've got a bite!"

She watched her son reel in his fish, a fine walleye. Samson lunged forward, barking at the flopping fish, and she quieted him with a word. It was a good thing Davy hadn't talked like this in front of Kade. It would hurt him to know Davy still longed for his father enough to create monsters where there were none.

She watched Davy take the fish from the hook—a task that would have required her help just last winter. She wanted to question him more about the baby but decided against it. She'd stop by Kade's office on the way home. He could reassure her that Davy was perfectly fine.

4

WITH THE COLLAR ON HIS COAT HIGH AND A HAT COVERING his ears, Kade hurried to the line of snowmobiles. He'd worked on the grant for an hour, dutifully padding the amounts needed for the study. At least he could leave his misgivings behind and do something useful now.

The Natives probably wouldn't tell him anything. An uneasy truce existed between those on the res and the whites. Hunters encroached on protected lands and fished in forbidden areas. For the most part, the Ojibwa bore the injustices with stoicism, but Kade was often ashamed of his race.

He started the snowmobile and mounted it, then crossed the parking lot. He was about to pull out onto the snowmobile path when he saw a familiar red Jeep come tearing up the lane. Spitting snow from the studs on the tires, the vehicle was going too fast for the slippery conditions. He saw Bree's set face behind the wheel.

He killed the engine and dismounted, waiting by the fence until she pulled into a spot in the parking lot. She got out, then climbed back in when she saw him hurrying toward her.

The heater blasted warm air into his face when he got onto the passenger seat. "Where's Dave?"

"I dropped him to play with Timmy."

He slid over and embraced her with his left arm. She nestled her head against his shoulder. "So, what's wrong?" he asked.

"Davy just told me he saw a windigo who looks like Rob put a baby in the snow." Her voice quavered.

"Whoa, that's a weird tale."

"I know. I tried to argue him out of it, but he was adamant."

He hugged her tighter. "What's riling you the most? The fact that he's seeing his dead father or that he believes in the windigo?"

The frown between her eyes eased. "The father thing," she admitted. "I thought we'd gotten past all that."

"A boy never stops missing his daddy. I still miss mine. I try to make up for it with Dave, and you know I love him, but he knows the difference, deep down."

Her green eyes pleaded for understanding. "He loves you, Kade."

He traced her jaw with his fingertips. "I know he does. There's room for two dads in his heart. You wouldn't want him to forget all about Rob, would you?"

Her face softened. "No, you're right. But don't you think it's worrisome that he equates his father with a scary monster? You think there's anything to the baby story?"

He shrugged. "Maybe it's how he's dealing with his dad's death. Take him to see the doctor if it will make you feel better, but I think he'll be okay."

The monsters lurking around the corner in their lives were huge—the possible loss of their house, their security. If he lost his job, how would he support them? Bree's insurance money from Rob's death was long gone, and the dog training didn't bring in much. The grant was his only hope.

He gazed into the eyes he loved, such a clear green, like glass. He could see all the way down to her soul. No sacrifice would be too great to keep her happy and content. It was his job to provide for her, and he meant to do it. No matter what it took.

He brushed her lips with his and withdrew. "I have to get back to work, babe."

She returned his kiss, then stared into his eyes. "Is there something wrong?"

"Just busy. You'd better let me get back to work." He knew his brusque tone had hurt her when she dropped her gaze.

He should tell her about the job situation, but the words stuck in his throat. He got out without saying another word. Only when her Jeep disappeared around the bend in the lane did his mind turn to the baby part of Dave's story. What if Dave really had seen someone dispose of a child? Two babies were missing. He pulled out his cell phone and dialed Bree's number, then ended the call before it could ring. No sense in worrying her. Mason would be the better person to contact. He punched in the sheriff's cell number.

"Hey, Kade," Mason Kaleva answered. "How's it going?"

"Fine. Hey, listen, Dave told Bree something weird." He related the story about a windigo who looked like Rob burying a baby in the snow. "I hear there are a couple of babies missing from the res. Been talk of some screams. I'm thinking it might be a cougar."

"I'm heading over to talk to them. You want to come with me?"

"You don't mind? I was hoping to hear their story too."

"Nope. I'll pick you up in two minutes. I'm just down the road."

"I'll be ready." He closed his phone. Bree would want in on this if it might affect Dave at all. He punched in her number and told her what was happening. Before he got it all out, she was turning her vehicle around.

"Be right there," she said.

By the time Kade put the snowmobile back into place, Mason's SUV was pulling in the lot with Bree's Jeep right behind him.

Kade jogged across the lot and held the back door open for Bree and Samson.

Bree reached the SUV with the dog. "I'm going too, Mason, you mind?"

"Nope. Hop in the back."

Bree climbed into the backseat while Kade took the copilot seat beside Mason. Kade stared out the window while Mason filled them in on all he knew. They were at their destination in minutes.

The Keweenaw Bay Indian Community had been here since 1854 and was as much a part of Michigan culture as the big lake itself. The kids went to public schools but still headed home to the res. It created a subtle class difference that disturbed many on both sides.

Mason drove to the house where the woman lived who had lost the child. Along the way, Bree ran her window down to throw out a handful of pistachio shells. She tipped her head to the side. "What's that?"

"What?" Kade asked.

"I thought I heard something. Like a baby crying." She paused. "There. It came again. You think it's a cougar?"

Mason ran down his window, but the only sound was the wind scooting along the icy cliffs above their heads.

"I didn't hear anything," Kade said. He ran his window back up.

"Maybe it was the wind," she said.

Mason continued to their destination. He parked in a pullout that had been cleared. Nearly buried in drifts, the modest ranch home sat back off the road. Someone had managed to shovel a path to the front door from the parking spot. To protect the walk from the next snowfall, sheets of plywood made a covering over the top of the walkway. Kade took Bree's hand so she wouldn't slip. They had to duck under the low-hanging plywood roof to scuttle up to the door.

Mason raised his gloved fist and knocked on the door. Kade stayed back two feet to give him space. Here out of the wind, the temperature wasn't too bad. The door was opened almost immediately by a woman. Her dark eyes were full of hope that quickly faded when her gaze went to their empty hands.

"You have not found my baby?" she asked.

"I'm sorry, but no," Mason said. "You're Ms. Meadowlark?" When she nodded, he added, "I'm Sheriff Kaleva, and this is Kade and Bree Matthews. I wondered if we could ask you some questions."

She stood aside with obvious reluctance, and they entered. The house was spotless, though the furniture, clearly from the fifties with a square shape, was sparse and worn. Kade kept hold of Bree's hand and let Mason take the lead. His gaze wandered the room and lit on a snapshot of the woman with a blond man. She held an infant on her lap, and she and the man were smiling.

"That the baby's father?" Kade asked, then wished he'd kept his mouth shut when Mason glared at him.

"Yes. Jarret Smith."

"Any chance he took your baby?" Bree put in.

The woman frowned. "He says he did not. The tribal police have followed him. There is no sign he has my William."

"You're not married?" Mason asked, clearly intending to take charge of the questioning.

"No." She looked down at the carpet. "But I love my boy. I want him back. I didn't hurt him."

"Why do you think a windigo took him?" Bree asked, her voice urgent. "My son says he saw a windigo." Mason sent a sharp glance her way, but Bree didn't seem to notice.

"I have heard it screaming by the barn last week. The winter has been very hard on us. Some have been hungry. A windigo appears in such circumstances."

"Any tracks in your yard?" Mason asked, his gaze intent on her.

"The wind has covered them now. They were large though." She measured out nearly twenty inches with her hands.

Mason and Kade locked glances. Kade saw the doubt on Mason's face, but Kade himself heard the ring of truth. Did this have anything to do with what Dave saw? "You mind if I take a look outside for signs of the windigo you heard?"

"You will not see anything now, but look."

"I'll come with you," Bree said.

They left Mason to finish talking to the woman. "You think this baby is connected to the one Davy said he saw?" Bree asked. "I was on my way to talk to Florence when you called."

"I think she should be the next stop," Kade said. There was nothing here but wind and snow. "I need to get back to work though."

"I'll go see her. Will you pick up Davy at Naomi's?"

"No problem. Call when you're done." He studied his wife's face. She wore that expression of determination. The windigo didn't have a chance.

⁂

The quaint village on the south shore of Lake Superior never changed. Quinn parked his truck on Quincy Hill and stared down at the sleepy town where he'd ridden his first bike and kissed his first girl. He'd always intended to come back someday, but he never dreamed it would be under these circumstances.

Though he'd dropped Jenna at the nicest hotel he could find in Houghton, he almost wished she were with him. Her chatter would provide distraction. His gaze pinpointed the house that was his target. He let the truck coast down the hill until he reached some snow-covered shrubs that partially hid his vehicle. Florence had managed to find out where the kid would be, and sure enough, there he was in the backyard with the O'Reilly children. He wore the same bright red parka and ski mask as last week. The kid's name was David Matthews, not a familiar name.

Pulling up his coat collar, he put on his ski mask, then got out of the truck and walked briskly toward the fenced yard. He let himself through the gate and moved toward the swings. All the kids wore ski masks, but he recognized the coat David wore.

He heard barking but kept his gaze on the kid. The dog could be a problem he hadn't counted on. All the possibilities raced through his head as he closed the last few steps to reach the boy.

The kids looked up and saw him. He saw his target's eyes blink, then Quinn snatched the boy up and tossed him over his shoulder. The children began to shriek, and David struggled to get away. Quinn held him fast.

The dog barked and ran around in circles before planting himself between Quinn and the gate. Every time Quinn shifted, the dog did the same, blocking his access to the gate. He heard a woman scream and glanced toward the house to see Naomi Heinonen brandishing a baseball bat and running toward him. What was she doing here?

David squirmed in his arms again, and Quinn lost his grip on the small, wiry body. He made a last grab at the boy, and Quinn's fingers snagged the kid's ski mask. The knitted covering slid from the boy's face, then Quinn was looking down at a face he'd seen a million times in his dreams. Davy.

Quinn stumbled, and his arms dropped to his sides. The boy raced away toward Naomi, who still approached with the bat.

The dog ran at him again, and Quinn recognized Samson. He kicked at the animal. "Get back, Sam," he yelled.

The dog veered, then raced after Davy. Quinn took the opportunity to rush for the gate before Naomi could identify him. Or beat him with the bat. He reached the safety of his truck and gunned it away. Glancing in the rearview mirror, he saw she was already on her cell phone. Calling the sheriff, no doubt.

He drove away with his thoughts in turmoil. Nothing that had just happened made any sense, and if not for the cold piercing his bones, he'd think he'd dreamed seeing two people from his past. A past he'd buried along with his emotions about it.

⌘

The paneled room had been recently waxed, judging from the odor of lemon in the air. It was all Lauri Matthews could do to keep from jiggling her leg. She crossed her ankles to settle her nerves, but it didn't help. Peeking at her watch, she saw it was nearly five. She flipped open her notebook and clicked her pen a few times until a woman appeared in the doorway.

The tall, elegant blonde's skin showed sure signs of a face-lift. She carried a manila folder, and her eyes were red as though she'd been crying. Lauri guessed her age at about forty-five.

Lauri sprang to her feet. "Mrs. Saunders?"

The woman extended her hand. "You must be Ms. Matthews. You're very young."

Lauri drew herself up to her full height of five-four. "I'm twenty."

Mrs. Saunders consulted the folder. "Your grades are good, but you college students seem to get younger all the time. Or maybe I'm just getting older." She gestured to the sofa. "Please, make yourself comfortable. Tell me why you want to work for me."

Lauri marshaled her thoughts. "My major is accounting, and your firm is known all over the UP. You keep the books for all the biggest companies. I can learn a lot from working with you. Not that I'd be working directly with you, of course," she added.

Mrs. Saunders scribbled something on the paper in her file. "Actually, you would be working with me for a little while. My assistant just quit and I need a fill-in until we can hire someone. Once we have that person in place, you'd move to the accountant pool."

Lauri's elation expanded. She wanted to ask why the woman didn't promote someone from the pool, but she wasn't about to blow her chance.

Mrs. Saunders closed the file. "Your credentials look good. Gordon Kievari has given you a stellar recommendation. When can you start?"

She had the job! Lauri tried not to show any unprofessional enthusiasm. "Right away. Today if you like."

Mrs. Saunders smiled. "Ah, the exuberance of youth. Tomorrow is fine. Eight o'clock sharp. The receptionist will show you to my office. You'll work four hours a day, five days a week. You're sure your classes are set for afternoons only?"

"Absolutely. Thank you for giving me this opportunity."

The conference room door opened, and a man stepped inside. About fifty, he wore a distracted air. Dark skin circled his eyes, and she wondered who he was.

Mrs. Saunders sprang to her feet and rushed to him. Lauri caught only a few snippets of words: "he called" and "oh no." She tried not to listen, but it was clear from Mrs. Saunders's clenched fists and rigid backbone that something was wrong.

The man kissed her, then backed out of the room. Must be her husband, Lauri decided. Mrs. Saunders turned back toward Lauri. The muscles in the older woman's throat convulsed, and her eyes were full of moisture.

"Sorry for the interruption," she said. "A personal matter. I'll see you tomorrow." Her tone dismissed Lauri in no uncertain terms.

Lauri headed for the door. "Thanks again, Mrs. Saunders." But the woman was already turning away. Lauri pulled the conference room door shut behind her. The latch barely clicked before the sound of muffled sobbing slipped faintly through the door. Poor woman. Lauri had no idea what could be wrong.

She wanted to skip to her car, but that would draw frowns from the receptionist and others she passed. Holding her head high, she walked the long, carpeted hall to the elevator and punched the down button. There was no one around to see her goofy smile.

When she reached her vehicle, she realized she'd left her notebook on her chair, where she'd laid it while she slipped on her coat. She hurried back through the parking lot to the building and stepped inside. The receptionist waved her back when she explained. Lauri hoped Mrs. Saunders had left the conference room. The last thing she wanted to do was bother the upset woman.

Good, the lights were out. She flipped on the light in the room and grabbed her notebook. Shutting off the light again, she approached another door and heard the murmur of conversation. As she neared the room, she realized two men were arguing.

"You won't get away with this."

Was that the voice of the man who had come in to see Mrs. Saunders? It sounded like it. Curiosity getting the better of her, Lauri glanced through the sidelight of the door and saw her boss's husband.

Lauri reared back as steps came nearer to the door. If they thought she'd been eavesdropping, she might lose her job as quickly as she'd found it. She glanced around for somewhere to hide and tried the closest door, one she'd already passed. Locked.

Putting on a smile, she walked briskly toward the door that was opening. A slim man with a bent nose stepped out. He was dressed in pressed black slacks, a leather jacket, and expensive shoes. She nodded and smiled and kept on going. She caught his suspicious stare as she passed, but he said nothing and continued to stand in the doorway.

She escaped down the elevator and gained the sanctuary of her car. She told herself to keep her nose out of her boss's business. Do her job and curb that curiosity.

5

THE WIND BIT THROUGH BREE'S JEANS AS SHE STOOD ON
the stoop of Florence's porch. She pressed her finger to the doorbell button and heard the peal from inside the house, but there
were no sounds from inside, though Florence's car was parked in
the drive. Bree rang the bell again, then decided to check the back
when no one answered.

Slogging through the high drifts, she made her way around the
side of the cottage to the tiny backyard, where she saw Florence's
prize-winning roses covered in winter mulch. And Florence lay
stretched in front of them.

"Florence!" Bree leaped to the woman's side. Florence didn't
respond to Bree's touch on her arm, but her head lolled to the side
and the movement revealed matted blood in her hair.

Bree quickly called for an ambulance on her cell phone, then
put it away and touched Florence's cheek. It was cold. Too cold.
Her fear mounting, Bree pressed her fingers to Florence's wrist.
There was only the barest flutter of a pulse. "Hang on, Florence,"
she muttered.

She needed to get her warm. Bree took off her coat and tucked
it around the injured woman. The wind dove down Bree's back
and poked icy fingers through her sweater. She shivered and her
gaze roamed the yard. Someone had attacked Florence. That someone might still be around.

The snow around the fallen woman was trampled with foot-prints. A dusting of pipe tobacco darkened the snow. Bree knew better than to touch it. The steps led off toward the pond and the woods. Her gaze followed the prints and landed on a figure.

Victor Pelton stood in the shelter of barren trees. He swayed where he stood. Bree thought he might have been muttering, but the wind snatched away his words.

She motioned to him. "Victor, come here. Miss Florence needs help."

At first he only stared at her, but when she motioned again, he moved toward her, shuffling his booted feet through the snow clogging the path. When he neared, she saw he clutched a paper in one hand. Her gaze went to the other, and her breath caught in her throat when she saw what he held. A bloody shovel.

He stared at her boots. "You have to get the baby, Miss Bree."

For a long moment, she thought he could read her mind—that he knew how she longed for a baby. Then he thrust the paper into her hand. Sudoku? He was out here working sudoku? "What baby?" she asked, her gaze on the shovel. Had he killed Florence? She couldn't wrap her mind around the possibility.

His stare went past her feet to where Florence lay. He backed away with his hands hiding his eyes. "The windigo is after the baby." He turned and bolted toward the woods.

Kade glanced at his watch when Mason dropped him back at the ranger station. Just enough time to get Dave, then meet Bree at home for dinner. When he pulled up in front of Naomi's house, she came flying out the door, pulling on her coat as she ran. Her face was as pale as the snow.

He got out of the truck and met her halfway up the walk. The wind blew the snow into eddies across the shoveled sidewalk. "What's wrong?"

She seized Kade's arm with both hands as though she needed steadying. "Kade, someone tried to grab Dave just now."

The blood drained from his head to his feet. He stared down into her eyes, and the desperation he saw there convinced him this was no joke. "Is he all right?" He started toward the house, but she tugged him back.

"He's fine. Samson drove the guy away."

Thank God for that dog. The Lord had used Samson more than once. "What happened?"

She gestured to snow bricks. "The kids were making a snow fort. I heard Samson barking. I ran to the back door, and this guy was right there in the yard with him. He had Dave over his shoulder and was heading to the gate. Samson was blocking the gate and still barking. He moved to block the guy every time he tried to get around the dog. I screamed and ran outside with a baseball bat. He saw me and dropped Dave, then ran past Samson and out the gate to a car."

"Did you get Bree?"

She shook her head. "I called Mason first. He's on his way over here. I was about to call Bree."

Bree would freak. And truth be told, he was freaking himself a little. Then what Naomi said soaked in. "I'd better call her."

Naomi's gaze went over his shoulder. "There's Mason."

Kade turned to see the sheriff jump out of his SUV and stride up the walk. What had almost happened here? A pedophile in Rock Harbor? Or something related to what Dave said he saw in the woods?

Mason reached them. "Dave okay?"

Naomi nodded. "Shook up. He's having cookies and milk with my kids. Samson saved the day."

Kade was going to stop on the way home and get the dog a steak. "I'd better go talk to him, reassure him."

Mason took Naomi's arm, and they fell into step with Kade back to the house. "I need a description of the attacker."

Naomi held open the door for them. "I didn't see his face. He wore a bulky goose-down coat and had the collar pulled up. He had on a ski mask, I think. He kept his head turned away."

"What about his car?" Mason's voice was full of resignation.

"A black truck," Naomi said.

Black truck. That was a world of vehicles out there. "Maybe Dave will remember something," Kade said. "But go gentle with him."

Mason walked through the living room to the kitchen. The aroma of chocolate-chip cookies would have made Kade's mouth water under other circumstances. He hurried to see his boy. The thought of someone evil putting his hands on Dave made him want to break a chair over the guy's head.

"Dad!" Dave saw him and jumped up from the table. He knocked over his glass of milk, and it ran onto the floor where Samson was happy to clean it up. Dave leaped into Kade's arms.

Kade held him close. Cold air and cookies clung to his boy's hair and clothes. "Are you okay?"

Dave buried his face in Kade's neck and spoke against his collar. "The guy was big, Dad. Like a house. Maybe it was the windigo."

"If it were a windigo, Samson couldn't have scared him off," Kade said, holding the boy tight.

At the sound of his name, Samson lifted his head from the milk on the floor. "You're a good dog, Samson." The dog's tail began to wag, and he came to Kade and pushed his nose against his hand. Kade rubbed his head.

Naomi scooped up Matthew from the high chair. The toddler

was a chocolate mess. Emily and Timmy were both wide-eyed at the table.

"Hey, buddy," Mason said, touching his nephew on the arm. "Did you see anything that might help me catch this guy?"

Dave lifted his head from Kade's shoulder. "His coat was black. And he smelled like Juicy Fruit gum. My daddy used to give me Juicy Fruit so I know what it smells like." He leaned closer and whispered in Mason's ear. "It was the same windigo I saw put the baby in the snow. I recognized his coat."

"I'd like to hear more about that," Mason said, his voice calm. "Was he as tall as your dad here or more like my size?"

"He was tall like Dad. Only skinnier, I think. It was hard to tell with that coat. And he had on a ski mask. It was red."

"You're going to make a good detective like your mom," Mason said. He roughed the boy's head. "Anything else, Davy?"

"Don't call me Davy," the boy said under his breath.

"Sorry, buddy," Mason said. "I'll try to remember next time. Anything else?"

Dave shook his head.

Mason put away his pad of paper. "You've been a big help. Make sure you don't go outside without an adult, okay? I'll see if we can find this guy."

"Khaki pants," Naomi put in. "I just remembered."

Mason scribbled it in his notebook. "Any letters or numbers from the license plate?"

"It didn't have a license plate," Dave said. "I looked so I could tell you."

Mason raised his brows. "So the guy had this planned," he muttered. "Did he say anything?"

"He yelled, 'Sam, get back!'" the boy said. "And he kicked at him."

"So he knew Samson's name." The hair on the back of Kade's neck stood at attention. Had the guy been watching his family?

"I guess." Dave kept his arms locked around Kade's neck. "I want to see Mom."

"We'll go in a minute."

The color was beginning to come back to the boy's face. Kade set him on the floor. "Go get your stuff and we'll head home." He waited until Dave reluctantly walked away to start packing his backpack with Timmy's help. "You've got to find this guy, Mason. If he knows the dog's name, he's been watching the house. This wasn't a random grab by a pedophile."

"I'm going to have a deputy drive by your place every couple of hours," Mason said. "We'll be looking for him."

That wasn't good enough, but Kade knew it was the best the sheriff could do. Protecting his family was going to be up to him. He and Bree would have to be vigilant. Dave wouldn't be allowed outside without an adult.

"What about the baby incident?" he asked. "Maybe it's related. Dave might have actually seen something. Victor too."

Mason's mouth turned grim. "I need to bring Victor in for questioning anyway. I was on my way to find him when you called. Bree found Florence Hawkins unconscious in the yard, and she died before she was transported to the hospital. Victor had a bloody shovel in his hand."

Kade needed to get to his wife. She'd be upset. "I can't see Victor being violent."

"Me neither, but I have to go with the evidence, and he was likely holding the murder weapon."

"You've got a description of the guy Dave saw. See if you can get a reaction from Victor when you talk to him."

Mason nodded and headed for the door. "I'll be in touch."

Kade thanked Naomi, grabbed Dave's backpack, then herded

the boy out to the truck. "Buckle your seat belt," he told him. He needed to tell Bree about what happened, but maybe it would be better in person, where she could see Dave was all right.

Dave turned his green eyes in Kade's direction. "Dad, I'm not a baby. I know."

The boy was growing up too fast. Nearly eight already. Where had the time gone? Samson nuzzled at Kade's ear as though he sensed his pain and commiserated.

"You deserve a steak dinner, big guy," he said, rubbing Samson's ears again. "Such a good boy," he crooned to the dog's obvious delight.

"Can we stop and buy him something special?" Dave said. "I'd have been a goner if Sam hadn't been there."

Thinking about what might have happened hurt too much. "The butcher might have a nice big bone for him. He'd like that." And it would be free.

⁂

Bree's eyes burned, but she dammed back the swelling lake. Florence was dead by the time the EMT arrived. She didn't know how she was going to tell Davy. After telling the deputy all she'd seen, she bolted. She expected Mason to be along with questions shortly. And he would want to talk to Victor for sure.

She pulled the Jeep into a vacant space by the coffee shop. As she neared the door, reality slammed into her again, and she nearly took her finger out of the dyke and let the tears go, but she somehow managed to hold on.

Preparations for the winter festival were in full swing around town, but the world had lost its gold-tipped glow for her. She stumbled into the coffee shop. The aroma of freshly ground beans cleared her head. She ordered her usual, then took it to a back table to nurse her wounds.

A woman's voice interrupted her. "Bree? What are you doing here?"

Bree glanced up into Hilary Kaleva's face. The mayor of Rock Harbor and Mason's wife, Hilary was also Bree's sister-in-law—or at least she was when Bree was married to her brother, Rob. "Have a seat, Hil."

Hilary continued to stand, her blue eyes shocked under the sleek bob she wore. "Aren't you going to go check on Davy?"

Every nerve ending in Bree's body sprang to attention. She sat up straight. "What do you mean? He's at Naomi's. Or he was. Kade was going to pick him up." Even as she spoke, her hands grabbed for her purse.

"Someone tried to kidnap him from Naomi's backyard. In broad daylight and inside the fence! Samson drove the guy off."

The air rushed out of Bree's lungs and rasped past her throat. She found it impossible to draw in more oxygen. "Wh-what are you saying?"

Hilary's gaze raked Bree's face. "He's fine now, don't panic. Kade got there right after the guy ran away. So did Mason. Mason's got his men looking for a black truck with no license plate."

Bree scrambled to her feet. "Why didn't they call me?"

Hilary followed her to the door. "I don't know. Maybe Kade wanted to tell you in person."

She didn't say good-bye to Hilary, but instead rushed to the Jeep and barreled toward home. She didn't pause long enough to snap her seat belt. The SUV fishtailed on the slick roads, and she barely noticed. All she wanted was to see her son's face.

When she reached the lighthouse, Kade's truck wasn't there, and her slow burn, ignited by his failure to contact her, received a dose of gasoline. Soon she was flaming brighter than the Fresnel lens in the lighthouse tower. How dare he not call? And then to take his time about getting home when he needed to explain things to her as soon as possible. She tried his cell phone but got dumped into voice mail.

She paced the floor. It had been a long time since she'd let her red-haired temper out of its cage. When she finally heard the rumble of Kade's truck outside, she sprang toward the door. In the deepest part of her heart, she knew she was overreacting, but by then she'd lost her hold on the tail of the tiger.

Davy came through the door first with Samson bounding after. "Mom, I was almost grabbed by this big guy! Sam saved me, didn't you, boy?" He skidded to his knees and threw his arms around his happy dog.

Kade came in right behind the exuberant twosome. He carried two bags of groceries. His gaze locked with Bree's and she let her anger show in her tight mouth and a glare that should have fried him on the spot.

"Davy, go get cleaned up and I'll fix dinner," Bree said, her voice level.

"Mom, don't call me Davy!" He got up and ran up the stairs with Samson on his heels.

Kade walked past her to the kitchen and she followed. "Kade, how could you let someone else tell me what happened?" she demanded. "Do you have any idea how I felt when Hilary told me about it in the coffee shop? The coffee shop? I had no clue. You should have called me."

He put the bags on the counter. "After the day you'd had, I thought you should hear this in person when you could see he was fine."

Her anger struggled to survive the revelation. "I'm his mother! You should have called me."

He folded his arms over his chest. "Don't you want to hear what actually happened instead of reaming me out? Dave is fine. Samson was there."

Her knees went weak as she thought of what could have happened. She would have fallen if he hadn't grabbed her arm and pulled her to him. The steady thump of his heart under her ear calmed her until she remembered his decision not to call her. She pulled away.

He dropped his hands. "I heard Florence died today. I'm sorry, hon."

The lump in her throat grew. First Florence, now this threat to Davy. "Tell me what happened."

"Naomi heard Samson barking. She ran out and saw a guy with Dave over his shoulder making for the gate. The dog barred his way. When he heard Naomi scream, he dropped Dave and bolted." He turned toward the grocery bags and drew out a package. "This is for our hero. He saved our boy."

My boy. The words trembled on her tongue, but she knew if she uttered them, things might change forever. With a supreme act of will, she managed to stuff them down where they'd come from, a dark place she hadn't realized existed. She'd thought of Kade as Davy's father for so long now, she'd forgotten there had once been another man. With that fact rising to the top of her memory, she found Rob's face floating in her vision.

"Say something," Kade said. "He's fine. Mason has his guys watching. There will be a deputy coming by every few hours."

"That's not enough," she said automatically.

"No, it's not." He squatted in front of her and lifted one of her hands to cover it in his. "I'm not going to let anything happen to our son."

She let him console her and lay out the promises, but she began to realize her past wasn't a riverbed washed clean. Ripples and eddies etched tracks in the ground that she found herself following subconsciously, even though she wanted to put the past away and only take it out when she was ready.

Rob really was a ghost, and his memory was going to sweep away the pleasant life she'd created for them here.

⌇

Davy was subdued through supper. He probably sensed the tension between his parents. Bree stood to clear away the dishes when the doorbell sounded the opening line of "Hound Dog." Samson raised his head and woofed.

"I'll get it," Kade said. He hurried to the front door.

Bree heard the murmur of a woman's agitated voice. She took Davy's hand and went to the living room. Sara Westola followed Kade into the room. Gray streaked her blonde hair, and her skin was tired and sallow. She was about sixty.

"Please, Bree, you've got to find Pia," Sara said. "She was supposed to come for lunch today like she does every Monday. She was going to make me fish soup and promised to be there by eleven, but she never showed up. She isn't answering her cell phone and I got worried. I went to her house and let myself in with my key. There's no sign of her, but her car is in the garage, and her skis are gone. I'm afraid she's had an accident out skiing in those woods behind her house. Her cell phone was on the kitchen counter too."

"Calm down, Sara," Bree said. "Maybe a friend stopped over." She didn't know Pia well. She was in her midtwenties and was the Children's Protective Services employee who had done the home study required for Bree and Kade to become foster parents. It wasn't unusual to see her scooting around town with her Mini Cooper crammed with children.

"Could we get Samson to look for her?" Sara asked, wringing her hands. "This isn't like Pia."

Bree bit her lip. "We've had a bit of an upheaval this afternoon, and I hate to leave. Someone tried to take my son."

Sara's gaze went to Davy. "Oh no! Did you catch the guy?"

Maybe she could get Naomi to go on the search. "Not yet. Listen, let me see if I can get some members of my team to find her." She grabbed the phone and made a few calls. Naomi didn't answer, and Bree's other three searchers were either out of town or tied up.

Kade interpreted the way she slowly set the phone down. He stepped to her side and slipped his arm around her. "Go ahead, babe. You know I'll take good care of him."

She stubbornly held on to her anger, even though she knew he'd give his life for her son. "I don't want to leave."

He shrugged. "Do what you do best. I'll lock up the house. He won't be alone for a second."

She knew she needed to go. Pia could be in trouble, and there was no one else. "Call me if anything happens, anything at all."

"I will." He brushed his lips across hers. "Be careful."

She had yet to tell him what the doctor said. Turning to Sara, she called, "It's all set. My husband will keep an eye on our boy." Bree snapped her fingers at Samson. "Let me get my dog ready."

She went to a closet and pulled out a backpack and a vest. Samson began to prance around the living room with his tail held high. He crouched and barked, then ran to Bree. She slipped the vest over his head. "Sara, did you think to bring an article of clothing that belongs to Pia?"

Sara nodded. "I put it in a paper bag, is that okay?"

"Perfect. Did you leave it in the car?"

"Yes, I'll go get it." The older woman hurried toward the door.

Bree slipped into her coat, grabbed her backpack, then clipped a leash to Samson's collar. He strained eagerly toward the door and practically dragged her onto the porch. She frowned at the quickly falling darkness. It would be pitch black by the time they got back to the woods. The dog leaped into the backseat as soon as she opened the door.

Sara handed the bag to Bree. "I got socks from the laundry basket."

"I think we should start at Pia's house, since it looks like she went out on her skis," Bree said. "Shall we ride together?"

"I'd better take my car separately in case she's hurt and I need to stay at the hospital with her," Sara said. She hopped into her Lexus.

Bree accelerated the Jeep down the driveway after her. Several men were carving ice sculptures in the park she passed. One was the spitting image of Samson. "Hey, boy, there you are," she told him. He woofed, then laid his head on her shoulder.

The thermometer read five degrees, even colder with the wind chill. They reached Pia's cottage at the edge of the Ottawa National Forest. The one-bedroom home was white with green shutters and sat back off the road. Sara pulled into the driveway and parked the car. The red Jeep rolled to a stop behind it. It was nearly dark.

Sara clambered out and ran to the house while Bree got Samson ready.

Sara unlocked Pia's door and went in.

Bree got out her ready pack and shouldered it, though she hoped Sara would return with the news that Pia was inside. When she approached the porch, the older woman reappeared.

"No one there," Sara said, her mouth turned down. "Let's check the back."

The women went around to the backyard. Bree saw the ski tracks sloping off toward the forest. Two sets.

"Could she have come back?"

"There aren't any skis in the garage," Sara said.

"Then maybe someone went with her."

Bree had the paper bag clutched in her hand. She knelt beside the dog and opened the bag. The dog thrust his nose into the bag and whimpered. His tail wagged in a frantic wave.

"Search, Samson!" She let go of her dog, and Samson leaped away through the snow.

His nose high, he crisscrossed the backyard. "What's he doing?" Sara asked.

Bree kept her gaze on her dog. "People give off skin rafts, microscopic particles of skin. They are unique to the individual. Samson is an air-search dog, so he's trying to pick up Pia's scent. Once he homes in on it, he can follow it like we would a whiff of perfume." She began to smile. "He's got it!" She put on her snowshoes, flipped on her flashlight, and followed Samson as he waded through the snowdrifts into the woods.

"I'll wait here," Sara called after her.

The sting of the cold wind on her face and the warm stretch of her muscles would have been enjoyable at another time, but the inner urgency to find Pia drove her on in a race that left no time for pleasure. The snow pack was heavy and she moved quickly on her snowshoes.

Bree reached the ski path through the woods, and the gloom deepened. The bobbing beam of light was easy to follow. Bare trees seemed to reach their limbs for her.

"It's creepy out here," she told Samson, just to break the silence. "I'd forgotten how scary the forest can be at night." At least she had the dog with her.

Bree paused to catch her breath. Out here in the dark, she could almost believe what Davy said about a windigo. She glanced around the black forest, and her laugh held an edge of unease.

She and Samson moved farther along the ski path. They reached the top of a rise and started down. Samson bolted away from her, and his howl echoed back. Bree caught her breath. "Oh no," she whispered when the howl came again.

She ran after the dog. The moon shone through the bare tree limbs and illuminated her path. At the bottom of the hill, she stopped and began to tremble. A body lay crumpled on the ground, and the bright splash of blood on the snow made her retch. Pia's sightless eyes stared up into the tree above her head.

Bree didn't have to touch the woman's cold body to know Pia's spirit had flown to somewhere else.

6

IT NEVER GOT EASIER TO BE ON THE FRONT LINES OF tragedy. Bree rubbed her stinging eyes and tried to comfort Samson, who lay panting at her feet. Finding a dead body was hard on him too. He'd vomited, then cried for several minutes. Bree expected Mason soon. After he told Sara the news. It appeared to Bree as though Pia had fallen onto a jagged branch that impaled her.

Samson's ears flicked, and he rose with his nose up. His dark eyes were worried. "It's okay, boy," Bree said, rubbing his ears. He whined and his dark eyes stared at a spot farther down the trail. "What is it?" Bree tried to see what had caught his attention, but her beam of light didn't push back the edges of the darkness enough.

She rose as a plaintive cry echoed through the darkness. The sound held an edge of wildness that made her shudder. A big cat? She'd have to tell Kade. Samson whined again and strained away from her. He seldom reacted to animals, so Bree's curiosity was caught.

She rose and let go of his collar. "Show me, boy." The dog leaped away from her until he disappeared into the darkness. Bree shined her light along the path and followed. "Samson, speak!"

The dog woofed ahead of her, and she moved the flashlight beam in the direction of the sound. She saw Samson standing by a pile of fallen trees just off the ski path. The pool of light caught him as he flattened onto his belly and nosed through the snow toward an opening in the jumble of wood. As Bree got closer, she heard a faint sound on the wind. The cry came again.

She hurried to join her dog. "Move away," she commanded, pulling on his collar. Samson sat back on his haunches, and she aimed her light into the cavity formed by the fallen trees. Bree caught her breath at the sight of an infant backpack carrier with a quilted cover. Weak cries came from the hidden baby. Kneeling, she pulled the carrier free of the trees and peeked inside.

A tiny baby in a pink sleeper wailed her misery to the world. Her tiny face was red and screwed with outrage. How long had she been here? Bree touched her. The baby's sleeper was totally soaked. Bree focused her light under the tree trunk again and saw a diaper bag. She pulled it out. How had the child gotten here? And who had hidden her like this?

"There, there," she soothed. Surely there were bottles and formula in the bag, though it might be frozen, depending on how long it had been out here. She touched the baby's cheek, and the infant turned her head hungrily. Her cheek was warm though. The insulating cover had done a good job of keeping her protected from the wind. The fallen trees where she'd been hidden had helped too.

Bree shined her light into the recesses of the bag and began to dig through it. Her fingers touched a wallet, and she flipped it open. Pia's face on a driver's license smiled back at her. Bree's throat closed, knowing the young woman would never smile again. She sat back and the light shone on a piece of paper lying on the ground. She picked it up and held it under the light. A sudoku, handwritten. She thrust it into the bag.

Her gaze went back to the child. A foster child in Pia's care? The baby mewled again, and Bree went in search of food. Her hand dug past diapers and sleepers. The formula inside was very cold but not frozen. At least the baby's tummy would be full. Bree didn't dare pull the infant from the warmth of the carrier. She shook up the formula, pushed the air out of the bag, then popped the nipple into the baby's mouth. The tiny girl made a face at the cold rubber, then began to suckle weakly.

How long had she been out here? Hours? Over a day?

Samson looked on and whined. He sensed Bree's agitation. "She'll be okay, boy," she said, looping her other arm around the dog.

How was she going to burp the baby? Bree couldn't expose her to the wind. The best thing to do was to get her to the hospital. It wasn't far. Bree could call Mason and explain why she couldn't wait.

The baby finished the bottle, and Bree lifted the covering over the carrier again. The baby whimpered inside. Rising, Bree slipped her shoulders into the carrier and went back the way she'd come. She whispered a prayer for Pia's family as she passed the woman's crumpled body. She stayed on the packed ski trail, which made walking in her snowshoes easier than what she might face on the surrounding heavy snow.

Her breath fogged out of her mouth, and the extra exertion caused her to pull more cold air into her lungs. She was already tired from the trek in, and the extra burden wore her out even more. Her cheeks burned from the cold, and she realized she should have worn a ski mask.

She reached the edge of the woods and saw bobbing lights moving toward her across the dark field. It had to be Mason. She paused in the shelter of the trees until the sheriff reached her.

Mason's gaze flickered to the baby carrier and he raised his brows. "Is that a baby?"

Bree nodded and drew in a deep breath. Carrying the extra weight had winded her. "I found her hidden in a pile of downed trees."

"Where'd she come from?"

"I don't know. I found Pia's driver's license in the backpack with her formula and diapers. If Pia hid her, this little one has been out here all day. I have to get her to the hospital."

"I'll check with Children's Protective Services. They'll have a record of which babies were in Pia's custody for placement."

Bree glanced back toward the house. "Did you tell Sara?"

He nodded. "She went to her sister's."

The baby began to whimper. "I need to get this little one checked out." She studied Mason's face an instant longer. "Kade and I have been approved as foster parents. When you call CPS, would you ask if I can keep her?"

"You think that's wise?" Mason's voice held unusual gentleness. "You'll have to give this baby up eventually. I'd hate to see you get hurt."

"I'm a big girl, my friend. You don't have to worry." The moment she'd heard the infant cry, her heart longed to care for the baby. What would Kade say? He might have the same concerns as Mason. Davy would be ecstatic though.

Mason shrugged. "Okay, I'll have them meet you at the hospital. You'll have to jump through their hoops, but it shouldn't be a problem."

The baby wailed louder. "She's soaked. I'm going to take her to the hospital first and make sure she's okay, so call my cell if you need me." Bree wouldn't rest easy until a doctor confirmed the baby was only suffering from hunger and mild exposure.

Mason nodded, and Bree hurried as fast as she could across the deep snow in the field. There were no lights on at Pia's house, other than the back porch light, so she went around to the front and found Sara's car gone. Bree tried the door and found it unlocked. Just as she'd hoped, she found an infant car seat inside. She installed it in the Jeep, then secured the wailing baby.

She had Samson get in the backseat, then she drove to the hospital. The baby's whimpers grew more plaintive, and Bree's palms grew moist with the desire to tend to the infant. She stopped at the emergency entrance to the hospital, retrieved the crying infant, then rushed her inside with Samson on their heels.

A nurse took Bree and the baby back right away. The baby's cries weakened. "There, there, precious," Bree crooned. The sleeper was dripping wet, all the way up to the neck. She changed the diaper and wrapped her in a dry receiving blanket. Humming "Can't Help Falling in Love with You," she cuddled the smelly infant and rocked on her feet.

The baby cried even louder when Bree unwrapped the blanket so the doctor could examine her. At the hoarse sobs, Bree rubbed the baby's soft head. "It's okay, precious. It's almost over."

By the time CPS arrived and filled out all the forms, the female doctor pronounced the baby fit and suffering only from mild exposure and hunger. The CPS worker mentioned that she had no record of the baby in Pia's care and would dig into it more in the morning. Bree carried the baby back to the Jeep. When Bree pulled up to the lighthouse, the clock on the dash read eight o'clock, but it seemed much later.

The lake ice gave a loud crackle when she got out of the Jeep and removed the infant carrier. Samson beat her to the porch, and Bree rushed to get the baby inside. The warm air was a welcome stream over her face when she opened the door. She carried the infant to the living room, where she set the carrier on the floor and peeled back the cover.

Samson pranced around the table as the baby's cries grew more insistent. "There, there, sweetheart," Bree said, lifting the infant out of the carrier. At the sudden human contact, the tiny girl turned her face into Bree's neck. Her fist went to her mouth. "Are you still hungry?" Bree said. "You're soaked again."

"Bree, is that you, *kulta?*" Anu Nicholls appeared at the bottom of the steps. Nearly sixty, she was a trim, soft-spoken woman with soft blonde hair streaked with gray. She was Rob's mother and still as close to a real mother as Bree had ever known. Her presence always calmed the family. "What are you doing with a baby?"

"I don't know. I found her hidden in the woods. Where are Davy and Kade?"

"David is in bed," Anu said in her faint Finnish accent. "Kade went to town for some formula. When Mason called and told him you were bringing home a baby, he asked me to come since David was already asleep." She approached Bree and touched the infant's cheek. "She is hungry."

"I gave her part of a bottle in the woods. I don't know how long she's been out there." Bree nodded toward the backpack. "Could you warm another bottle? I'll get her bathed and changed."

She carried the baby into the kitchen, and Samson followed anxiously on her heels as though the baby were his responsibility. He'd been this way with Davy too, Bree remembered, though he'd only been a puppy. She turned on warm water and let the sink fill. "You need a bath, baby girl. You'll like the warm water." Cradling the child in one arm, she put a dishtowel on the counter and undressed the baby quickly.

The tiny girl's thin wails cut off in a gasp, and she threw out her arms. Bree quickly tossed a corner of the towel over the infant's chest. "It's okay," she crooned.

Samson put his front paws on the counter and watched with anxious eyes. "Get down, boy," Bree said. The dog dropped back onto all four paws. She transferred the baby, still on the towel, to the sink. The infant's tender skin was red and raw from the extended contact with her dirty diaper.

"We'll be done soon," Bree said in a soothing voice. She became aware of Anu moving up behind her. Bree turned the water on in the other side of the sink so Anu could fill a pan with water to warm the bottle. She used gentle hand soap to wash the infant.

"Could you grab me a hand towel from the drawer?" she asked Anu.

Anu did as she was asked and also laid out another hand towel on the counter. "Here are the clothes from the bag. My, she looks quite new."

"I don't think she's more than a couple of weeks old. Maybe not even that." Bree lifted the screaming infant and wrapped her in the hand towel. She dried her, then put a clean diaper, onesie, and sleeper on her. The baby began to quiet in the clean, dry clothes. Bree cuddled her close and turned to see Anu checking the temperature of the milk.

"It is not quite as warm as she might like it, but the cold edge is off, *kulta*," Anu said, drying the bottle and handing it to Bree.

The baby sucked greedily at the bottle, and her translucent eyelids began to close as the lukewarm milk slid down her throat and filled her tummy. When was the last time Bree fed a baby? Maybe not since Davy was this age. The warm weight of the baby's relaxed body filled a need in Bree's heart.

Still holding her close, she carried the infant to the living room and settled into the rocker. The baby girl's mouth slackened as she sank deeper into sleep, and a dribble of milk spilled from it. The sweet scent of baby skin drifted to Bree's nose. There was no better fragrance.

Anu sat on the sofa opposite Bree. "*Kulta*, you will have to give her up. Do not be too quick to love her."

"Too late." Bree managed a smile. "But I know it's temporary."

"What do you know about this little one? Did not Kade say some babies were missing from the reservation?" Anu studied the infant's sleeping face. "Though she looks Caucasian."

Bree ran her palm over the baby's thin blonde hair and studied her translucent skin. "I don't think she's Ojibwa, but I'll check it out." She glanced over to see Anu lifting items from the backpack. "Maybe God heard my cry for a child," she said.

"God always hears the cries of his children," Anu said. "But do not be too quick to jump to a conclusion the Father never intended." She frowned. "What is this?" she asked, holding out a paper. "One of those sudoku things."

"I found it on the ground by the baby." Bree glanced at it. The top numbers were familiar. "Grab that sudoku Victor gave me at the cabin, would you? It's there on the coffee table."

Anu smoothed the paper and laid the other sudoku beside it. "The top numbers are the same. And the handwriting appears identical."

Victor had left a sudoku in the woods? Bree's mind made connections she didn't want to make. He'd been on the scene when Florence died too.

⁂

Light spilled from the lighthouse windows in a welcoming glow. The wind drove needles of icy snow into Kade's skin as he hurried inside with the formula. He'd grabbed disposable diapers as well, then stopped at Naomi's and borrowed a bassinet. He and Bree had made preparations to be foster parents, but he hadn't expected their first child to show up so quickly or under such dramatic circumstances.

He found Bree nestling the infant in the living room. Samson lay curled at her feet. "Where's Anu?" he asked, shrugging out of his coat.

"I sent her home." Bree's green eyes stayed focused on him. "Thanks for getting the formula. She's sleeping now."

He sat beside her and studied the baby. "She's tiny."

Bree smoothed the infant's soft hair. "Newborn."

"I'm sorry I forgot your doctor appointment." He ran his hand through his hair. "Man, was that only this morning? So much has happened. What did she say?" He watched the muscles in Bree's throat convulse as she swallowed hard, and he knew the news wasn't good.

"The doctor thinks we should go to in vitro."

"What does that mean?"

She raised her gaze to meet his. "She'll give me high-powered drugs to help me make more eggs than usual. They'll extract them, fertilize them, then implant them. But it's expensive."

His mouth tightened. "How much?"

"Five thousand dollars." Her gaze stayed on him. "Per month. I know it's a lot, but it might be the only way to get pregnant."

"You got pregnant a few months ago."

"And lost the baby."

"What would keep you from losing it again, even after spending all that money?"

"I forgot to ask her," Bree said. "I guess they'll give me something to help me carry the babies."

"Babies? As in more than one?" His brain tallied the cost.

She nodded. "Probably."

He winced. "Let's just try it on our own, babe. I don't think we can swing that now."

Disappointment darkened her eyes. "Maybe I could get a part-time job."

"Your work with training search dogs is important."

"But it doesn't bring in much money," she reminded him. "I want to give you your own child, Kade."

He cupped her chin in his fingers. "Dave *is* my own. I've got you and him, and if we don't have more, it's enough."

"You're a good man, Kade Matthews," she said, her voice husky.

Kade smiled. "I *know* we'll have our own baby, Bree."

Her smile returned. "I'm sure I'll be able to find this girl's parents, but if Pia had her, they might be unfit."

"We'll cross that bridge if we have to."

Her gaze turned thoughtful. "It's late, but Mason might know who she belongs to by tomorrow."

He could only hope this little one's parents were located before Bree grew too attached to the girl. "Seems strange Pia would hide the baby like that. You think she was being chased and was murdered?"

"The thought crossed my mind." Bree's head fell back against the sofa. "Something about the way she was lying. She'd fallen uphill too, as though she'd been shoved."

"I know it's useless to warn you not to get involved." Kade grinned and dropped a kiss on his wife's check. "But be careful."

"I've got Davy to think about too. He'll have to stay close to one of us." She shuddered. "With Florence and Pia both dead, I have to wonder about his story. Maybe there's a killer out there after all, human or otherwise. I need to talk to Victor."

Mason called Bree's house at nine the next morning while she was getting dressed. CPS had no record of the baby they'd found by Pia. He hadn't been able to find Victor, either, and wanted her team's assistance. She left the baby in Kade's care, assisted by Davy, who had barely left the infant's side. Kade had called in to take a few hours off work and had been strangely silent when he got off the phone, but she didn't have time to probe.

The sheriff and his men waited for her at Florence's house. The temperature stood at ten below, and the wind whistled through the treetops after zooming off Lake Superior. She stood with Samson on his leash and listened to the sheriff outline what he needed.

Mason's skin was sallow, and his eyelids drooped. "We suspect

Victor Pelton is hiding in the woods somewhere. I want us to find him before anyone else is hurt."

"Mason, Victor is autistic, not a murderer." She tried not to remember her fear when she saw the bloody shovel in Victor's hands.

Mason shrugged. "Let's just say he's a person of interest right now."

The wheels of justice sometimes crushed the innocent, and she was afraid that was about to happen to the gentle twenty-five-year-old man. He mowed their yard, and she'd often baked him cookies and had him stay for dinner. It was hard for her to believe he could have hurt Florence or Pia.

But he might know who did.

Her team today consisted of Naomi and her dog, Charley. No one else was available. They stood at the edge of the Ottawa forest. The most recent storm had dumped another six inches onto the twenty already on the ground. Luckily, a hard crust had formed over the snow, so they should be able to walk on the top with snowshoes.

"Let's head away from the lake," she told Naomi.

"You're worried, aren't you?" Naomi asked.

Bree nodded. "I'm afraid Florence's death is connected to that guy trying to grab Davy from your place yesterday. I wish you'd caught a better look at him."

"Me too, but he had on that ski mask. Something about his walk seemed familiar, but I can't put my finger on it."

Bree knelt and had the dogs sniff the scent article—Victor's socks—that Mason had obtained. "Search, Samson," she said, releasing him from the leash. She watched as Naomi released Charley and the two dogs bounded away. Naomi's golden retriever was a world-class search dog too, and she had every confidence Samson and he would find Victor.

Bree plodded along on her snowshoes. Only occasionally did she break through into thigh-high snow. She kept her vision glued to the animals. Charley and Samson crisscrossed the open meadow with their noses in the air as they tried to pick up the scent.

Samson's tail stiffened, and his head came up. "He's got the scent!" she shouted to Naomi.

She and Naomi moved as fast as they could through the forest. A small cabin lay just ahead, a hunter's cabin. A wisp of smoke trailed from the chimney. Samson and Charley ran to the door. Her dog whined and pawed at the door, and she knew Victor was inside. She called Mason on her cell phone, and he told her to wait outside.

She would rather talk to Victor, but she closed her phone and told Naomi they had to hold back. Bree called to the dogs. Samson's tail sank but he obeyed her command to come. Bree fed him a treat and rubbed his ears. "Good boy," she said.

His ears pricked and he turned to gaze back at the cottage. She stared too and saw the door opening. Uncertain what might be happening, she fell back another step, tugging Samson with her.

Victor, dressed in a blue parka and rubber boots, stuck his head out the door. When he saw Bree, he exited the cabin and came toward her with a paper held out in his hand as though he wanted to give it to her.

"Stay here," she murmured to Naomi. She advanced to meet him. "Hi, Victor, we've been looking for you. Are you okay?"

He said nothing but continued to approach her. Bree knew Mason would be alarmed at Victor's expressionless face and vacant eyes, but she still didn't believe he would hurt anyone.

The first thing she needed to establish was control. "Victor, look at me," she said in a commanding tone.

He was staring above her head. At her order, his gaze didn't shift, and his eyes retained their emptiness. He reached her and stopped with the paper still extended.

"You want me to take this?" she asked. Her gloved fingers touched the paper, and he released it. He was still staring above her head, not making eye contact. "What's this all about, buddy?"

He turned and trudged back to the cabin. Bree started after him, then heard the buzz of Mason's snowmobile behind her. He'd be here in minutes.

"What did he give you?" Naomi asked, joining her.

Bree handed it to her. "It's just another puzzle. He's crazy about sudoku."

"I've never figured it out," Naomi said.

"I've dabbled with it."

"Did he say anything?" Naomi asked.

Bree shook her head. "And he wouldn't look at me. He just came out, handed me the puzzle, then retreated back to the cabin. His eyes looked funny. Shocked and distant or something."

Naomi glanced toward the cabin "You said he had that shovel. Maybe he found it by Florence's body, and it traumatized him."

"Maybe." Bree watched Mason and one of his deputies approach on their machines before she glanced at the puzzle in her hand again. The sudoku grid had been drawn in red ink, then filled in with black ink. Her gaze traced the numbers, and it appeared he had done it correctly. At least as far as she could tell with a quick scan.

The whine of the engines quit, then Mason and Deputy Doug Montgomery thrashed through the snow. Without snowshoes, their weight sent them crashing through the crust on top of the drifts. They were panting by the time they reached the women.

"He's in there," Bree said, pointing to the cabin. "He came out a minute ago and gave me this." She handed the puzzle to Mason.

He frowned. "What is it?"

"Sudoku." She could tell he'd never heard of it from the way his brows drew together. "It's a number puzzle. The basic has nine boxes in a three-by-three grid. You can use each number only once in every column, each row, and each of the nine boxes. It's based on Latin squares."

Mason raised his thick brows, graying now that he was nearly forty. "Did he say anything?"

"No. This is the third puzzle I've seen." She quickly told him about the one she'd found in the baby's backpack and the one Victor had given her after she found Florence's body.

"Maybe he's trying to tell us something. Is it a code or something?"

"I don't know. The numbers on the top row are the same in all three sudokus."

He nodded, then pocketed the puzzle and started toward the cabin. Montgomery hurried after Mason as fast as his bulk would allow. Bree wanted to be in on the questioning, but she knew even Mason couldn't allow it.

"Let's get back." Bree called Samson to her, and the team trooped back through the forest to her Jeep. Kade had wanted her to call when she found Victor, so she paused on the road to dial while Naomi loaded the dogs.

His voice came on at the second ring. "Hey, babe. You done?"

"Yes, he was hiding in the hunter's cabin out near the gully."

"That's good," he said as though he hadn't even heard her.

She tried to read his distracted tone. What was going on with him? "We're heading home now. Everything okay with the kids?"

"Sure. Anu offered to take the baby home with her, so I let her. Dave and I are playing Uno."

"You didn't want to keep her?"

"She cried a lot and I didn't know what to do."

Or he didn't want to try. She didn't argue about it. "I'll stop by the store and get her." Then she was going to dig around a little until she heard what Mason found out from Victor. Someone had to know something about a missing baby girl. How did Pia come to have her if CPS had no record of it?

7

TUESDAY MORNING QUINN SAT ON HOUGHTON STREET with the car turned off and held the phone away from his ear. Yelling wasn't going to change anything. Florence had gotten cold feet, and he'd had to deal with her. Unfortunately, he hadn't realized how much his partner had cared about her. His thoughts drifted to the boy. If he'd managed to take Davy, he could have gotten to the bottom of what had really happened four years ago.

"What's done is done," Quinn said when the shouting ended. "I have to go now." He clicked off the phone without waiting for more anger.

"He's mad about Florence?" Jenna asked.

"Furious. I'd say our partnership is about at an end."

She shrugged. "I don't like the way he bosses you around anyway. He doesn't treat Rosen like that."

Quinn stared at the jail. On his way through town, he'd seen Mason driving in the other direction. No one else would be likely to recognize Quinn in the wig and beard, but no sense in taking any chances, though he wasn't too worried. People saw what they expected to see.

When Jenna had heard her brother was picked up for questioning in a murder, she'd freaked. Normally she was cool as an ice princess, but she'd talked him into coming downtown with her. He hadn't put up much of a fight, because he needed to know more himself. He couldn't stop his gaze from sweeping the figures on the sidewalk. Could Davy be here with his mother?

"I'll wait here," he told Jenna as he unlocked the doors.

Jenna clutched at his hand. "I need you with me." Her coat was sleek and more for style than to bar the cold, and her red hat perched on one side of her head.

He would have to give in now or listen to her whine. "Let's get in and out quick."

"You never said who might recognize you here."

"And I'm not going to. You don't need to know." He shoved the door open without acknowledging her wounded glance. Two minutes later they were in the deputy's office. Quinn didn't recognize the big man sitting behind the desk.

The man's badge read Montgomery. He heaved himself to his feet. "Thanks for coming, Ms. Pelton." He indicated the seat across from the desk, then settled back into his own chair. His stare lingered on Quinn. "And you are?"

"Quinn Matilla."

"My boyfriend," Jenna said in an imperious voice. "What do you have on my brother?"

Montgomery rubbed his ear. "Plenty, eh?" He glanced at his computer screen. "Florence Hawkins was bludgeoned with a shovel, and Victor also had her blood on him. He was seen on the property with the shovel in his hand, and his prints are the only ones on it. We also found one of his puzzles by a baby that had been hidden in the woods."

Quinn's attention sharpened. "A baby? Dead?"

Montgomery shook his head. "The child is all right but her caregiver is dead."

Jenna's eyes were wet. "He did yard work for Florence, but he wouldn't hurt anyone. His prints would be on the tools. And it's likely he just found the body and that's why her blood was on him."

She leaned forward. "Deputy, Vic is autistic. Violence among autistics is very rare. And I know my brother—he won't even step on an ant. He didn't do this."

Montgomery shifted in his seat and dropped his gaze. "We have to go with the evidence, eh, Ms. Pelton."

Quinn leaned forward. "What about motive?" How could he find out from this big dumb guy just where the baby was *now?*

"We don't have a motive yet," the deputy admitted. "Victor isn't talking."

"He hasn't said how he happened to find Florence?"

"He's not talking at all. Not a word. All he does is work sudoku. Over and over. He makes them up on sheets of blank paper." Montgomery rose. "I'll take you to him."

The deputy led them to a small interrogation room that stank of sweat and desperation. The once white walls had turned a dingy yellow, probably from cigarette smoke. A battered table sat in the middle of the room, and four chairs surrounded it. The industrial gray tile on the floor made the room seem even more lifeless.

"I'll get your brother, eh?" the deputy said.

Quinn glanced at Jenna. She was pale. He wanted out of this place. It was only by fate that he'd avoided being in one of those cells back there. He tugged at his hat and adjusted it to cover more of his face.

"I never thought Victor would get in this kind of trouble. Growing up, I always looked out for him. When people stared at Vic's awkward movements and his monotone voice, I explained." Her voice broke. "Sometimes I was embarrassed by his strangeness, but I always loved him."

Quinn had never seen Jenna show such sentimentality, and it caught him off guard. When she reached over to take his hand, he squeezed her fingers.

"I have to get him out of jail. Victor will go crazy penned up.

He loves to walk, even in bad weather. Nothing keeps him inside—not snow, ice, or rain."

The door opened, and a young man stepped inside. Montgomery poked his head in. "I'll lock the door. Use the intercom if you need me." He pulled the door shut, and the latch clicked.

The man's dirty blond hair obscured his face, which was turned toward the ground. When Jenna spoke his name, Victor didn't look up. She rose and went to hug him. Victor's gaze stayed on the floor, and his arms hung slackly in front of him, still in cuffs. He held a sheet of paper.

Quinn had never met an autistic person before, so he didn't know what he'd expected, but it wasn't this.

"It's good to see you, buddy," Jenna said, her voice shaking. She led him to the table. "I'm here to help get you out of jail. Tell me what happened."

Victor threw the paper at her, but he still didn't raise his head. She caught the paper and glanced at it.

"What is it?" Quinn asked. Rows of numbers in squares had been scrawled on the yellow sheet.

"What's this about, Vic?" she asked.

Victor rose and went to the door. He began to bang his head against it. Jenna went after him. "It's okay. I'll call the deputy to take you back to your bed."

"Does he always do that? Bang his head, I mean?"

Frowning, she said, "He hasn't done that since he was five or six. And he's not talking. He always talks about whatever his current interest is."

When Victor left with another deputy, Quinn clasped her hand and led her down the hall back to Montgomery's office. There had to be a way to find out the baby's location.

Montgomery closed his file when he saw them in the doorway. "He talked to you, eh?

"He wouldn't say anything, and I didn't press him. He gave me this though." She held up the sudoku.

"We've got more in his file."

"Can I have copies?"

The deputy nodded, then extracted several sheets from a manila folder, stepped to the copier and copied them, then handed them to Jenna. "Any help would be appreciated. When did you last talk to your brother?"

"Probably three weeks ago. I've called him several times since but he was out, so I've left messages."

"And when you last talked to him, he didn't say anything about his new hobby of sudoku?"

"No. All he talked about was how early the snow had come this year. He said he hadn't been ready and some of Florence's roses might have been damaged because he didn't get all of them mulched in time."

Quinn wished she hadn't said that. Didn't she realize that the deputy might consider it a motive if Florence had yelled at Victor?

She must have caught something in his expression, because she quickly added, "But if you're thinking she might have criticized him and triggered rage, that doesn't happen with Vic. When people get mad at him, he hides. Sometimes under the porch, sometimes in the attic. He's such a gentle soul, Deputy. This is all wrong."

Montgomery's expression turned pained. "I, uh, I don't think he's guilty, Ms. Pelton. But we're just doing our job. The evidence points to your brother."

"Have you called a lawyer for him?"

Montgomery nodded. "As soon as he was arrested. He hasn't talked to the lawyer either."

"Where is his cell? Can he see the sky from there? Is he getting outside at all?"

The deputy fiddled with his pen. "No, ma'am. The cells with

windows are all taken, and the weather has been too bad to let the prisoners out for exercise."

"Can you do anything about that? Exchange a cell with another prisoner? Get Victor outside some? He can't stand being cooped up. Maybe if he feels more comfortable, he'll talk to me and we can get this cleared up."

"I don't think I can move him, but I can see he gets outside, eh."

Quinn fidgeted. Mason could come back any time, and they'd been here way too long. He cleared his throat. "I noticed a lighthouse out by the bed-and-breakfast. They don't take in boarders, do they? I noticed the Blue Bonnet isn't open right now."

"No sir. Kade Matthews, he's a ranger out at the forest, and his wife, Bree, trains search-and-rescue dogs. They don't take boarders."

"I thought I saw a kid and a dog in the yard," Quinn said, keeping his voice casual. So she'd married someone. Figured.

Montgomery nodded, but his gaze sharpened to suspicion.

Quinn shut up. He couldn't have asked more questions if he'd tried. The news Bree had married was enough to take in. Good riddance, he told himself. Back outside he turned to Jenna. "I want you to stop by that lighthouse. I have a feeling they will know where the baby is."

The tiny office Lauri occupied barely held her desk and chair, but she didn't mind. She was working for a prestigious company. Her first day of real work. She couldn't wait until Kade heard the news. He wouldn't think his baby sister was such a major screw-up. Maybe she could live down all her past mistakes after all.

The intercom on her desk beeped, then Mrs. Saunders's voice blared. "Lauri, in my office please."

Lauri's first summons of the day. She wiped suddenly moist

palms on her black A-line skirt and grabbed her notepad on her way out the door. The thick carpet muffled her steps to the big office at the end of the hall. She tapped on the door.

"Come in."

Lauri stepped inside and closed the door behind her. She waited for Mrs. Saunders to acknowledge her. The woman wasn't her put-together self this morning. A tight bun contained hair that was usually coiffed and stylish. She wore no makeup or jewelry, and the harsh hairstyle accentuated the lines around her eyes and mouth. Wrinkles marred her lime green pantsuit.

Mrs. Saunders quit reading her computer screen and glanced at Lauri. "Sit down, Ms. Matthews." Lauri sat with her notepad in her lap and her pen ready. Mrs. Saunders shook her head. "You won't need that. I want you to run an errand for me before you leave for the day."

"An errand?" She prayed she wouldn't be asked to go get lunch or buy a shower gift. She'd hoped to have a real job learning more about accounting, not be a glorified gofer.

"What can I do for you?"

Mrs. Saunders reached under her desk and lifted a briefcase into view. "I need you to deliver this."

Lauri wanted to ask what was in it, but the closed expression on her boss's face warned her not to ask too many questions. "Where am I to take it?"

"A man is waiting for it at the library. He'll be wearing a Red Sox cap. Simply walk up to him and give it to him. His name is Bill Jones." She shook her head. "He's on a tight time schedule today. I know this is outside your normal duties, and I'll make sure you don't turn into a delivery girl. This kind of thing doesn't happen often. Call me when you've done it."

Lauri grasped the handle of the briefcase. Heavy. What was in it? She tried not to imagine the worst: drugs, guns, papers for industrial espionage. Kade would tell her to squelch that vivid imagination, but the older woman's furtive behavior had Lauri's mental antenna at full alert.

She grabbed her coat from her office and hurried to her car with the briefcase. The Portage Lake District Library was on Huron Street. Lauri navigated the icy roads and parked in the lot before slipping and sliding her way to the building. The briefcase grew heavier with every step, maybe because her reluctance weighed it down.

The worker behind the circulation desk smiled at her, and she returned it automatically as she scanned the library for patrons. At eleven thirty in the morning, only a few people browsed the shelves. She knew the man wouldn't be in the children's section, so she headed for the adult fiction.

Then she saw him. Seated at a table, he held an open book in front of him. The bill of the Red Sox cap shaded his face since he was staring down at the book. When she approached, he glanced up, and she realized it was the same man she'd overheard talking to her boss's husband. He gave her the creeps, but she had a job to do. "Mr. Jones?" she asked when she was a few feet away.

He nodded and his gaze never left the briefcase she carried as she walked to the table. He rose when she stopped and held out his hand. "I think that's for me."

Lauri's grip tightened on the case. If he hadn't smirked, she would have passed it over without a word. "What's in here?"

"None of your business." His fingers closed over hers. "What's your name?"

"Lauri. Lauri Matthews."

"Any relation to Kade Matthews?" He held on to her hand.

"My brother. You know him?"

"Not personally."

The touch of his hand made her shudder, and she let go. It

wasn't her concern, she told herself, bolting for her car. She was just doing her job.

Driving away from the library, she decided to swing by her apartment and eat an early lunch before class instead of buying something. When she parked on the street in front of her apartment, Lauri saw Wes's car. She climbed the outside steps to her apartment, wishing for the umpteenth time she could afford one that had an inside hallway. And maybe she could soon.

As she approached her door, she heard the pulse of rock music. A smile stretched across her face. His presence always did that to her. She hurried the last few feet and turned the knob to her apartment. He never locked it behind him. Zorro met her at the door and she put her hand on his head, so he didn't bark.

The pulsing beat of his Kenny Chesney CD pounded through her veins. It was so loud he hadn't noticed her arrival. Her lips curved as she watched the man she loved. Lauri enjoyed watching him when he thought he was alone. He bobbed and weaved in a jerky dance on her scarred wooden floors. She thought maybe he was trying an old Michael Jackson move, but on Wes's frame, the jerks were weird.

She put a gloved hand over her mouth to stifle her giggle. Careful to keep her expression nonchalant, Lauri moved into his eyesight and waved. Wes stopped what he was doing, and the grin that always stole her breath appeared. The love she felt for him always took her by surprise, and she wasn't sure when it had first happened.

He met her before she'd taken five steps and swept her into his arms. She burrowed against him, relishing his warmth. His lips brushed hers, and she closed her eyes. He drew away and led her to the sofa.

"Did you tell her yet?" Lauri asked. She knew the answer when his smile faltered and a shadow darkened his hazel eyes. "Oh Wes, you promised."

He glanced away from her gaze. "I tried, Lauri, really. But I hate to hurt her. I'll be disappointing our parents as well as Maura."

They'd been over this time and again. He was such a—a *guy*. "The longer you wait, the harder it will be for her to stop all the wedding plans. You don't want her buying a lot of stuff for something that isn't going to happen."

"I know, I know. I'll tell her soon."

Yeah right. How many times had he told her that? For six long months, ever since Wes first told her he loved her, he'd been saying he'd break it off with Maura. Tears burned Lauri's eyes, but she wasn't going to let him see. She wanted to believe him, but it was getting harder and harder every day.

"I don't want to force you into doing something you don't want to do."

He pressed his lips against her hair. "It's not that. I want to be with you, but I have to choose the right time. If I do this wrong, Dad will cut me off, and how will I even support you? I'd like to start my own outfitters but it takes money—preferably Dad's."

At first she'd had cozy visions of setting up a small house with Wes with the two of them always together. But he was a man's man. Into sports, hunting, fishing. He was happiest when he was in the wilderness. How could she even ask him to change his life so drastically by settling down with her?

She'd messed up her life so badly. Ever since her parents died, she'd made one mistake after another. Wes was the best thing that had ever happened to her, and she didn't want to ruin this relationship too. Her dream of a new car vanished. She'd start giving money to Wes. Eventually it would be enough for him to break free from his father. He could buy the equipment for his outfitting business and make a name for himself. She wouldn't be under her brother's eagle eye anymore and could have a real life with Wes.

The thought of Kade made her wonder if she could talk her brother into a loan.

Watching Wes, she knew he'd had no intention of breaking away from his dad or Maura without another plan in place. Wes was a pragmatist. He'd always known where he wanted to go. There had to be a way to accomplish their dreams.

She thought of Zoe, her daughter. Mason and Hilary adored that little girl. Every time Lauri saw her—and she tried to make sure it didn't happen often because it hurt too much—she knew she'd done the right thing to give Zoe up for adoption, but the sacrifice had made her long for a family of her own. A good man, another baby—one she could keep this time. But first Wes had to break it off with his fiancée and make their relationship a priority.

It would be up to her to figure out a way to make her dreams happen.

Her cell phone chirped in her purse, and she turned away from Wes's pleading face to dig it out. The generic ringtone told her it was someone who didn't know her, but she glanced at the screen anyway. Her boss's cell phone number flashed across the screen.

"Hello, Mrs. Saunders." She turned her back to Wes's questioning expression.

"How—how did the meeting go?" Mrs. Saunders asked. "I wanted to catch you before class."

"What meeting do you mean?" Lauri tried to think if she'd forgotten a meeting for today.

"The delivery you made for me."

"Fine. I did what you asked."

"Did he say anything?"

"No. He just took the briefcase."

"Strange. He still hasn't . . ."

Lauri wasn't following any of this. "Hasn't what?"

"Never mind. I'll have to wait. I must call Mike." The phone went dead.

Lauri hung up. "That woman has been so weird," she said.

Wes reared away from the sofa. "Who was that?"

"My boss." She told him about the errand she had run and what Mrs. Saunders had said.

Wes pulled at his chin. "You think she's running drugs or something?"

Lauri shook her head. "Not Mrs. Saunders. But she's been really upset since I met her yesterday. I don't know what it's all about."

"What's her husband do?"

"I don't know. I never asked."

He flipped open his laptop and called up the browser. Lauri watched him type in the name. She leaned closer when the results came up. "Her husband is Mike Saunders. He owns Kitchigami Mining Corporation." She vaguely remembered hearing of it.

"I wonder if the briefcase had something to do with him. Maybe he's about to go bankrupt or something."

"That doesn't explain what I delivered."

"Maybe it was a payoff or a kickback to let him open a new mine somewhere."

"You've got a wild imagination." She shrugged, her interest waning. "I think I'll heat up some beef pasties for lunch." She leaned into his embrace. He smelled of wood chips and snow. And he was hers.

"Sounds great. Don't forget the ketchup."

"I won't. You want anything else?"

"A Dr Pepper. I have to be at Mom's in fifteen minutes so better hurry."

"What? I've got two hours before class."

"She needed me to help Dad move the living-room furniture around. She's got a euchre club meeting tomorrow."

Why did his mother's stupid meeting come before her? Lauri stormed off to the kitchen. Maybe it would always be this way. Ever since she'd met Wes, it seemed he put his family and everyone else first. She should insist on meeting his family. They were going to have to know about her sooner or later. If she left Wes to his own devices, she'd be eighty before he married her.

8

THE CHILDREN'S PROTECTIVE SERVICES EMPLOYEE HAD already come and gone this afternoon. With the baby sleeping in the carrier by her feet and Davy playing beside them both with a fire truck, Bree launched the Web browser on the computer and typed in another search for missing babies in the UP, Michigan, or Wisconsin. No new Amber alerts had been posted since she'd first searched over the weekend, only the ones she knew about for the reservation babies. She clicked to the next page and found an article about a woman who had been stolen from a reservation and was being reunited with her birth parents. Old news.

"Nothing," she told Samson, who stood guard over the baby. Her gaze lingered on the infant's face. "Who are you, little girl?" she asked softly.

The doorbell pealed out its Elvis tune, and she rose to answer it. She left the baby sleeping, but Samson padded after her. "Come with me," she told Davy.

He made a face. "Aw, Mom. No one is going to grab me in the hallway. Besides, I need to look after her."

They were on the second floor of the lighthouse, and the doors were locked. "Okay," she said, touching his hair. "Take good care of the baby." She jogged down the steps as the doorbell song restarted. "Coming," she called.

Through the window in the door, she saw a woman standing

on the porch. Blonde, about twenty-five, maybe a little older. Beautiful bone structure and dressed in a stylish coat with a red beret perched on her head. Even from here, the outerwear looked expensive.

Bree pulled the door open. "Can I help you?"

The woman clasped her hands together and focused tear-filled blue eyes on her. "I'm Victor Pelton's sister, Jenna. I'm here to try to clear him, and I'd heard you were a friend of his. I need your help."

"I was sorry to hear about Victor. Come in." Bree stepped back to allow the woman to enter.

"I don't suppose I could use your bathroom?"

"Sure." Bree shut the door and locked it. "It's this way."

The woman's high-heeled leather boots clicked across the oak floor, but she stopped when Samson nosed at her hand and whined. "Gorgeous dog," she said, rubbing his ears.

"His name is Samson. He's a search dog."

"I've heard of him."

Bree showed her to the powder room, then checked on Davy and the baby before going back to the hall to wait on Jenna. The woman was very different from her brother. She'd be more at home in New York than a small town in the UP.

The powder-room door opened. Jenna had removed her hat and coat, and her blonde hair curled around her shoulders. She wore impeccably pressed gray trousers and a pink blouse under a tailored jacket. "Thanks for seeing me. I just got to town."

Jenna followed Bree into the living room, where flames leaped in the fireplace. Samson followed close on Bree's heels. "Sit down," Bree said, indicating the chair by the fire.

"The fire is lovely." She sniffed. "Your candle smells wonderful." Jenna sank into the chair and crossed her legs.

"How can I help you?" Bree asked.

"Did you see anything that might help me clear my brother?" Jenna asked.

Bree hated to disillusion the woman. "I'm afraid not. I actually saw him with the bloody shovel in his hand."

"He probably found it and picked it up," Jenna said.

"I thought it likely."

Bree noticed her staring at the pictures. "That's Davy, my son."

"Cute kid." Jenna turned away.

Bree heard a faint cry. "Just a moment." She ran up the stairs. Davy was talking to the infant, showing her the pieces of his puzzle. The baby's blue eyes stayed fastened on his face. Smiling, Bree lifted the baby from the carrier. Glancing at her watch, she saw the girl couldn't possibly be hungry. She checked the diaper. Dry. "Faker," she scolded, carrying the child back to the living room.

"Oh, such a darling baby," Jenna said when Bree stepped back into the living room. "How old is she?"

"We're not really sure. Less than two weeks," Bree said. She told Jenna about finding Pia's body and the baby in the woods. "One of Victor's sudokus was in her bag."

Jenna bit her lip. "So you're saying Victor might have had something to do with that woman's death too?" She rubbed her forehead. "Oh, what am I going to do?"

Poor woman. Bree reached over and took her hand. "Sheriff Kaleva will sort it out. He has to follow the leads, but he's smart and intuitive. He'll find whoever is behind the murder."

Jenna clung to her hand. "Thank you," she whispered. "I didn't know where to turn."

"Where are you staying?" Bree asked. The woman's vulnerability touched her.

"I-I don't know. I tried the hotel downtown, but it's full."

"The festival is this weekend. It's always sold out early with vendors hitting town to get stuff set up." The Blue Bonnet Bed-and-

Breakfast next door was closed while Martha was out of town. There was nowhere else to recommend. "You're welcome to stay here. I've got a guest room with your name on it." It might not be up to Jenna's city standards, but it was clean.

"I wouldn't want to be a bother to you or your husband. Are you sure he won't mind?"

"I'm sure. Mason will have this squared away in a few days. You'll see."

The baby whimpered, and Bree rocked her a bit. Mason would be busy investigating the murders, but she was determined to find this little one's family.

Kade stopped the snowmobile and consulted his map. The report of the screaming last night had been just over the next hill. Any evidence he could find of cougars here would bolster the chances for the grant. If he could find a den, he'd have proof of a breeding population. His goal was to get a picture of cubs.

Driving forward slowly, he scanned the ground for evidence like tracks or scat, but all he spotted were fox tracks. Until he started down the slope. At the base of a large maple tree, he saw a pile of droppings. Dismounting his sled, he knelt and examined the excrement. His excitement rose when he realized it belonged to a big cat. It might be that of a lynx, but he couldn't help the surge of hope. Grabbing a plastic bag from his snowmobile, he collected the scat and started deeper into the forest.

Snow pillowed bare branches. The sound of the sled's engine hit the trees, then bounced back louder to his ears. The frigid air burned his lungs, but Kade pressed on. The roar of the motor gradually subsided to another growl. He rounded a boulder and saw two men cutting up fallen trees. Their chainsaws blatted and belched smoke.

He cut his sled's engine and dismounted. The closest man,

bearded and swathed in red and black plaid, glanced up. The sound of his saw stopped. He jabbed the other man, whose stringy blond hair hung out from under a duck hunter's hat. The sudden silence when the blond guy shut off his saw threw an eerie quality over the clearing.

"Howdy," the bearded man said. He eyed Kade's park service patch.

"You have a permit to cut here?" Kade asked. He knew the answer. Permits for firewood were only issued after April 1.

The bearded guy tightened his grip on the chainsaw. "These trees are downed."

"Doesn't matter. You need a permit to cut."

"Look, ranger, I got four kids at home and heat the place solely with firewood. I'm just a family man trying to do the best I can. Can't you help me out?"

Judging by the rusty pickup on the fire trail, Kade didn't doubt him, but the law wasn't his to change. "I have to cite you," he said, pulling out his pad. "I'm sorry."

The men moved closer together. The blond guy clenched his fists, and the bearded man held out his hand and smiled. "I know you. You're Kade Matthews. You're the guy looking for cougars. If I tell you where to find a litter of kittens, will you let me off this time?"

Kade's senses went on full alert. "You've seen cougars?"

The man's expression turned crafty. "Maybe I have and maybe I haven't."

The firewood was unimportant. "Load up whatever wood your truck will hold. Where did you see cougar kittens?"

"We got your word?"

"Yes. No citation. Tell me where you saw them. How many? What all did you see?"

"You know Kitchigami Crag?"

Kade nodded. "How'd you shimmy up there in the winter?" It would take a mountain goat to scale that trail. The howling wind scoured the path, only a foot wide in some of the worst spots.

"I wore crampons and took an ice pick. I've done it plenty of times."

Kade studied his face. There was a valley on the other side of the crag where elk roamed. If the guy was poaching, Kade would bust him, information or not.

"It's not what you think. I climb for sport," the guy protested. "I'm not a hunter."

Kade chose to believe him, though he wondered if the decision would come back to haunt him. "Go on."

"On the backside of the crag, there's a small cave. A big boulder overhangs it and it's hard to find. In this heavy snow, you may have trouble, but it's there. That's where I saw the kittens. Two days ago."

"How many?"

"Four. Cute as all get-out with their blue eyes. I wanted to pick one up, but I figured mama would come flying out of nowhere so I skedaddled."

It would take Kade an hour to get up there. He'd be crazy to try it in this wind. He warned the men not to steal firewood again and headed home.

The events of the past few days plus the baby's soft noises from the bassinet kept Bree from sleeping. Kade snored, but Bree lay with her eyes wide and unblinking in the dark. She'd wanted Davy to sleep with them tonight, but Kade convinced her that Samson would protect the boy. Keeping to a regular routine was healthier for their son too.

She'd checked on Davy before she turned out the lights, and

her son had his arms around the dog. Samson was on his back with all four paws in the air.

A creak came from the hall. Was someone in the house? She leaped from the bed and rushed to the door. Silence. Tiptoeing down the hall, she peeked into Davy's room. Samson still lay sprawled and intertwined with her boy. The dog opened his eyes, looked at her, then closed them again. He would be alert if there were any danger.

She was overreacting. Again.

The glint of moonlight on snow illuminated Davy's room a bit. A picture of a much younger Davy with Rob was on the bed-stand. A glow highlighted Rob's face, and Bree's gaze skirted it. She stepped closer to the window and looked out. The moon gilded the snow and ice with crystals of light. It was beautiful yet terrible, and she was thankful to be inside where it was warm.

Her gaze lingered on the window. It was unlocked. Unease rippled up her spine as she locked it. Not that anyone could get up here very easily without a ladder.

She heard a noise behind her and turned to see Samson jump from the bed. He came to her side and nudged her hand so she would pet him. Spoiled thing. She started to rub his ears when she heard a low rumble from his throat. He put his front paws on the window and stared down into the yard.

"What is it, boy?" she whispered, her back prickling. "What do you see?"

His tail was wagging, yet he was growling as well, which was odd. Either he was alarmed or he wasn't. She strained to see what or who was in the yard but all appeared calm.

Samson dropped his paws from the window, then went to the door. He turned to see if she was coming, and when she moved toward him, he vanished on down the hall. His toenails clicked on the hardwood steps.

Following Samson's lead, she went down the stairs in bare feet. The house seemed to sleep as well. Nothing stirred on the first floor. She heard the clock on the mantel ticking, the thump of the furnace kicking on, but nothing that put her senses on red alert.

Samson went to the back door and whined. Her hand touched the lock, and she realized the dead bolt wasn't thrown, yet she'd locked it herself before coming to bed. Leaving the light off, Bree peered through the curtains and saw a movement. She gasped and stepped back, then forced herself to look again.

Jenna. Relief coursed through her. What was she doing outside in the middle of the night? No wonder Samson was confused. He didn't know the young woman well, but even he knew her foray into the night wasn't normal.

Bree flipped on the outside light and opened the door. "Jenna?"

The woman whirled. Her coat was over her nightgown and her feet were in slippers. Her eyes went wide. "Bree, you scared me."

"What are you doing out here?" Bree squinted.

"Ju-just getting some air."

Was that a figure in the shadow of the garage? Samson pressed his nose against the door as though he wanted to go out. Bree opened the door, and the dog dashed from the house. He stopped long enough to nose at Jenna's feet, then moved toward the garage.

Jenna caught his collar. "Let's go back inside, boy. It's cold out here." She glanced behind her.

"Who's there?" Bree called.

"Just me," Jenna said, dragging Samson with her toward the door. The dog kept whining and struggling to get away. His tail was going fast enough to cool Bree's cheeks. He must know the person.

Bree peered toward the shadows. She could have sworn she saw a movement.

Jenna pulled Samson inside with her. "We're letting out all the heat."

Bree gave a final sharp look toward the garage but didn't see anything out of the ordinary. She reluctantly stepped back. Samson managed to escape Jenna, and Bree grabbed him. "Oh no you don't." She shut the door before he could wiggle through.

Ignoring his reproachful gaze, she turned him loose. "Go watch Davy."

With a last hurt glance, he left the room with his tail hanging low. She turned and studied Jenna's face. The other woman was pale, and her gaze avoided Bree's.

"Are you okay?" Bree asked.

"I'm fine. Just upset about my brother. I thought the air might clear my head. I need to figure out how to help Victor."

"Who was the guy by the garage?"

Jenna's eyes grew wide. "What guy?" Her voice trembled.

"I know someone was out there. Samson was eager to go see whoever it was, and I saw his shadow." She didn't know how she knew the person had been a man, but she was confident.

Pink crept into Jenna's cheeks. She scuffed the toe of her slipper. "It's a guy I'm seeing," she admitted. "He heard about Victor's arrest and wanted to make sure I was all right."

Bree wanted to believe her, but so many strange things had been happening. "You could have invited him in."

"We didn't want to awaken anyone. Guess we did anyway, huh?"

"I wasn't sleeping."

Jenna must have heard the stress in Bree's voice. Her gaze lingered on Bree's face. "I guess you don't ever get used to finding a dead body."

"No, you don't. That poor woman was so young." In her mind's eye Bree saw Pia's face. She'd been pretty, vibrant.

"So is Victor. And his life is going to be ruined." Jenna's voice broke.

Poor girl. Bree hugged her. "We love Victor. You know I'll do whatever I can to help him."

Jenna's hug was stiff as though she wasn't used to being touched. "Thanks." She stepped away.

Bree stretched and yawned. The clock on the mantel read nearly eleven thirty. "We both need to get some sleep."

"Right." Jenna headed toward the stairs.

Bree followed until Jenna turned left to the room where Lauri usually stayed, then she peeked in on Davy. He was still asleep and Samson had settled down. She tiptoed back to her room. The baby was asleep too.

Kade rolled over when she sat on the edge of the bed. "What's wrong?"

"Nothing. I just couldn't sleep." She slipped under the covers and moved closer to Kade. He'd already turned his back to her. He gave off a welcome warmth, and she flung her arm around him and curled against him, spoon fashion. To his credit, he didn't stiffen, but she could sense him waiting to see if she would say anything.

"I'm sorry I overreacted last night, Kade." There, that wasn't so hard, was it? With the apology over, the last of her tension melted. She buried her face in his back and let his warmth ease the cramps from her legs.

"You were right, babe. I should have called you."

Though his words were right, he still didn't roll over and take her in his arms. A few moments later, she heard him begin to breathe slower and easier. He was asleep and he hadn't even kissed her.

9

THE CABIN WAS AT THE END OF A LOGGING TRAIL THAT was impassable except by four-wheel drive. Wednesday afternoon, Quinn parked the big truck, a white one he'd rented while he left his black one parked. "Home sweet home," he said to Jenna.

She sat huddled in her fur coat. "Why'd you have to get such a remote place?" she asked. "This is totally in the boonies, Quinn. Why did you have to come all the way out here?"

"I don't want anyone seeing us together, especially now that you've gotten into the Matthews house and have access to the baby." He climbed down from the truck and went to the cabin. She followed. He clicked the latch and stepped inside. The fire he'd built before leaving sputtered, but just barely, in the fireplace. The chill had begun to take over the room. He stepped to the hearth and threw some more logs on, poking them until they caught the blaze.

Jenna shut the door and sat on the rocker. She grabbed a throw from the back of the chair and curled up under it. "It's freezing in here!"

"It will be warm soon." He took off his coat and sat on the sofa. "What have you found out so far?"

"Nothing much. Bree has the baby. She's looking for the parents."

"What about Bree and her family?"

She shrugged. "Typical small-town folks. She's all wrapped up in her family. And the dog. He's a pretty cool dog. He found the baby, did you know that?"

He hadn't heard that news, but he wasn't surprised. "They have a kid, right? Davy?"

"He doesn't like to be called Davy. He likes Dave or David." She yawned, then smiled. "Hey, you didn't tell me Bree's husband was such a hunk. He's a really great guy. Strong, caring, a good dad. She's lucky to have him."

Was that emotion welling in his throat *jealousy*? Surely not. He'd murdered too much of his own past to feel anything when confronted with it. He grunted and didn't answer.

"I really need to get a manicure," she said, studying her nails. "So what's the plan?"

"Nothing for a few days." Not until the baby's father did what he was told. And Bree caring for the baby solved the problem of what to do with the infant until her parents complied with his demands. The bigger issue was Davy Matthews. The ranger was working on adopting Davy, and Quinn found himself resistant to the idea. While adoption made sense, Quinn decided he couldn't let it happen.

With Jenna on the inside, he'd grab both kids when the time was right.

⁂

Kade and his boss rode snowmobiles off-trail through the forest. The snow buried fallen logs that would have blocked their passage through the trees. The men shut off their machines and dismounted near Kitchigami Crag. Kade put on snowshoes, then made his way along the base of the cliff, where he peered at the ground and into every nook and cranny.

Landorf tromped up behind him. "See anything?"

"Nope." The wind had swept the area, and the only tracks he saw were those of a couple of rabbits. Then his gaze caught a red tinge on the snow. "What's that?" He made his way toward the stand of sycamore trees, where he found the body of a rabbit. All that remained were fur and feet. A cougar? He studied the mussed up snow for a clear print.

His boss joined him. "A cat?" His voice was eager.

Kade caught sight of the footprints and tried to keep the disappointment from his voice. "Wolf." Once upon a time, he would have been excited to find wolf prints here, but he now knew of several wolf packs roaming the area. In 1989, gray wolves had been verified to be living again in the UP. But a glimpse of a timber wolf was still a thrill.

It was not the thrill he sought. His gaze scanned the area. "It's a good habitat for cats though. The men might be right."

"Eagles too," Landorf said, pointing to the tall crags. "I bet there are nests up there."

Kade gazed at the terrain. "This is near where the new mining operation is scheduled to begin. Cubs won't have a chance when that gets underway come spring."

"Don't remind me. The eagles and our other birds will have problems, too, with the pollution."

Kade glanced around at the trees glistening with ice and snow. "Let's get up this cliff and see what we find."

He kicked snow over the remains of the rabbit, then started toward the path. Landorf followed close behind. They'd only moved ten feet or so when a movement caught his eye from above. He squinted against the glare of sunshine on snow. A guy in a black puffy coat and a red ski mask stood atop the promontory. It took a second for the guy's attire to hit Kade's awareness. The guy who tried to grab Dave was dressed like that.

"Hey!" Kade yelled. "I want to talk to you." Too late he realized he should have tempered his tone.

The man leaped away from the edge, but Kade knew this forest. The only way up or down from there was via a long trail on the north side of the rock face. He ran for the trail.

"What's going on?" Landorf shouted.

"It's that guy—the one who tried to grab my son!" This man had tried to hurt their boy, and Kade wanted to put an end to the danger. The trail up Kitchigami Crag was just ahead. He spared a glance up the path to the top. No one there.

Kade huffed from the ten pounds he'd gained over the winter and paused to catch his breath. He reached the base of the narrow trail. Where was the guy? Kade expected to see him come hurtling down the icy path any minute. He glanced back the way he'd come and saw Landorf following him. When he saw he had Kade's attention, Landorf waved him back.

Kade wanted to ignore the summons, but he retreated five feet. It wasn't like the guy could get away. There was no way off that ledge unless the man had wings.

Landorf glanced at his watch. "Are you sure it was the same man? We've got that meeting in an hour."

"This'll only take a minute." Kade turned and stared up the deserted path. Could the guy have reached the bottom of the trail on foot before Kade got there? It didn't seem possible. He walked along the base of the cliff. No way down these jagged rocks. Something blue caught his gaze over the sheerest rock face. He stepped closer and saw a rappelling rope dangling from tree roots from above.

"Well, I'll be," he said. The guy must know this area well. "He was here." Kade pointed to the rope. "He escaped that way."

Landorf frowned. "Maybe he was just out here climbing. He scaled the rock face, then went back down."

Landorf might be right, but Kade's gut said otherwise. If the guy were out on an innocent rock climb, he would have waited to talk. And his clothing alone raised Kade's suspicions.

Landorf checked his watch again, then jerked his head back toward the trail. "Let's go."

Kade followed Landorf to the snowmobiles. The men got on their sleds and headed back to headquarters. As they neared the trail that ran beside the highway, Kade glanced to his right. There was the black truck, and a man at the wheel. Unable to let Landorf know, Kade followed his gut. He veered into the road and blocked the truck's path.

From what Kade could see, the man's eyes behind the windshield widened. He stepped on the brakes, and the truck fishtailed on the snow-covered pavement. Kade tensed as the truck veered closer. It was stupid to sit here where he might be struck, but if he got out of the way, the man would flee. Kade held his breath.

The sun glinted off the windshield and obscured the man's face. Kade could smell the hot vapors off the truck engine. Then the truck rocketed toward the ditch. Everything moved in slow motion. The studded tires spit up gravel, and the bumper plowed through the high drifts of dirty snow before coming to a stop with steam spilling from under the hood.

The guy jumped out. "Are you crazy?" he demanded.

Kade looked him over. Black hair. Brown eyes. It was a different guy. He was so in trouble.

Davy was gone for a visit with Anu. Though Bree knew Anu would watch the boy closely, she was nervous about being away from him. The baby had cried most of the morning, and Bree couldn't find a cause. She got the infant settled down, then saw Mason's SUV stop outside. She met him at the door. "Come on in," she asked, stepping aside to let him into the warm lighthouse. "I've got fresh coffee."

"I'll take some." He patted Samson on the head, then followed her to the kitchen, where she poured him a cup, then to the living room, where he dropped onto the sofa in front of the fire.

"Any news about the murders? Or about the baby's parents?" she asked, unable to stand the suspense. Before he answered, she heard the front door open and Jenna's voice call out.

The young woman entered the living room. She dropped onto the sofa beside Mason. "I hope you're here looking for me. Are you releasing Victor?"

Mason shook his head. "I'm afraid not. We've found evidence tying him to the Westola scene too."

"It was murder?" Bree asked. "You got the results back from the autopsy?"

"It was inconclusive," the sheriff said.

"What evidence?" Jenna demanded. "I know he's innocent."

"One of his puzzles was at the Westola scene," Mason said. "And we found his tennis-shoe tracks near the body."

Jenna sank back against the sofa. Her lips trembled.

The baby began to fuss. Her cries grew more powerful as Bree tried to comfort her. Samson whined and danced around her. "The baby is proof Pia's death wasn't an accident. If there was no danger, Pia wouldn't have hidden her," Bree said. The baby found her thumb and settled down again. Samson lay on the floor watching.

Mason pressed his lips together, then gave a reluctant nod. "I agree. What I'm saying is the coroner found no sign of foul play. Pia could have fallen on that jagged limb. But there were bigger footprints around her body. It looks suspicious."

Bree winced at the reminder. She jiggled the infant up and down. "So what's next?" Bree asked.

"I'm keeping the investigation open-ended as to the cause of death. I'll investigate it like a murder." Mason glanced at the baby. "CPS been here?"

Bree nodded. "I jumped through their hoops so I have her for now. I'm going to call her Olivia since I found her under an olive tree." But she wasn't about to tell them the idea to adopt the baby had already sprouted. She could only hope and pray Kade had the same idea.

"I'd like to get a copy of all the sudokus Victor has given out," she said.

Mason put down his coffee cup. "What good will that do?"

"Don't you want her to clear my brother?" Jenna burst out.

Mason glanced at her, then back to Bree with a question in his eyes.

"I want to compare them with the copy I found in Olivia's backpack," Bree said. "I think Victor is trying to tell us something."

Mason shrugged. He pulled out his cell phone and punched in a number. "Margaret, would you fax a copy of the sudoku evidence we have on the Pelton and Hawkins cases to Bree Matthews?" He talked to the clerk a few more moments, then put his phone away. "She's faxing it over. Don't investigate anything without me."

"I won't. I just want to do some research online." She glanced at the baby. "What about Olivia?"

"No reports of missing babies other than the two from the res. But I did find something interesting. A pregnant woman over in Ontonagon has disappeared. Ellie Bristol."

"Disappeared? Do you know if she delivered? Or when she was due?"

"She was due about two weeks ago and disappeared about that time. Her mother reported her missing when she didn't come home from a doctor's visit."

Bree glanced again at the baby. "Do you have a photo of her?"

"Yeah. Stop by the office."

"Wa-was she blonde?" Bree hoped he'd say she was swarthy with black hair, and the realization that she really didn't want to have to hand over the baby shocked her.

"Light brown hair, blue eyes. About twenty-five."

"Have you talked with her mother?"

Mason nodded. "The mom says she was giving the baby up for adoption, but she doesn't know who was making the arrangements. It was a private adoption."

"Sounds fishy to me. Wouldn't a mother know what her daughter was doing?"

"I wondered about that," Mason said. "I ran a check on Mrs. Bristol, but she came up clean. When I talked to her, she said her daughter wasn't one to confide in her."

"What if we take Olivia over and see if she'll tell us anything more?"

"That's really why I came by," Mason said. He glanced at the clock over the mantel. "There's enough time to run down to Ontonagon and still be back by suppertime. You game?"

"Of course, but I'd like to run by Anu's and just make sure everything is okay."

"No problem. I talked to my deputy an hour ago. He's keeping an eye on the store. Everything's quiet."

"I'd just feel better if I checked."

He nodded and rose. "We go right by there anyway."

"I think I'll stay here," Jenna said. "It's cozy by the fire. And Kade will be home in an hour."

Bree disliked the self-satisfied expression on the young woman's face. She wanted to ask how she knew Kade's schedule, but she didn't want to sound like a jealous shrew—though she could feel her claws starting to come out. She nodded and said nothing.

Mason stopped in town long enough for her to run in and

check on Davy. He didn't see her as he munched on some of his grandmother's famous *pulla*. Her worry eased, Bree hurried back to Mason's SUV. Olivia's cries were escalating when she reached the vehicle. Samson barked when she got in the back with the baby. She popped a bottle into Olivia's mouth.

Neither she nor Mason had much to say on the drive. He turned into a mobile home park, then stopped in front of a dented home that looked at least twenty years old. The steps to the front door sagged, and one shutter on the front window hung by one screw.

Bree unclasped the belt and retrieved Olivia's carrier. The baby had fallen asleep. Samson leaped out to follow her to the mobile home.

Mason led the way to the door. "Careful," he said, pointing to a broken board on the step.

She avoided the weak spot and tried to shield the baby as much as possible from the wind. Mason's knock was answered almost immediately by a woman in her forties. A rubber band held back dull brown hair streaked with gray. She wore jeans and a plaid shirt, wrinkled so badly she must have slept in it.

Her gaze locked on Mason's face. "You've found Ellie?"

"No, Mrs. Bristol, I'm sorry." He introduced Bree and Samson, but her gaze dismissed them.

Until Olivia made a squawk. "Is that a baby?" She stepped away from the door. "Come in."

Bree followed Mason inside. The interior was neat with a threadbare brown carpet and worn sofa. Photos of a young woman decorated the coffee table. The tousled brown hair and bright smile brought a lump to Bree's throat. "Is this Ellie?" she asked.

"Yes. She's my only child. Raised her on my own when her daddy decided he wasn't cut out to be a father. She's always been a good girl. It was the biggest shock of my life when she got into trouble." Samson nosed at her hand, and she rubbed his ears, her shoulders relaxing. "Nice dog you've got here."

"Yes, he is." Samson had that way with people. Bree hoped he brought some comfort to the woman. Uncovering the carrier, Bree lifted Olivia in her arms, waking her. "This baby was found in the woods. We've had no success in finding her family. I wondered if she might be Ellie's baby."

Mrs. Bristol came closer, then knelt by Olivia. She stared at the baby. Olivia's blue eyes locked on to the woman's face. Mrs. Bristol touched her hair. The reserved expression on her face vanished. "She doesn't look like Ellie." Her voice held doubt. "She's got light hair and blue eyes. Ellie had greenish-blue eyes. But it's possible she's Ellie's. I wouldn't want to say it's impossible." But her voice held doubt.

"I'd like to get a DNA sample," Mason said. "Maybe some hair from Ellie's hairbrush."

Mrs. Bristol scowled. "If you're planning on foisting her off on me, don't go there. I barely have enough money to feed myself, let alone a baby. I don't have the energy to care for a baby anymore. My job at the diner takes all my time. When Ellie told me she was pregnant, I told her in no uncertain terms how it would have to be."

"So Ellie was okay with that decision?" Bree asked. She watched the woman wind her arm around Samson's neck.

"She wanted to go to college, and I had no money to send her. When she found out the adoptive parents would give her so much money, it seemed they were heaven-sent."

Bree nearly gasped. "You-you mean she *sold* her baby?"

The woman's relaxed manner vanished. She dropped her hand from Samson and straightened. "It wasn't like that. The people are well-off and wanted to show their gratitude to Ellie by paying for her college and living expenses."

"How much money did they pay her?" Bree didn't think the woman would say.

Mrs. Bristol's gaze darted from Bree to Mason. She bit her lip. "I have to say, don't I? It was forty thousand dollars."

"Did she get the money before the baby was born?"

"Part of it. Twenty thousand, I think. Some guy brought it over. He was a bit off. All he wanted to do was talk about sudoku."

Bree's gaze locked with Mason's. *Victor.*

"How did she hear about this couple?" Mason asked.

"A woman in Rock Harbor. Older woman with dyed red hair. She drove a bright yellow convertible."

Could she be talking about Florence Hawkins? Bree struggled to make sense of it all. Was fun, helpful Florence involved in some kind of black market adoptions? Could this be at the root of her death?

10

Rock Harbor bustled with activity on this sunny Saturday morning. The winter festival was the highlight of the cold months. It marked the halfway point until spring vegetation would come bursting through last year's dead leaves. Bree didn't mind winter though. There was always something to do, and frozen Lake Superior was otherworldly.

Davy kept looking in the bed of the truck behind them. "I've got the best outhouse ever, Mom. Me and Timmy are going to win." He leaned over and spoke to the baby. "Are you going to root for me, Olivia?"

"I'm sure you'll win," Bree said, glancing into the backseat of the truck at her son and Olivia.

Kade had the outhouse strapped down to the bed. The skis they'd mounted it on used to be her favorite cross-country skis, but Kade had promised her a new pair. They'd painted it a bright red. Across the top of the door in blue paint, Davy had written MATTHEWS PRIDE. Samson rode in the back beside it and wore a smug expression.

Kade's adoption of Dave wasn't final yet, but the boy couldn't wait to announce to the world that his name was Dave Matthews and had been calling himself by that name since school started.

Olivia fussed a bit, but the infant's eyes were still closed. Davy guided her hand to her mouth, and she settled her fist there and quieted. Davy's grin held triumph.

"You're really good with her," Bree said.

"She's cool," Davy said, watching her.

Kade parked by the open snowy field where other children gathered with their families. Bree saw outhouses painted every shade of the rainbow lining up along Main Street, which was closed to through traffic today. One particularly handsome one boasted a black-and-white checkerboard design.

"Let's go, let's go," Davy chanted, bouncing up and down on the seat.

"Hold your horses," Kade said, laughing. He pulled up his collar and jerked the flaps on his hat down over his ears and got out, then unlatched the back door. Davy leaped from the truck and ran around the back.

Bree climbed into the back, then tucked the cover around Olivia and climbed out with the infant. She recognized Kade's boss, Gary Landorf, who wore a judge's badge. He'd gone a little grayer since the last time she'd seen him.

Gary noticed her and moved in her direction. Kade stiffened at his boss's approach, and Bree glanced up at him, but he said nothing.

"I might as well check you in," Gary said. "The outhouse meets all the specs?"

"Yes," Kade said. "Made only of wood and cardboard." He lowered the tailgate, then leaped into the back of the truck, where he opened the outhouse door. "Got a toilet seat and a roll of toilet paper inside."

Gary lifted the seat and grinned when a jack-in-the-box dog popped up. He marked a couple of ticks on the paper he carried on a clipboard. "Best of luck to you," he said, touching Davy's hair before moving on to the next entrant.

Kade scooted the outhouse to the edge of the tailgate, then leaped to the snowy ground. "I'd better wait until Donovan gets here to help get it out," he said.

Davy began to wave. "There they are!" He ran through the crowd to Naomi and Donovan, who were approaching with the children.

"Everything okay at work?" Bree asked quickly before the O'Reilly family could reach them.

"Just the usual," Kade said, not looking at her.

She frowned, but there was no time for more probing, because their friends had reached the truck. Timmy's face was flushed with excitement. So was Emily's. Even their toddler in Naomi's arms was looking around wide-eyed and smiling. Bree smiled at Matthew, and he ducked his head into his mother's neck.

"Let's get this bad boy down," Donovan said. His color was high too, and his blue eyes sparkled with excitement.

Samson jumped out of the way and came to stand beside Bree. Bree and Naomi exchanged amused glances as their husbands hauled the outhouse to the starting line. "They're more excited than the boys," Bree said.

Naomi shifted Matthew to the other arm. "I don't think Donovan slept a wink last night. Which meant I didn't get much sleep either. Hey, Timmy left his sled in your garage the last time he was there. You mind if we stop over and get it when we leave?"

"Nope, it's unlocked. Help yourself."

The sheriff striding through the crowd caught her attention. "Mason, over here!" she called.

He made his way to her. "I thought you'd be here somewhere," he said. "I was watching for you."

"Any word on Pia's death? Or Florence's?" Bree found she both dreaded and longed for the answer.

Mason shook his head. "I've talked to all their neighbors. No one saw anything."

Bree tightened her grip on the baby carrier. "Do you think Olivia is in danger?"

Mason's gaze bored into her. "Don't take any chances, Bree. It's a possibility we can't ignore. It's a weird situation."

"I've wondered about a black-market baby ring."

He raised his brows. "The missing babies from the res?"

She nodded and told him about finding some news stories about babies being stolen and adopted. "What if Florence cared for the babies as they were being funneled to their new parents?"

"And Pia helped?"

"That's what I wondered."

"I'll see what I can find out," he said. "Maybe you should run for sheriff in the next election cycle, Bree."

"Not a chance." Bree caught sight of her son, and pride filled her chest. "The race is starting."

Ten children were lined up with five outhouses, one child on each side. Each structure had a push bar on both sides so two children could maneuver it down the snowy street. Boys and girls hopped up and down with excitement as they waited for the starting whistle.

Gary waved a flag in the air. "We're about to get started," he called. "Remember the rules—you'll each have your turn and you'll be timed. Whichever outhouse gets to the finish line fifty feet down there"—he turned and pointed to the line in the street—"in the fastest time wins the race. And the prize this year is a Newfoundland puppy. One for each racer."

Naomi and Bree stared at one another. "Do you know how big they get?" Naomi whispered. "I hope our boys don't win."

"But they're so sweet," Bree said.

"And the size of a black bear," Naomi said. "What were they thinking?"

Samson whined at their feet. "You'd like a new puppy, wouldn't you, boy?" Bree asked, resting her hand on his head. "But he'd swallow you up by the time he was six months old."

Gary gave all the entries a number. Timmy and Davy would go last. Bree nearly groaned. She wanted it over for the boys. They came to stand out of the way while the first outhouse made its run.

The two girls were off at the blare of Gary's whistle. The girls were about twelve, but they lacked good coordination of their efforts. At one point they had the outhouse sideways on its toboggan and heading for a tree. With everyone screaming instructions, they managed to get their outhouse turned. They took nearly two minutes to reach the finish line, not nearly well enough to place. Their crestfallen faces made Bree's heart hurt.

The next three teams did better. Two ten-year-old boys finished at just under sixteen seconds, which was going to be the time for their boys to beat. "You're up, Davy," Bree said. "I mean Dave," she added when Davy sent a scowl her direction. She'd never remember.

The boys sprang to their outhouse. Their faces flushed, they wore identical expressions of determination. Davy glanced over his shoulder at his mother, and she gave him a thumbs-up. He grinned, then turned his attention back to the judge.

Gary blew the whistle. The boys strained a bit to get the outhouse moving, then it slid forward easily. Samson ran alongside, barking his encouragement, while Bree and Kade yelled at the top of their lungs. She kept an eye on the sweep of the second hand. Close, so close to winning.

Then the outhouse slid over the line at sixteen seconds on the dot. They'd barely missed beating the other boys. Bree considered it a win, since Davy and Timmy were only eight. "Great job!" she called, but Davy's face looked dejected.

She watched Kade hoist her son onto his shoulders in triumph. Davy's scowl changed to a cheeky grin atop Kade's broad shoulders.

Bree's gaze lingered on her handsome husband. Was there anything more attractive than a man who shouldered a responsibility that wasn't his?

~~~

Quinn shivered when a stream of cold air blew down his neck from his open window. He wore a dark brown wig over his short hair. He had a fake beard on as well. The leather doo-rag and jacket plus boots completed the biker look. He'd always heard it said if you want to be disguised, be blatant about it. This was about as blatant as possible.

The pavement was surprisingly clear of snow, but high piles left from the snowplows reached nearly to the eaves of the garages along the streets that he passed.

Maybe he should have stayed away, just in case, but where better to hide than in plain view among a throng of people? After being ignored after umpteen calls to his partner's cell phone, Quinn planned a face-to-face visit in town to see what was going on.

Folks out for the Heikinpaiva Festival crowded the streets. The Finnish winter festival had always been his favorite time of year. Parka-clad spectators watched as artists created ice sculptures near the old wishing well. He saw a lifelike ice statue of a dog. It couldn't be any dog but Samson.

Quinn parked and got out. His mouth watered at the scent of *pulla* on the cold air. Tonight there would be a Finnish smorgasbord of all kinds of delicacies. His favorite was the smoked lake trout and the *leipajuustoa*, or squeaky cheese. But he wouldn't dare show his face to that.

He kept his gaze on the sidewalk though he wanted to gawk at the familiar sights: men lining up for the wife-carrying contest, bathers in Speedos ready for their polar bear plunge, the partygoers raising their glasses of cold *kalia*.

Someone shouted, "*Talven selka poikki!*" and pounded on his back. The words rolled off his own tongue before he realized how they might give him away as he returned the greeting that meant, "Winter's back is broken."

Luckily, whoever he'd just talked to hadn't thought anything of a biker knowing Finnish. The man continued on his rolling course down the sidewalk. He'd definitely had too much *kalia*.

Quinn quickened his pace. He passed so many familiar faces, but he kept his expression impassive behind his sunglasses. As he hoped, no one gave him a second look as he blended in with other biker types. The sun turned the ice and snow into a glittering playland. The brilliant light made him glad he wore the glasses.

Ahead of him, the crowd broke, and the sun shone onto red curls under a knit cap. Quinn recognized the walk instantly. The tilt of the head, the pointed chin as she glanced up and laughed at the man who walked next to her. A young boy clung to her other hand, and his gaze focused on the boy. Alive. He still couldn't take it in.

He realized he'd come to a stop when someone jostled him. He stepped out of the flow and around the corner away from her. His heart was pounding. If she'd turned her head to see him . . . But no, she'd never expect to see him and wouldn't recognize him in this getup. He was safe.

Fumbling in his pocket, he couldn't get his packet of pipe tobacco out. Swearing, he tore off his glove and drove his hand into his pocket for it. His hands shook. He grabbed a pinch, stuffed his pipe, and lit it. The first pull of the aromatic vanilla and maple Cavendish blend soothed him immediately.

The smoke curled around his head, and he leaned against the block building and surveyed the waves of humanity moving around him. Nicholls' Finnish Imports was across the street. From here, he could look in the window at the sweaters and Finnish items for sale.

This town was too familiar for his peace of mind. The coffee shop, his favorite café, the library where he'd gone for story hour.

Sweat broke out on his forehead, and nausea churned in his belly. He took one last pull on his pipe, then tapped the contents into the snow. He stepped out into the crowd again.

And came face-to-face with her. She was still laughing. That's how he remembered her. Laughing with the joy of life. Something nudged his leg, and he looked down. Her dog pressed against his calf and whined. Samson knew Quinn.

Wheeling, Quinn ran for his truck. He hadn't seen his partner anyway.

The scent of the pipe tobacco brought back memories. Bree inhaled it, tasting the vanilla and maple sugar. Rob had smoked that same tobacco, and she hadn't smelled it in years. Samson nudged her leg, and she looked down. He was staring at the biker who'd been in front of her a minute ago. He whined, clearly wanting to follow the man.

Bree studied the man's back. Something about him held her attention. His walk maybe. She couldn't put her finger on it. He stopped by a truck, and she caught a good look at his profile. A gasp escaped her.

"What's wrong?" Kade asked.

"No-nothing," she stammered. He'd think she was crazy if she said the guy reminded her of Rob. It was probably because she'd smelled that pipe tobacco. Her mind was playing tricks on her.

"Hey, there's a wife-carrying contest going on," Kade said. "You game?"

"If you want to risk a hernia," she said, deciding to put the worries away for a while. She wanted to devote the day to Rob and Davy. Er, Kade and Davy.

Why had her mind slipped Rob's name in like that? The fertility hormones she was taking were making her crazy and reminding her of when she was pregnant with Davy—and married to another man.

"I think I'll pop in and see Anu," she said.

"Good idea. I'll take Dave over to watch the polar plunge," he said.

"Meet you at the Suomi in half an hour," she promised. She watched Kade take her son's hand and lead him and Samson off toward the lake. He'd been a good father to her boy, even though Davy had given him a hard time at first. Davy hadn't wanted anyone to take his father's place. Kade had patiently worn down the boy's defenses, and Davy rarely mentioned Rob until just lately, and then only in the context of being afraid. Bree found she was a little sad about that. She'd hoped to keep Rob's memory alive for his boy, but it was a good thing that Davy trusted and loved Kade.

The traffic had nearly stopped with cars and trucks jamming the street. Lugging Olivia in the carrier, she jogged between the vehicles to the other side of the street and pushed open the door into Nicholls' Finnish Imports. Shoppers filled the store, lines in every aisle. Anu wouldn't have time to talk.

Anu saw her and waved from behind the cash register. "A break I am needing," she told her assistant. "I will be back in fifteen minutes." She slipped around the counter and took Bree's elbow. "Back here, *kulta*. I have coffee and rolls just out of the oven."

"I smelled the *pulla* the minute I opened the door," Bree said. Her tummy rumbled. "Coffee sounds good too."

"Never have I known you to turn down coffee." Anu led her to the break room and had her sit. "Rest. You are having a good time, yes?"

"Wonderful, though Kade is trying to talk me into the wife-carrying contest." Bree laughed at the inner picture it conjured. "I can't imagine him even being able to lift me, let alone carry me," Bree said, laughing. "Not in all these winter clothes. They have to weigh at least fifteen extra pounds with my boots." She accepted the bread Anu offered and took a bite of the warm, yeasty goodness. "Delicious," she muttered through her full mouth. "I'm famished."

"Eat, eat," Anu urged. She poured out the coffee and handed the cup to Bree.

"Thanks." Bree took a sip and set it down. "Anu, I'm having the weirdest sensations today."

Anu settled into the chair at the table. "What is wrong?"

"I keep thinking about Rob. Just now I smelled that pipe tobacco he used and thought I saw a guy who looked like him. Very strange."

Anu's smile faded. "I, too, miss him. Every day I think of my son. How he would look if he had lived. What he might have done with his life. Always, I carry this sadness."

"Me too," Bree said softly.

Anu watched her. "What of your house guest?"

"She's still with us."

Anu pressed her lips together.

"What?" Bree demanded.

Her mother-in-law shrugged. "This murder her brother is accused of, Pia's death. And you, right in the thick of things as always."

"It's where I like to be." Bree swallowed the last of her coffee. "I'd better go find my family." She rose and dropped a kiss on Anu's powdered cheek, then grabbed the baby carrier.

Walking back across the street, she found herself watching for the biker again.

11

KADE HELD TIGHT TO DAVE'S HAND. "YOU DID REALLY well in the outhouse race. I'm proud of you, son."

The boy gave a little skip. "I wanted to win."

"Next year. Mom was glad you didn't win that Newfoundland puppy."

"He was cute. I want to get one."

They reached the Suomi Café. The bell on the door jingled when they entered.

"There's Jenna," Dave said, pointing to the blonde woman in the booth in the back corner.

Molly saw them and waved. Samson started toward her, but Kade stopped him with a word. The dog fell in at their heels as they walked back to join Jenna. Her reddened face and tear-filled eyes made him pause.

"You okay?" he asked.

"Fine," she said.

Davy tugged at his hand. "Can I go pick out a roll?" he asked.

"Sure." He watched the boy run to the display case, then slid into the seat across from Jenna. "You're crying. Anything I can do?"

"Boyfriend troubles," she said, dabbing at her eyes.

"I'm sorry." He shifted uneasily. "Bree is a good one to talk to about stuff like that. I'm hopeless."

His hands were on the table, and she reached over and cradled one of his hands in hers. "It helps just to know you care," she said.

He started to pull his hand away. Surely she didn't mean anything by it. At least that's what he told himself until he caught the come-hither expression in her eyes. It shocked him so badly, he sat there like a lump and left his hand in hers.

"What's going on here?" Bree asked to his right. Her gaze was on their linked hands.

Kade snatched his hand out of Jenna's. "Jenna is upset. I told her she needed to talk to you."

Jenna smiled. "Kade is such a sweetheart to try to comfort me. You're so lucky, Bree."

"What's wrong, Jenna?" Bree's eyes remained skeptical.

"Just boyfriend trouble. Not all men are like Kade."

"No, he's one in a million." Bree's words held a cold edge.

Davy ran from the pastry case and tugged on his mother's hand. "Mom, can I have some grilled cheese?"

"Sure, honey." Bree stepped over Samson, who had plopped on the floor, then slid into the booth beside Kade. "Sit down by Miss Jenna." She set the baby carrier on the floor.

Jenna scooted over to make room for Dave, but she wore a sulky expression. Molly came up to take their order. She put down a plate of food for Samson, who began to gobble it up.

"Hi, Molly, what's the special today?" Bree asked.

"How about some nice borsch, eh?" Molly said. "And I know your man. He'll want some smoked trout."

"I'll have both," Kade said, grinning. "You know me too well."

"Blech, borsch," Davy said. "Can I have grilled cheese?"

"You got it, little man," Molly said, scribbling down the order. "And that pastry with thimbleberry jam, right?" Davy nodded.

Bree ordered borsch. Jenna studied the menu. "Nothing sounds very good. What are all these weird things? Cabbage rolls, pickled herring. Ick. I'll have grilled cheese too," she said, folding the menu and handing it back to the waitress.

Kade could sense Bree's displeasure coming off her in waves. He was relieved to see Mason's burly form enter the café and head straight for their table. He grabbed a chair and dragged it to the edge of the table, then sat. "Having a good time?"

"The best," Bree said. "Hilary around with Zoe?"

"They're over at the kids' games."

"Any word on my brother?" Jenna asked. "Is he talking this morning?"

"Nope. He did some more puzzles."

"It must be his way of coping with his circumstances," Jenna said.

"I went through your brother's room at the Blue Bonnet right after we arrested him. I sorted through it again this morning. Nothing much there. More puzzles. His clothing. An iPod shuffle and a few Madonna CDs. His toiletries. Nothing else."

"He hates clutter, and he prefers to spend his time outdoors." Jenna gawked at the men walking by the big plateglass window in Speedos. "He loves winter festivals. I'm sure he'd like to be here now."

"I managed to get him moved to a cell with a window," the sheriff said. "He seems more calm. No more head banging at any rate."

"Oh, thank you so much!"

Kade watched her glow at the news. Poor kid. She loved her brother very much. Mason glanced at Bree. "Hilary wanted me to invite you to dinner next Sunday. It's Zoe's third birthday."

"We wouldn't miss it!" Bree's smile was warm.

Mason rose and returned the chair to the table from where he'd taken it.

"Nice guy," Jenna said, watching him walk away. "He'd be nicer if he'd let my brother out of jail. It sounds like you're related or something."

"His wife is my first husband's sister," Bree said. "And they adopted Kade's niece. His sister, Lauri, had a baby at sixteen."

"Where is Lauri now?" Jenna asked.

"College at Houghton."

Molly brought their food, and nothing more was said as they dug into their lunch. When Jenna was done, she excused herself, saying she needed to run an errand. As soon as she was out of sight, Bree opened her mouth, glanced at Davy, then shut it again. Kade knew she wanted to ask what the hand-holding was all about.

He smiled at her. "It was nothing, babe."

Her green eyes clouded. "It looked like something."

"I know, and I'm sorry for that. She was just upset." His cell phone rang and he took it out, then smiled. "Lauri. I was just thinking about calling her." He punched the talk button. "Hey, sis, how's school?"

Lauri's voice was high with excitement. "Great, just great. But even better, Kade, I got a job! It's working for the top accounting firm in the UP. And I'm getting paid really well. No need to worry about your baby sister anymore. I can take care of myself from now on."

A pang squeezed in the region of his heart. "I never minded taking care of my baby sister. I kind of liked it, in fact."

"I'm grateful, too, but my life is changing for the better. No more pinching pennies. As soon as I get paid, I'm buying a different car. This old rattletrap is about to fall apart."

At least that would be one financial burden he wouldn't have to carry. His thoughts went to the grant application. The lies he'd told on it gnawed at him.

The chatter around the café faded to a distant hum. Bree knew this was her problem, not Kade's. He'd just been comforting Jenna. His kindness was one of the things that had drawn her from the beginning. She sipped her coffee, which had grown lukewarm. Was that happening to her marriage? Was the passion between them fading to a humdrum routine?

She dared a peek at her husband. He picked at his smoked fish with an absent expression. This was Kade, not some stranger. He'd never do anything to hurt her.

"Honey, I'm tired. Could we go home?" she asked.

He glanced up with worry in his eyes. "You okay?"

"I'm fine. Just ready for a nap."

Kade looked at Davy. "While Mom's napping, you and I will go make a snowman."

"Yay!"

Kade reached over and picked up Olivia in her carrier. She was wide-awake and looking around with big eyes.

Bree slipped her coat on and followed her husband and son into the driving wind. The fine day had turned more frigid. The sun slipped behind the gathering snow clouds, and a cold front blew from the northwest, bringing moisture from the lake. Kade held her hand so she wouldn't slip on icy patches. The sense that he cherished her calmed those nagging doubts.

The truck was like an icebox when she slid across the frozen seat. Davy got in the club seat behind her and she heard his seat belt snap into place. He was good at remembering to buckle up. Kade secured the baby in the middle of the backseat while she fastened her own seat belt.

Kade drove slowly out of town, and Bree stared out the window at the frozen landscape. As they rounded the curve out to the light-house, she saw the man in the biker gear along the side of the road. He was beside a white truck. Her heart jumped to her throat, and she strained to see him better.

"You should probably stop and help him," she told Kade, point-ing to the stranded man.

"Yeah, you're right." He eased the truck to the side of the road. "I'll leave the truck running so you'll stay warm." Kade got out and went to talk to the man.

Bree watched them through the window. The man had taken his glasses off, and she caught her breath again at the sight of his profile—so much like Rob's it was scary. But this guy had dark hair and a dark beard. Rob's were light brown that turned blond in the summer.

Then the man smiled at Kade, and her breath froze in her throat. That crooked smile. She stared harder, and the guy turned and looked straight at her.

Rob. It was Rob.

The certainty coalesced in her head, her heart. She couldn't breathe past the constriction in her lungs. When she stared harder, she became less certain. Didn't they say everyone had a twin somewhere?

Was she totally going crazy?

It was all she could do to swallow the fear in her throat. She watched Kade go around to the back and retrieve his gas can. He poured some into the biker's truck, and moments later, the big vehicle roared to life. The man drove off as Kade returned.

"Who-who was that?" she asked, trying hard to keep her voice steady.

"Said his name was Quinn Matilla."

"From around here?"

"He didn't say, but his accent sounded like it." Kade dropped the transmission into drive and continued on down the road. He glanced at her as he pulled into their driveway. "You okay?"

"Fine. He just reminded me . . . of someone."

"Who?"

She put her finger to her lips and mouthed, "Later."

But she doubted he'd remember later, and she wasn't about to bring it up. Often enough over the years, he'd seemed insecure about whether she'd truly gotten over Rob's death. And judging from her reaction today, she wondered the same.

A thump hit the back of her seat. "Don't kick the seat," she told her son.

"Mom, did you find Olivia's mommy?" Davy asked in a voice that was too nonchalant.

She twisted around to stare at him. His gaze was locked on Olivia. "Not yet, honey."

"You found her in the woods, just like me," he said.

She'd hoped those memories of his being lost had faded. "Yes, that's right. I'm trying to find her mommy and daddy though."

"Mother didn't try to find you."

The woman who had found Davy, Rachel Marks, had made no attempt to find Davy's family. She'd kept him for a year, and it was only because of Samson that Bree found her son again. And God, of course. Mostly God.

"No. No, she didn't. And that was wrong." Olivia began to cry, a thin wail that told Bree she was still half asleep.

Davy took her hand. "She's crying for her mommy," he said. "I hope God hears her. Grammy says God always hears. Do you think he hears Olivia?"

"I'm sure he does," Bree said, her eyes filling with tears. She hadn't been looking at the situation through Olivia's eyes, only through her own need for a baby. Whose cry would God answer?

Kade parked and got the baby out of the back. Olivia's cry was ramping up. Bree took Davy's hand and went to the lighthouse. The baby was wailing by the time they stepped into the house. She took the carrier from Kade and lifted the baby from it.

"So much for a peaceful afternoon," he said. "What's wrong with her?"

"She'll be all right. She sounds hungry." Bree tossed her coat at him, and he caught it and took it with his to the closet. She kicked off her boots and went on into the living room.

"There, there," Bree crooned, cradling the infant. Olivia gave a small hiccup and began to quiet immediately. Bree grabbed a bottle and put it in the warmer.

Kade followed her. "I saw you talking to Mason. Has he found anything about her parents?"

"Nothing." She hesitated, then told him of her suspicions of a baby ring. "I think maybe she's Ellie's baby."

"What about the parents who adopted her? Why did they never get her? And how do we find them?"

"I don't know. I hope we don't find them," she said. "I want to keep her, Kade."

He pressed his lips together. "Bree, we'll have our own baby."

"I want *this* baby. I love her."

"I was afraid this would happen," he muttered. "You have to give her up. For one thing, we can't afford a child right now."

"We're doing okay," she said.

"Have you noticed how much formula and diapers are costing us? We haven't gotten the first payment from CPS yet either, and it's all coming out of our pocket."

Was this turning into an argument? She'd thought Kade would be on board with the idea of adopting her. "I thought you loved her too," she said, her lips trembling.

His voice softened. "Babe, she's not ours. Someone is desperately looking for her."

"You don't know that!" She removed the bottle from the warmer and stormed back to the living room. The phone rang. Glancing at the caller ID, she saw it was Naomi. She composed herself and answered it. "Hey girl, what's up?"

"I'm not sure. We stopped over to get that sled, and I saw some guy in biker gear walking in your backyard."

The guy had come here? Her pulse ratcheted up a notch. "What was he doing?"

"Just standing out back. Looking at the water, then turning and looking at the house."

Ice moved through Bree's veins. What did this mean? Rob was dead. She'd overseen the removal of his body from the crash site into the graveyard here in town. Of course he was dead. If he were alive, wouldn't he have come back to her?

"Did you speak to him?" she whispered.

"No. He saw us and ran off around the other side of the house. Donovan ran after him, but he got away before Donovan reached him."

"Maybe he was just admiring the lighthouse." People did all the time. They stopped and asked to come in like it was some kind of tourist attraction. Surely that was it. She hung up the phone, her hands still trembling.

She took the warmed bottle and popped it into Olivia's rose-bud mouth. The baby began to suck. Her eyes closed. Bree had to keep Olivia. It was impossible to think of her life without this little girl. Bree fed her, then laid her in the bassinet, grabbed a throw, and curled up on the sofa. Kade and Davy clattered down the steps as they ran outside, where they shouted and laughed.

Alone for a few minutes, she went to the bookshelf and dug out a photo album. She'd put it on a low shelf so Davy could look at it whenever he wanted, but Bree hadn't seen him going through it in over a year. She probably hadn't looked at it since she married Kade.

She carried the book back to the sofa and flipped it open. Her younger self smiled at the camera. Dressed in a soft white wedding gown, she'd been impossibly young and happy. She hadn't known then what the future would hold.

She flipped the pages and stopped at the close-up of Rob. His eyes crinkled at the corners from his face-splitting smile. That crooked smile she'd seen fifteen minutes ago. Bree swallowed hard and told herself again it had to be her imagination.

Why had the biker come here if it was all in her head? Until she'd heard Naomi's news, she'd been able to convince herself he was a lookalike.

She closed the book and went to the back door. Wrapping herself in the blanket, she stepped out and stared at the man's footprints tracked there in the snow for all the world to see.

A dark blob caught her eye. Paulie, their resident cardinal, sat on it. She didn't have any shoes on, so she stepped back inside and slid her feet into Crocs, then went back out. As she neared the item, it registered. A pipe. His pipe. She stumbled and nearly fell but caught herself.

She didn't want to look at it, didn't want her world to crumble around her, but she forced her feet to move closer until she stood looking down at the evidence in the snow.

Pipe tobacco littered the white snow, but her gaze was frozen on the pipe. She knew that pipe well. Paulie tipped his head and sang out. He pecked at her fingers when she moved her hand toward the pipe. "Go away, Paulie," she said, shooing him away.

She reached down and picked it up. The bowl was an eagle's head, carved by Rob's grandfather. Anu had given it to him when her father died, and it was Rob's most prized possession. He would never have left it behind on purpose.

The biker couldn't be Rob. Someone was messing with her head. She put her hand to her cheek and moaned.

12

THIS HAD BEEN GOING ON LONG ENOUGH. QUINN DIALED his mark's number and listened to the ring. When the man answered, he let the silence hold a moment. "Hello?" the man said again. "Is anyone there?"

"I've seen no announcement in the news yet," Quinn said, his voice a growl. "You need more incentive?"

"I-I thought the money was what you wanted," the guy stammered.

Quinn frowned. "Money?"

A confused silence ensued. "Your partner asked for cash. I delivered it. Aren't we square now?"

"Money? How much?"

"Half a million dollars. I've been waiting on you to call and tell me where the exchange will be."

That double-crosser. Quinn literally saw red. This was no oversight. "The money was not what we agreed to," he said. "When the announcement hits the papers, you'll get the baby back."

"Bu-but . . ."

Quinn clicked his phone off. He hadn't been offered his cut. What was his partner trying to pull? And was this the reason none of his calls had been returned?

The hum of the digital clock mingled with Kade's snores. Bree lay with her eyes wide and unfocused. Her internal vision replayed the man she'd seen by the truck. The shape of the face, the mouth. The shoulders. Plus his pipe in the backyard.

Her eyes burned. Samson rose from his bed on the floor beside her. His cold nose nudged her hand. She rolled toward him and ran her hand over his silky fur for comfort. He always sensed when she was distressed. He pushed forward and nuzzled her neck. His hot breath gave her goose bumps, but breathing his good doggy scent calmed her.

This situation couldn't be what it seemed. She wasn't ready to swallow something so outrageous. She knew Rob. He would never have walked away and left Davy in the woods alone. Never. He'd adored his son.

What if it is Rob?

The question wouldn't let her alone. The thought of such a terrible possibility made her struggle to pull enough air into her lungs. She rolled away from Samson and faced Kade's broad back. The warmth of his body encompassed her. The threat of losing each other, or—even worse—of not being really married to each other would traumatize them both.

What would she do if Rob were alive?

She flung her arm over her eyes. Thinking about it was driving her crazy. She sat up and slipped out of bed. The baby still slept in the bassinet, so she padded down the hall to Davy's room. Samson followed her. Davy had managed to tangle the bedding into a wad at the foot of the bed. The room smelled of oranges, and she stepped on two orange peels by his bed. She straightened out the covers, pulling them up over him. Watching him a moment in the moonlight, she imagined his elation if Rob were to walk in the door.

After touching his warm cheek, she backed out of the room and went downstairs. Maybe a cup of chamomile tea would help. The wood floor was cool against her bare feet. The living room still held the aroma of the apple spice candle she'd burned earlier, and it made the tea sound even better. She went to the kitchen to put the kettle on the stove and turned the flame to high while she got out the tea bag and a cup. Her stomach rumbled, and she decided to have a piece of the chocolate cake she'd baked yesterday.

Samson followed her with his tail wagging. At least someone cared that she was awake. Kade hadn't budged when she got out of bed. The kettle began to hiss and steam. She removed it before it could start shrieking. As she poured the hot water over the tea bag, she glanced up. A light bobbed in the backyard.

Bree's pulse galloped, and she quickly flipped off the light. Peering through the window, she saw nothing, but Samson's ears perked up, and he went to the door. He whined and gazed up at her with expectation in his eyes.

He wasn't barking. Her alarm ebbed. She glanced at the clock on the stove. Midnight. Who would be out there at that hour?

Rob.

Why the thought rushed to mind she had no idea. What a crazy idea. She stared at the door. Samson whined at her knee, and she put her hand on his head. "It's okay, boy." Maybe there was nothing out there at all. Just an animal.

She squared her shoulders. The least she could do was check it out. The doorknob was cold under her fingers. She threw the dead bolt and opened the back door. As she did, she heard a creak from overhead. She quickly shut the door again.

She couldn't talk to Kade about this yet.

⤬

Kade walked to the door of the bedroom in his pajama bottoms and T-shirt. He looked at the clock. Just after midnight. She was probably downstairs. Since her miscarriage, she often couldn't sleep.

Pausing in the hall, he listened. The house was silent. Both kids still slept. He walked to the top of the stairs and saw Bree coming up. "You okay, babe?"

She lifted a cup of steaming liquid in the air. "I thought chamomile might help me sleep."

"I heard Olivia grumble a little like she was going to wake up."

"I'd better check on her." She came on up the stairs and passed by him to hurry to the bassinet.

Her sweet scent wafted behind her to his nose. Since the baby had come into the house, she didn't have much attention to spare for him. And maybe it was best that way. He didn't want her to notice how worried he was about his job. This new revelation that she wanted to keep Olivia depressed him more. He hated to disappoint her in anything, but he didn't see how they could do this.

He went to the kitchen and poured a glass of milk. Heat from the kettle where she'd fixed her tea radiated from the stove. Samson stayed on his heels. "No milk for you, big guy," Kade said. "How about a treat?" He got out the bag of venison treats. Samson took it with gentle care from Kade's fingers. "Good boy."

He rubbed the dog's head, then took a swallow of cold milk. It had barely hit his stomach when he saw Samson go to the door and whine. "I'm surprised your mom didn't let you out." He unlocked the back door, and Samson leaped out.

As the dog dashed past him, Kade saw a flashlight bobbing along the snowy ground in the glow of moonlight. He saw Samson run to a shadowy figure. Surprise held Kade still and mute.

"Hey, Sam," a muted male voice said. "You remember me, huh?" The dark figure bent over the dog. "You seen my pipe?"

Kade stiffened and stepped out onto the back deck. Who would be in their backyard at midnight? He squinted in the dark. "Who's there?"

The flashlight jerked, then began to move along the snow faster before winking out. Kade leaped into a snow bank. The frigid snow hit his bare feet, then he plunged thigh high into the icy stuff. He winced at the cold burn.

"Wait!" he called when he heard the sound of thrashing. Tree-filtered moonlight shone down on the outline of the dog. Samson had moved to the edge of the garage and stood staring after something. Probably the man who had just fled.

Kade struggled through the snow back to the deck. "Samson, come!"

He stomped the snow from his feet and pajamas, the wet coldness seeping into his bones. The door to the kitchen still stood open, and he hurried inside to the warmth he could feel pouring out of the house. The click of Samson's nails came up the steps to the deck. Kade waited to close the door until the dog was inside.

He threw the lock behind them. His feet left wet trails on the wooden floor. Snow clung to Samson's fur.

He touched the dog's head. "You didn't bark, boy. And the guy called you Sam, which I've only heard Davy say. Who was that?" Wait, Dave said the man who tried to grab him had called the dog Sam.

Samson gazed up with a steady expression as though he held the secret to everything and wasn't telling. Samson wasn't concerned about whomever had been out there, so Kade didn't think the person was dangerous, but why was he prowling around at this hour? And why hadn't he identified himself?

"Did you say something?" Bree stood in the doorway. Her gaze went from her snow-covered dog to Kade's wet pajamas and feet. "What happened to you?"

"There was someone in the backyard." An expression passed

over her face. A little bit fear and a little bit resignation. But no surprise.

Had she met someone out there?

He rejected the stray thought as soon as it came. Bree would never have an affair. This was no illicit tryst. He wasn't sure what it was, but he knew that much.

"The guy called Samson *Sam*, like he knew him."

Bree paled and wet her lips. "That's odd."

"I thought so too." He studied her downcast eyes and trembling lips. "Do you know who it might have been?"

"Not many people have ever called him Sam. Just Davy. And R-Rob." She stammered over her dead husband's name.

"Well it wasn't Davy, and it sure wasn't a ghost." He stopped when she swayed where she stood. "You okay, Bree?"

"Just tired." She passed a hand over her forehead. "I haven't been sleeping well."

She was as pale as the snow on his pajamas, and he could have sworn she was shaking. He put his arm around her. She *was* shaking.

"Are you getting sick? Let's get you to bed." He led her toward the steps. "Whoever it was is gone now. Maybe it was someone who heard Davy call the dog Sam. The funny thing is that Samson didn't bark. He ran right up to the guy like he knew him. Weird."

"Very," she said, her lips barely moving. She clung to his hand as they went up the stairs.

When they reached the bedroom, she turned and moved into his arms, laying her head on his chest. "I love you, Kade." Her words held a trace of desperation.

"I love you too, babe." He wet his lips. Their argument over Olivia must be bothering her. He needed to explain. "I'm sorry I can't agree to adopting Olivia, but things at work have been . . . difficult."

"Difficult how?" she asked.

"Layoffs, the usual. Lots of work." He brushed his lips over her forehead and inhaled the fruity scent of her shampoo. His hand smoothed her curls. They sprang right back with the same courage and spirit Bree possessed. His wife was the most precious person in his life. He'd do anything to protect her and keep her happy.

Bree clung to him with a grip that seemed desperate. He'd never seen her in such a state. She trembled as if she had the flu. "Are you okay?" he whispered.

"Love me, Kade, just love me," she said, backing toward the bed.

He glanced at the clock. "It's late," he whispered. "You'll have to care for the baby. Get some rest. Something has upset you."

But he couldn't resist the tug of her hands or the invitation in her eyes. They could sleep tomorrow.

Kitchigami Crag beckoned. Though the weather was still frigid, the fierce storm had settled to a mild gale, and the sun bounced off the snow. Kade stood at the bottom of the trail and stared up. The snow on the trail had turned to ice in the last twenty-four hours. The ascent wouldn't be as easy as last time.

Tribal policeman George DeCota stood nearby. Though in his fifties, he was as trim and fit as a man in his twenties. His dark eyes scanned the imposing rock formation. "Good day for climbing," he said.

"Thanks for coming with me." Kade seated his hat more firmly over his ears. "The trail doesn't look too bad." He'd been surprised the Ojibwa man had been willing to come out with him, but George suspected some of the screams his people feared might be a big cat. He wanted to set the rumors about the windigo to rest.

"Ready?" Kade asked.

George nodded. "I know this trail. I will go first."

Both men had put crampons in the soles of their boots. Kade ground his feet into the icy path with each step after George. As the ascent grew steeper, he used his ice pick for leverage and to keep from sliding off the edge. Ice glittered along the narrow path, and as they progressed higher up the crag, the way grew more slippery.

He was panting by the time he reached the summit. George stood watching him heave himself the last two feet. Kade couldn't see that the other man was even winded. As Kade paused to catch his breath, he watched George kneel and examine where something had churned up the snow and ice.

"Cat," George said, satisfaction rippling in his voice. "Could be lynx, but could be cougar." He pointed. "Went that way." He took off at a brisk pace.

So much for a rest. Kade jogged after him. Here on top of the crag, the wind tore through the material of his pants as if he wore nothing at all. He quickened his pace and soon caught up to George. The Ojibwa led him along a tumbled mass of rock close to the edge of the mountain. The track disappeared over the edge. Peering over, Kade saw more tracks along the rocky face. But it was much too dangerous to try to climb down from here.

While George continued to scan the ground, Kade moved back toward the trees. The men he'd found taking wood said the den was this direction. He studied the landscape for the cave they'd described, but the snow softened the edges of rocks and valleys and made it difficult to determine the terrain.

As he turned to see if George had found anything, he heard a shout. Squinting through the trees that blocked his view, he saw George throw up his arm as a dark shape leaped at him. It happened too fast for Kade to get more than an impression of bulk. George yelled again, then disappeared over the rock face. Kade couldn't see the animal any longer either.

He broke into a run, then slipped and went down on one knee. Praying for George's safety the whole time, he staggered to his feet. Pain pierced his knee from the fall, but he pressed on, hobbling as fast as he could to the spot where he'd last seen George. He flung himself onto his stomach and peered over the edge.

George's upturned face stared back at him. "I have broken my ankle," he said, his voice calm. "You will need to call the reservation for help. You cannot get me up by yourself."

Kade surveyed the situation. George lay on an icy ledge eight feet down. The sliver of rock barely gave him enough room to cling to the rock face. Dragging out his cell phone, he called up the number of the tribal police and reported the incident.

He put his phone away, then sat on the edge and dangled his feet over. "They'll be here as fast as they can. Can I do anything?" He wasn't sure the ledge would support both of them.

George shook his head and attempted a smile, but his teeth chattered. "Shock," he informed Kade. "You wouldn't have any whiskey on you, would you?"

"Sorry. I've got coffee." Kade shrugged out of his backpack and rummaged in it for the thermos. He attached it to a line and lowered it to George, who took it off the rope, opened the lid, and swallowed it straight from the thermos.

George put the lid back on and tucked the container against his chest. "Thanks."

"What was it that jumped you?"

"You didn't see? Big cat. Cougar."

"I caught a glimpse but wasn't sure." If he'd only gotten a picture. But even that wouldn't be enough. There had been cougar sightings over the years, but the official DNR stance was that only a breeding population was real proof of the species' return.

"You can do nothing while we wait," George said. "Go. Look around for the den." His glassy eyes closed.

He didn't like the way George's teeth continued to chatter. "I'm not leaving you alone." The words barely left his lips when he heard a scream behind him. It made the hair on the back of his neck stand at attention.

And it had been close. He rose and turned in the direction of the scream.

"Get out your Mace," George muttered.

"Good idea." Kade dug it out of his coat pocket and held it ready. He didn't think the cougar would come back. The trees and rocks might hide what he sought, and he took a step in that direction.

A rumble echoed through the snow-topped trees and grew louder. Snowmobiles. He gazed down the rock face and saw four snowmobiles pull up to the base. The men riding them dismounted. They began climbing the path to the top.

"Help has arrived," Kade said.

George waved a hand weakly. "Go, go. Check for the kittens. My friends will be here any minute."

Kade stayed until the men reached him and he could point out George's location. "What can I do to help?" he asked.

"Just stay out of our way. I'm going to rappel down and attach a harness to him, then lower him to the ground," the youngest man said.

Kade stood aside and watched. They knew what they were doing. Their movements were practiced and efficient. He glanced back at the trees and the tumbled rocks beyond. "I'll be over there a few minutes," he mumbled.

He dug out his camera, then dropped his backpack into the snow. With his load lightened, he jogged to where he'd been when he heard George yell. The snow pack seemed pristine and untouched, but he wandered farther away from the rescuers. There. The remains of an animal. And paw prints.

He snapped some pictures of the prints and followed them.

They led to a tree, not a den. He circled back again and studied the rocks for the opening the woodcutters had mentioned. Nothing. Maybe they'd been pulling his leg.

Disappointment left a bitter taste in his mouth when the rescuers called for him. The hunt would have to continue another day.

BREE RUBBED BLEARY EYES. IT WAS GOING TO TAKE awhile to track down what the specific number across the top of Victor's sudoku puzzles meant. The fact that the same number recurred every time told her it was important.

But who would have guessed there were so many nine-digit numbers? She'd spent the morning running a computer search and found many references. It could be a bank deposit box account, a prisoner number, an ISBN, a bank routing number, the Standard Point Location Code for delivery, a driver's license number, a bird banding by the park service, an American Society of Reproductive Medicine member number, a college student number, an EIN, a library ID number, a specific zip code, a job code from the Dictionary of Occupational Titles, a UPC code, a hunting or fishing permit, a park service animal tag, or a juror number. The list seemed never ending.

Her gut told her to pursue the line of the young woman who was missing, Ellie Bristol. If only she could figure out the sudoku thing. It would take a lot of digging, but she was sure everything—the deaths, the puzzles, the missing mother—were connected to Olivia in some way.

Olivia was asleep in the bassinet, and Bree hated to awaken her, but she couldn't sit here and expect the answers to drop into her lap. The baby's head lolled as Bree lifted her and slipped her into the carrier.

"Are you going somewhere?" Jenna stood in the doorway.

Bree was so ready to get the woman out of her house. It was clear Jenna found Kade attractive. Normally Bree would have found it comical, but her emotional state was too fragile right now.

She zipped up the carrier cover around the infant. "I'm going out to check on what Victor's puzzles might mean."

"I've wracked my brain and I can't imagine what that number is," Jenna said. "A Social Security number?"

"Mason ran it through the system," Bree said. "A dead woman came up. She's been deceased for ten years."

"Any connection to Florence at all?" Jenna asked.

"Not that Mason could tell. She had spina bifida and lived her entire life in a nursing home. She wasn't related to Florence."

Jenna watched her bundle the baby. "You can leave Olivia here. I'll watch her."

Nice of her to offer. Bree hesitated. It would be much easier if she could just scoot in and out of the places she needed to stop. She should be ashamed of her antipathy to Jenna too. Pure jealousy, that's all it was. But no matter how she tried to talk herself into it, she couldn't bring herself to leave the baby.

"I'll just take her, but thanks for asking." *Invite her to come.* Bree wanted to ignore the inner prompting but she forced herself to smile. "You want to come with us?"

"It's so cold." Jenna shuddered, an exaggerated movement. "My new boots are already ruined from all the snow."

Didn't she care about clearing her brother? Bree tried not to judge her, but the woman made it hard. She was such a city girl, and Bree had nothing in common with her. "Suit yourself."

"Want me to get Davy from school for you?" Jenna asked.

Bree barely kept the frown from her face. If the woman didn't want to go out, why would she offer to get Davy? Did she hope to run into Kade? "Kade is picking him up."

"Oh. Well, maybe I'll come with you after all. There's nothing to do here."

Bree nearly rolled her eyes at Jenna's petulant tone. She wanted to tell her to get a life and not be so self-centered. "Fine. I'm leaving now so grab your coat and boots."

Samson rose and stretched, then padded after her when she snapped her fingers. Bree clicked her Jeep's automatic starter, which Kade had bought her, and waited. She didn't want to subject the baby to the brutal cold. Ten minutes later they were on the road.

"Where to first?" Jenna asked.

"The courthouse," Bree said. "One possible nine-digit number is a juror number. Also a license number, though Mason has already run it for that and found nothing. It could be a prisoner number too though."

She drove downtown and parked in front of the courthouse. When she turned the Jeep off, Jenna reached over and tried to grab the keys from her hand. Bree reacted by jerking her hand away. "What are you doing?"

"I'll wait here with the Jeep running. It's better than taking Olivia out in the cold."

Though the young woman had a point, Bree disliked the highhanded behavior. "I'm going to check in with CPS while I'm here. They'll want to see her." Tucking the keys into her pocket, she slid out and retrieved the baby and Samson. "But you're welcome to wait."

Jenna sighed and got out. What were they—two children having a spat? Bree hurried inside as fast as she dared on the icy sidewalk. Ten minutes later she was able to rule out the possibilities she'd hoped to find there. After stopping at the CPS office and letting them ooh and ah over Olivia and Samson, she headed toward the exit.

"Oh Bree, what is that little bundle you've got?" Tina Watson's rotund figure blocked her path. She had a silk rose tucked into the hat that covered her gray curls, a sign of her passion for roses. The color in her cheeks matched the pink in the flower.

Bree pulled back the cover. "I'm calling her Olivia." She told the older woman about finding the baby in the woods. "You haven't heard about any missing babies, have you?"

Tina's smile vanished, and she glanced from Jenna to Bree. "This has to be tied to Florence's death."

Bree's pulse rocketed. "Did Florence tell you something about Olivia?"

Tina pressed her lips together. "Florence and I were hardly, friends, God rest her soul. We had an argument at the fair this past summer over the prize for Best Rose. I normally wouldn't mention it, but we, ah, raised our voices, and the deputies came. Mason could tell you. I was sure the committee that looked into it would realize she'd stolen a cutting of my rose." Tears flooded her faded blue eyes. "They found in her favor. I went to her house to reason with her, to ask her to withdraw her entry. I saw that young man Victor walking toward her car with a baby carrier."

Bree frowned. "That would have been late last summer. We just found Olivia."

"I know. But there was something fishy going on. When I asked Florence about it, she told me to mind my own business." Tina's voice rose with indignation.

Tina's reputation as a busybody was known all over town. Bree couldn't decide whether to believe her or not. Still, it wouldn't hurt to tell Mason, so she hurried across the street to the jail.

The sun shone from a pale blue sky. The bitter wind swept

through Bree's jeans. She hurried to get the baby out of the gale. Jenna barely kept up.

The deputy at the desk smiled and buzzed them back to Mason's office. Mason still wore his coat but shucked it and tossed it over the back of his chair as they entered his office.

"Sorry to bother you," Bree said. She set the carrier down and unsnapped the cover so the warm air could get to Olivia. The baby still slept.

"You're never a bother," Mason said, dropping into his chair. He pointed to the seats on the other side of the desk. "Sit." Samson went around to Mason, and the sheriff rubbed the dog's head.

Bree and Jenna sat down and Bree took off her gloves. "I heard a rumor about Florence and an argument she had with Tina Watson. I guess it's more than a rumor since Tina told me herself. Have you heard about it?" The more she thought about what Tina said, the more skeptical she became.

"The roses caper?" Mason grinned and leaned back in his chair. "Come on, Bree, you have to admit it would take a crazy person to murder over roses."

"Stranger things have happened." Bree leaned forward. "Did you talk to Tina?"

"Sure. She claims she and Florence made up two weeks before the death."

"Any evidence that it's true?" Bree asked. She glanced over to see Jenna examining her nails.

"I need a manicure," Jenna muttered.

Mason leaned forward, ignoring Jenna's self-absorption. "No one overheard them talking, if that's what you mean. Watson claims Florence called her up and apologized for stealing a rose clipping. Said she was going to give an interview to the paper and confess." His voice held amusement.

"Did she? Call the paper, I mean?"

"I talked to the editor and he said he had no story like that in the pipeline. But maybe Florence hadn't gotten around to it yet."

It sounded fishy to Bree. She told Mason what Tina said about seeing Victor with a baby. "I wondered if she was trying to smear Florence's name."

Mason's mouth went tight. "There's more to it than you know, Bree. I checked some local and out-of-town stores. Victor had been buying bottles and diapers. For at least a year."

Jenna gasped. "What are you accusing him of?"

"We don't know yet."

Aware her mouth dangled open, Bree gulped and closed it. "The description Ellie's mother gave us sounded like Victor. You think he's been involved all along in the adoption thing?"

"Your guess is as good as mine."

Olivia began to fuss. Bree lifted her from the carrier and jostled the baby on her knee.

Bree leaned forward. "Could I see Victor?"

"Not with the baby. It's not safe."

"I'll keep her," Jenna said. "I just saw him yesterday. You go on back and I'll wait here with Olivia and Samson."

Bree raised a questioning gaze to Mason, and he nodded. "I'll take you to an examination room and go get him," he said, rising from his chair.

Mason led her to a room at the end of the hall. Bree dug out the sudokus Victor had done and spread them out on the table. They didn't tell her anything, but she hoped when he saw them, he might react. She didn't have to wait long before she heard steps and the key at the door of the room.

Victor shuffled in. There was a stubby pencil behind his ear. Mason glanced at his watch. "Ten minutes?"

"That should be fine," Bree said. "Hey, Vic, sit down a minute.

I thought maybe we could do some puzzles together, just like old times. You game?" She watched for a reaction, but he simply shuffled to the other chair and sat in it with his head down.

Bree studied him: lank blondish hair that needed a trim, a spotty complexion that the garish color of the jumpsuit only emphasized, and downcast blue eyes. In the past she'd seen him animated and talkative, waving his hands as he spoke. This young man seemed to have had the life drained out of him. It hurt her to see him this way.

She slid a puzzle across the table to him. "Buddy, did you create this?"

He didn't nod or shake his head. His hands clasped in his lap, he stared at the sudoku.

"Do you have any new ones?"

Slowly his hand went to his chest, and he reached into his jumpsuit and pulled out a folded piece of paper. He unfolded it and smoothed in down on the table.

Bree leaned forward. The page was blank, but Victor took out a pencil and began to draw lines that soon became boxes. His long fingers moved quickly and the grids appeared. He began filling in some of the boxes but left most of them empty, so Bree knew he was creating a puzzle for her to do. He put the pencil behind his ear again, then slid the paper across the table to her.

She studied it and realized the top row would form that same number again. "What do the top numbers mean, Vic? I don't understand."

He stood and shuffled to the door, where he laid his head against the door. Bree went to join him. She touched his arm. "Vic? Please explain. Jenna and I want to get you out of here."

He began to bang his head against the wall. "Don't do that!"

she said. She tried to pull him from the door, but he thumped his head even harder. "Mason," she called.

The key scraped in the lock, and the sheriff peered inside. "Ready to go back to your cell, Victor?" he asked.

Victor hung his head, and she knew this puzzle was the only clue she was going to get.

Lights shone in a welcoming halo from the windows of the lighthouse. The day had seemed unending to Bree. She hurried with Olivia up the path to the house. Samson followed. It was like walking through a snow tunnel with the high piles of shoveled snow on either side. If they had another storm, Kade wouldn't be able to heft the snow high enough. Her gaze swept the yard. No new footprints.

Since she'd found the pipe, she'd watched for another sign.

The baby was wailing when she reached the living room where Kade sat on the floor playing Uno with Davy. "There, there," Bree crooned, smoothing the fuzz on the infant's head. "Don't cry, Olivia."

Davy jumped up and ran to the baby. "Hey, Olivia," he crooned. "You just missed me, didn't you?"

Surprisingly, the baby quieted at Davy's voice. Bree smiled. "I think she did miss you."

Kade glanced up. "She probably has another name. You have to be careful not to get too attached, Bree." His voice was stern.

She pressed her lips together, unsure how to convince him the baby needed them. The tension in the room escalated. Bree didn't want to admit, even to herself, that she would have to give up this tiny girl. She snuggled the infant and inhaled the sweet aroma of baby powder. She'd been quick to buy her favorite—

Baby Magic. The scent brought back many happy memories of when Davy was born.

Samson shook the snow from his fur and came to lie down at Bree's feet.

Davy took the baby's hand, and her fingers curled around his thumb. "Hi, Olivia," he crooned. He looked up at his mother. "Did you find her mom and dad today?"

Bree shook her head. "I'm still working on it." She watched her son turn back to make faces at the baby. Was Olivia's mother somewhere mourning her loss the way Bree had mourned that year for Davy?

Davy tickled the baby under the chin. "Do you like living here, Olivia?" He glanced up at his mother. "We'll try to make it nice until we find your mom."

Her urgency to find Olivia's parents flared again. Though she'd investigated today, she secretly hoped to find nothing. Davy's reminder that someone might be searching for the baby kicked up her anxiety.

Kade went down on one knee by Davy. The seven-year-old looped his arm around his father's neck and leaned against him. One day soon the adoption would be final.

The doorbell rang, and Kade sprang up. "I'll get it."

Moments later, she recognized Mason's deep tones. He had said nothing about stopping by. He must have news.

The sheriff's burly figure stepped into view behind Kade. He carried his hat in his hands. "Evening, Bree."

She stood with her fingers tightening around Olivia. "Is there news?"

He nodded. "Another missing baby report filed in Marquette. Chuck Loonsfoot and his girlfriend, Mandy Walker."

Bree glanced at the sleeping child in her arms. "Olivia isn't Native American. Besides, I think she is Ellie Bristol's baby."

"The mother is Caucasian. We have to check it out. I want to take the baby to the couple and see if they identify her."

Bree's face went hot, then cold. "I'll go with you."

"Bree, I'm not sure that's wise," Kade said.

"I have to go, Kade!" Bree swallowed hard. "If-if we have to give her up, I'll want to say good-bye."

"We'll all go then," Kade said. "Davy will want to give her a last kiss."

Did he even care they might lose Olivia? Bree swallowed down her tears and put a few extra diapers in Olivia's bag.

Davy's eyes grew round. "Uncle Mason, you mean you found Olivia's mommy?"

Mason touched his nephew's red hair. "I don't know, Davy. Maybe. Maybe not. We can only go check it out."

The boy blinked his eyes fiercely but smiled through his watery eyes. "Okay. I'll get my coat. And her teddy bear."

The lump forming in Bree's throat became a boulder. She laid Olivia in her carrier and tucked the cover over it, then slipped on her coat. Kade grabbed the diaper bag, and they all went out to Mason's SUV. Even Samson tagged along. Mason let the dog into the back hatch. Kade took the baby from Bree and secured Olivia's car seat carrier.

All the way to the reservation, Bree alternated between the unselfish hope that Olivia's parents would be found and a plea to God that she and Kade be allowed the keep the baby. When Mason's SUV rolled along the roads to Marquette and stopped at a block building, she took a deep, calming breath. Whatever happened next was what God knew was best. Hard as it was, she needed to keep that truth in mind.

She freed Olivia's carrier and climbed out of the backseat with the baby. Davy slid out after her and took her other hand. She squeezed his fingers. "We'll be all right, no matter what."

"I know," he said. "She needs her mom. Just like I did."

She knew he loved the baby as much as she did. How could a child show the way to such an unselfish path?

"Want me to carry her?" Kade asked, joining them on the sidewalk.

"No, I've got her." She wasn't taking in the diaper bag unless they had to. Her pulse hammered as Mason led them into the police headquarters. The parents were supposed to be here waiting.

As soon as they entered with the baby carrier, a man and woman shot to their feet and rushed toward them. Chuck and Mandy.

"I want my baby," the woman cried out. In her midtwenties, she was beautiful with big blue eyes. Her straight blonde hair fell nearly to her waist.

Her boyfriend touched her arm. "We don't know if this is our baby," he reminded her. About Mandy's age, his coloring was as dark as hers was fair.

Bree exchanged a glance with Kade and Mason. It was possible the woman was Olivia's mother. Bree peeled back the cover to expose Olivia's face. "Is this your daughter?" she asked.

The bright hope in the couple's faces drained away. Mandy closed her eyes briefly, then opened them and shook her head. "No," she whispered. "Our Ruth has black hair that sticks up like a woodpecker's feathers. Her cheeks are fat and round." She sank back onto the bench by the door and buried her face in her hands.

Her sobs broke Bree's heart. She handed the carrier to Kade and went to Mandy. "Is there anything I can do?" she said, sitting beside the stricken mother.

The woman raised her head. "No." Her gaze locked with Bree's. "Who would do this—steal a baby?"

"What happened to your baby girl?" Bree asked.

"I carried her outside with me to the backyard to feed the

chickens. I put the carrier down on the porch a minute to get the feed, and when I turned back around—she was gone." Her voice broke, and tears slipped down her cheeks.

"I'm so sorry." Who would have taken an infant when the mother's back was turned? "Do you have any idea who might have taken her?"

Mandy's eyes widened. "Chuck says it was a windigo," she whispered, her eyes darting to the dark window. "But they're not real, are they? He's so superstitious."

Under normal circumstances, Bree would have laughed, but the fright in the woman's eyes made the chuckle die in Bree's throat. "Why does he say that?" she asked.

"I-I heard a scream. Strange and terrifying. It made me shudder and run to get Ruth. That's when I found out she was gone." Mandy clasped herself. "I hope I never hear that sound again." She rose and went to Chuck, who stood talking to the men. When she touched his arm, he nodded to them, and the two of them went out into the cold.

Bree joined the men where they stood talking to the policeman. "Did you hear what she said?" she asked. Kade shook his head. "She said Loonsfoot thought her baby had been taken by a windigo. She heard a weird scream."

The policeman nodded. "I have had several of these reports. And I heard a scream myself, just last week. It was enough to make me run for the house."

"What did it sound like?" Kade asked.

"A wild, lonely sound. Full of rage and hate," the man said. "I gotta admit, I was looking over my shoulder."

Kade glanced out the window into the dark yard. "Where did you hear it?"

"From the woods behind my house. Around midnight. I was on the porch smoking."

"You said you'd had other reports," Mason said.

"Reports of the screaming."

Bree knew her husband—he was on the trail to discovering what animal would make that sound. She didn't believe in the windigo, but the longer the man talked, the more uneasy she grew.

Kade shoved his hands in his coat pockets. Davy sidled closer to him, and Kade took out his right hand and put it on the boy's head. "Any tracks?"

"There was nothing I could determine."

"I'd like to see," Kade muttered.

The officer shrugged. "Nothing to see, but you're welcome to look." He gave Kade the address to his house.

Olivia began to cry, and Bree glanced at her watch. Feeding time. A good distraction from the fear that had begun to creep up her neck.

14

HER FIRST PAYCHECK. WEDNESDAY MORNING, LAURI CLUTCHED
the envelope in her hand and turned on her computer. Only for a
few days' pay, but the money held the promise of a new life for her
and Wes. She jiggled her mouse and checked her e-mail. Nothing.
The day's work consisted of working on quarterly reports for several clients so Mrs. Saunders could pay the taxes.

She bent to her task and several hours passed before she knew
it. Rubbing the ache in her neck, she decided a cup of coffee
would give her a boost. Starting to the door, she glimpsed a man
stride past. It was Mrs. Saunders's husband. She faltered at his grim
expression.

Her phone rang, and she stepped back to grab it. Mrs. Saunders
demanded her presence. Now. Maybe Lauri would get to hear
what Mr. Saunders had to say. Aware she shouldn't be so nosy, she
rushed down to her boss's office with her notepad. Raised voices
echoed into the hallway, and she paused, uncertain about entering
Mrs. Saunders's office.

"I'm doing all I can," Mr. Saunders said.

"It's not enough!" Mrs. Saunders's voice vibrated with anger. "Do
what they want, Mike. You have no choice."

"I hate giving in to blackmail."

Mrs. Saunders's voice softened. "We already gave them the

money. Just withdraw the mine and it will be over. I want it to be over."

Blackmail? Was that what Lauri had taken in the briefcase? A payoff? She wondered why the Saunderses would be blackmailed and whether she should report what she'd heard. But really, it was no business of hers. And she might lose her job.

If she got a chance, she'd talk to Kade about it.

The cold wind blew off a frozen Lake Superior, and the sun tried to shine through the cloud cover. Quinn stood on the promontory behind the lighthouse and listened to the horn out in the bay. He adjusted the wig but took off the sunglasses. No one would see him today.

He wasn't here to moon over the past and what might have been. He'd made his choice, and now he had everything he wanted. Everything except his son, and he meant to remedy that.

His cell phone rang, and he saw it was Jenna. "Hey, everything okay?"

"I just left the jail. Victor still isn't talking. They're going to convict him, Quinn, I just know it. What can I do?"

"Have you talked to his lawyer?"

Her laugh was bitter. "The kid is fresh out of law school."

"Has Victor said anything at all?"

"Nothing," she said, her voice despondent. "He doesn't look at me, doesn't react. I can't even tell if he knows I'm in the room. And he's still doing those endless puzzles. It's driving me crazy."

The wind was freezing his butt off, and he was ready to end the call. Her whining didn't do anyone any good. "What do you want me to do?"

"Nothing, I guess." She sighed. "Where are you?"

"At the lighthouse. I'm just here figuring out how best to pull it off." And how to get the boy, but he didn't mention that part. He wanted to get inside and get this reconnaissance over with before Bree came back. "Listen, I've got to go."

"How long do I have to stay with Bree? I'm getting tired of lying to her. She's a nice lady."

"Not much longer. I'm guessing he'll cave in the next two days. Then we can grab the baby and go." She'd have to know about his intentions to take Davy sooner or later, but not yet.

"Do you have a heart at all, Quinn?" she asked, her voice soft.

"Where'd that come from? I'm trying to help you."

The click on the other end told him she'd hung up. He rolled his eyes. Women. He'd never figure them out. Jenna's moods changed faster than Lake Superior's weather.

The key in his pocket used to fit the door, and if he knew Bree, it still did. She would have seen no reason to change it. In seconds it was in his hand, and he was standing at the back door. His own back door. The lock accepted the key and turned easily, and he stepped into the kitchen.

Nostalgia caught him unawares. He'd walked away from his old life years ago. He moved to the sink and touched the faucet handles. The installation of these had been tricky, and he'd had to do it twice before he'd gotten them turning the right direction.

His gaze swept the refrigerator. Did she still drink root beer? He pulled the handle and looked. Six cans of Dad's Root Beer were on the bottom shelf. A smile tugged at his lips, but he couldn't afford to become sentimental. Leaving the kitchen, he found his way into the living room. A photo album was on the bookcase. He flipped it open. A picture of him with Davy and Samson was on the first page. It had been taken just before the plane crash.

Quinn stared into the face of the boy he'd thought never to see again. Davy had been the most important thing in his life. Quinn looked forward to getting to know his boy again.

Upstairs, he told himself. The door to the bedroom he'd shared with Bree stood open. Now another man's shoes were in the closet. Another man's toothbrush sat next to hers in the holder on the bathroom counter. The indentation on the pillow belonged to another guy. Matthews held her at night.

It was just as well. She was much too unsophisticated for the life he led now.

His gaze focused on the bassinet. Problem here. The baby must sleep in their room. It might make snatching her a challenge. He backed out the door and went to his son's room. Stepping to the window, he looked down onto the roof over the kitchen. It would be an easy matter to climb the roof and come in this window. Snatch Davy in the middle of the night.

He hurried down the steps, but stopped when he'd nearly reached the bottom. A woman stood in the living room. Though her back was to him, he'd know that stylish cut anywhere, though it had grayed more since he saw it last. He must have made an involuntary sound, because she whirled to face him.

"I came to borrow . . ." The words died on her lips as their gazes locked. The pink color in her cheeks faded and left her looking old and sallow. She slammed her eyes shut, holding them closed for a minute. "Dear Jesus," she whispered. "Now I am seeing ghosts."

Quinn should have run the moment she shut her eyes, but he found himself frozen in place. "*Aiti.*" The Finnish word for *mother* came out croaked and faint, but she must have heard it because her eyes flew open.

Her gaze roamed his face, his form. "Wh-who are you?"

Nothing could have made him lie with her blue eyes on him. "It's me. Rob." The unfamiliar name rolled off his tongue much too easily. He hadn't been Rob Nicholls in an eternity. But Anu Nicholls had ingrained certain morals in him. And not lying to his mother was one of them.

What dab of color remaining in her cheeks left her. Her eyes glazed over, and she swayed.

He leaped to catch her before she could crash to the floor. She was as light as a child in his arms. He carried her to the sofa and laid her on it. Water. He needed a cold cloth. Rushing to the kitchen, he found the dishtowels where Bree had always kept them. The cold water running over it revived him as well. If he were smart, he'd take this opportunity to run.

His mother might think she'd been dreaming.

Though the idea tempted him, he had to make sure she was all right. She was his mother, after all. Maybe he could talk her into keeping quiet. He ran back to the living room and laid the wet towel over her forehead.

She stirred, and her lashes fluttered, then opened. Her gaze was fuzzy until it focused on his face. The awareness in her eyes sharpened. "Rob?" Her shaking hand found his cheek. "I am dreaming, *kulta?*"

He forced himself to remember why he was here. "No, you're not dreaming. I'm really here."

She struggled into sitting position. The cloth fell from her head to the sofa. "Rob, you are alive?"

"Alive and kicking." He attempted a smile, but the ramifications of revealing his presence to her slammed into him.

She was going to want to know why he was back after all this time. And where he'd been. He couldn't tell her anything.

Her eyes narrowed. "Where have you been? Why did you let us grieve you?"

"It's complicated. I'll explain everything later. But for now, you have to keep quiet. Don't tell Bree."

His mother's face grew stricken. "Bree. She and . . . and Kade."

"I know she's remarried."

His mother's eyes filled with tears. "Oh *kulta*, this is so painful for you. It will hurt Bree too."

He shrugged. "I'm fine and she seems happy enough."

"She grieved you for many months, my boy. For a year she searched for the plane, for your body and that of Davy's."

"Did she ever find the plane?"

She nodded. "Who was in it if not you?"

He wasn't prepared to answer her questions yet. He rose, pulling away from her clinging hands. "I can't talk about it now. Wait for my timing. Don't mention this to Bree. Please?"

Her nod held obvious reluctance. "Very well. But I will not hold my tongue for long, Rob. You must tell the truth. To all of us."

He brushed a kiss across her soft, powdered cheek. "I'll be in touch."

She called after him, but he couldn't make out her words, and if he stopped to ask what she'd said, he'd never be able to leave. It was all he could do to walk back the way he'd come, to leave the place he'd once called home.

There was nothing he could do about it now but play the hand he'd dealt himself.

⌘

This poor child needed some clothes. Bree had alternated the three sleepers, but she was tired of doing laundry every day. Another outfit or two wouldn't hurt. The sun shone brightly on this Wednesday morning. The sun wouldn't have enough power to melt the piles of frozen waves in the lake though.

Naomi was already at the Suomi Café with Matthew in a back booth. The toddler was in a booster seat and chewing on a biscuit. The rich scent of *pannukakku*, *pulla*, and jam donuts teased Bree's nose. She was famished.

The waitress, Molly, saw Bree enter with Samson and the baby.

"I've got breakfast for you, my fine boy," she said, smiling at Samson. "The leftovers of a chicken omelet have your name on them. That's okay, eh?" she asked in her thick Yooper accent.

"You're a doll, Molly."

"I've already put in an order for *pannukakku*. Coffee's on the table, eh." She hustled off to the kitchen.

Bree walked toward the booth, but it was always like walking a gauntlet. Everyone wanted to greet Samson, and today they all asked questions about the baby. She finally reached the booth where Naomi sat waiting.

"I didn't think you'd be here yet," Bree said, putting Olivia's carrier on the table. She took off her coat and slid into the booth.

"Donovan had to go in early today, so I got around quickly." She poured coffee into a cup and scooted it toward Bree. "Coffee's fresh."

"I need it." Bree dumped creamer and sugar into her coffee and took a sip. "Fortification for shopping. You know how I hate it."

Naomi rubbed her hands together. "I love it." Her gaze went over Bree's shoulder. "Hey, there's Anu." She waved. "Anu, back here!"

Bree half-turned and smiled at her mother-in-law. Anu looked a little pale, and her smile was halfhearted, but she walked back to join the women. Dressed in crisp navy slacks, every pale blonde strand was in place this morning.

Naomi moved over so Anu could sit. "I love those slacks. I wish I could look so put together."

Anu smiled. "You must come by the shop. We have more colors of this same style."

"Good morning," Bree said, smiling. Anu hadn't yet looked at her, and unease began to work its way up Bree's spine. There was something rather off-putting about her mother-in-law this morning.

"I did not expect to see you girls here so early," Anu said. She poured herself a cup of coffee and sipped it. "I stopped by your house, my Bree, but I missed you there. I wanted to borrow some thimbleberry jam."

"Did you find it?"

Anu shook her head. "What are you girls doing out so early?"

"Breakfast out sounded good. Then we're going shopping for Olivia. I'm tired of seeing her in the same three sleepers. I thought we might come by your shop and see what you've brought in from Finland."

Anu smiled but still didn't look at Bree. "I have many new things. Stop and see."

Molly approached with a plate of leftovers for Samson and food for Naomi and Bree. "You want what Bree's havin', eh, Anu?"

Anu nodded, but Bree noticed her smile was still strained. Once the waitress left, she leaned forward. "You okay, Anu? You don't seem quite yourself this morning."

Anu stared into her coffee cup. "I . . . I did not sleep well, *kulta*. Many thoughts troubled me."

"Rob?" Bree asked, barely daring to breathe.

When Anu raised her gaze, tears shimmered in the depths of her eyes. "I remember so much about my son. But perhaps what I remember is a mother's longing. I'm sure he had many faults I did not see."

Bree raised her brows. In Anu's eyes her son had been pretty wonderful. Bree had tried not to go to Anu when she and Rob had problems during their marriage. "He was a good man," she said. "You can be proud of him."

"I am not so sure," Anu whispered. She gulped some coffee, and her hands shook.

Had Anu seen the biker who so resembled Rob? Bree reached across the table. "Why all this talk about Rob? Have you seen that guy?"

Anu clutched Bree's fingers. "What guy?"

She shouldn't say anything, but it was impossible to keep the words back. "I've seen a man around, one who looks so much like Rob he could be his twin." Her fingers itched to pull out the pipe, but she wasn't willing yet to accept what it meant.

"You didn't tell me that," Naomi said, her voice accusing. Matthew's biscuit fell to the floor, and Samson gobbled it up. Naomi scolded the dog, then got another biscuit for the toddler when he began to cry.

"I've tried not to think about it. It's a little disconcerting," Bree admitted. "I've wondered if someone is playing a game with me. It can't be Rob. We buried him."

"Perhaps that is it," Anu said, setting her coffee down. Some sloshed onto the table.

Bree thought Anu whispered, "Maybe I dreamed it," but she wasn't sure. Anu was normally the strong one, the rock everyone else leaned on. Something had disturbed her in a way Bree had never seen.

Anu's blue eyes focused on Bree's face. "You saw Rob's remains, did you not, my Bree?"

Bree shifted at the uncomfortable subject. She didn't like to relive those days. "Mason showed me the clothing left in the grave with the bones. The jacket was the one you bought him for Christmas that last year."

"Of course, of course," Anu murmured.

Anu was raising doubts in Bree's own mind. She'd been certain the other night that the man was Rob, but in the cold light of day, she knew it was impossible, pipe or no pipe. Now, talking it out with Anu reminded her again of the positive ID on the clothing. How certain Mason had been when he saw the bones.

Bree reached over and squeezed Anu's hand again. "Do you want me to work at the shop for you today? Maybe you need to get some rest."

Anu's smile was forced. "I am fine, *kulta*. I will go to bed early this night. My mind, it plays tricks on an old woman."

"You're not old," Naomi broke in. "I hope I look like you when I'm your age."

Amusement crinkled the edges of Anu's eyes. "Such a back-handed compliment."

"I didn't mean it like that!" Naomi rolled her eyes and took a bite of her omelet.

Anu patted her hand. "This I know, dear girl." The shadows cleared her eyes, and her smile seemed genuine this time.

Bree watched her through the rest of the meal, but Anu had managed to throw off whatever troubled her. When the women paid for their food and stepped outside into the sunshine, she heard the rumble of a big truck. All her certainty rushed to form a lump of doubt in her throat. She tensed and turned to look, but only a man and woman in a beefed-up pickup rumbled past. Red not white.

She wanted to laugh, but the haunted fear had returned to Anu's face, and Bree knew the expression mirrored her own. What was happening to them that they saw ghosts where none existed?

She took a tremulous breath and managed a smile. "We'll walk along with you to the shop."

"Very good," Anu said. "Come, Samson. Grammy has some treats for you." The dog padded at her heels.

Bree found herself staring at every male she passed and wondering if he was the man she mistook for Rob. They passed the jail, and she waved at Mason. He waved back but didn't stop before running up the steps, so something must be up. She wondered if it had anything to do with Victor. Or maybe Pia's death.

Anu unlocked the door and let them into the shop. The scent of new clothing mingled with yesterday's cardamom bread. Bree set the baby carrier on the floor, then went to the racks of baby clothing first. Anu didn't carry much infant clothing, but Bree picked out two new sleepers and a little cotton dress that would be cute when the weather broke.

If she still had Olivia.

Anu gave a choked sob, then turned and vanished through the bathroom door. The lock clicked.

Bree went to the door and shook it. She heard the unmistakable sound of Anu vomiting. "Anu, what's wrong?"

After a few moments, Anu's voice came through the door. "You go now, *kulta*. We will talk later. I am sick. The flu, I think. I will go home when Eino gets here. Go now."

Bree didn't believe for a minute that Anu had the flu. Was she going crazy or had a ghost taken up residence in Rock Harbor?

Did a ghost drive a pickup? Or leave footprints in the snow beside a well-known pipe? She didn't want to face those questions when the answers might turn her life upside down.

15

THE ROAR OF THE SNOWMOBILE SHUT OUT THE THOUGHTS in his head. Kade rode his machine along the groomed snowmobile trail. He managed to stay focused enough to note where shrubs needed to be trimmed back and where low branches overhung the trail. Reaching the pavilion at the end of the trail, he shut off the engine, then dismounted and walked down to the frozen pond to check out the report of a dead deer.

He saw the evidence in blood on the snow, but the carcass was already gone. Wolves, from the tracks. After jotting the incident down in his log book, he rode on to headquarters.

His gut tightened when the brick building came into view. Leaving the snowmobile in the corral designated for the machines, he walked into the building. Nodding at the receptionist in the public display area, he went through the door marked PRIVATE and down the hall past the bank of offices to his own space at the end of the hallway. Inside his office, he shut the door and dropped into his chair. He'd made it to safety. So far.

Before his relief had a chance to jell, he heard his boss's familiar tap at the door. The knot that formed in his belly nearly made him sick. "Come on in, Gary."

Landorf pushed open the door and walked in. His brows were

drawn together, and the way he avoided meeting Kade's gaze made the acid churn even more. Maybe today was the day.

Gary dropped into the chair opposite the desk. "You check out that dead deer report?"

"Yep. Wolves already disposed of it."

"You got that grant application ready?" Landorf said with no more small talk.

Kade swallowed hard. "Yeah, but I have to tell you, I'm not comfortable with skewing the numbers."

"It's not a big deal, Kade. Don't sweat it." Landorf held out his hand. "I'll look it over and give it back to you to send in."

Kade handed it over. "It's weak without proof of a litter."

"Couldn't find that den?"

He shook his head. "I guess they were lying."

Landorf already had his nose deep in the grant papers. "Take one more pass out there. If you still don't see anything, we'll send this in as is."

If everything worked out, the grant would be approved, and Kade would be called back to the park service before the grant money was gone. He should have been more forceful with Gary about lying on the application though.

Landorf didn't have anything else to say, so he backed out of Kade's office. Kade grabbed his coat and headed to the truck. His cell phone rang. He glanced at the display and saw it was Lauri and flipped it open. "Hey, kid sister."

"How's it going?"

Did her voice hold strain? "Good."

He accelerated down the drive. "You okay? You sound a little upset."

"I'm fine. I got my first paycheck today."

"Good for you! Ready to get that car?"

She didn't answer for a moment. "Well, that might have to wait. Wes, that boyfriend I've been telling you about, wants to start his own outfitting business. I'm going to save up to help him get started."

Like tracks worn in a dirt road, habit was hard to break. Kade knew she'd blow if he tried to advise her, but the words wouldn't stay in his mouth. "You think that's wise?"

"What do you mean?" Her voice was prickly.

"Just that the guy is supposed to take care of his girl, not the other way around. It's setting a bad precedent."

"Kade, you're so old-fashioned. It's a wonder Bree can stand to live with you. Listen, I have to go. I'll see you soon." The phone clicked.

He replaced his phone and shrugged. She was an adult, even if she didn't always act like one.

He turned on a dirt road packed hard with snow. It was probably a waste of time to go back to the crag, but he drove in that direction anyway. He passed a crossroad, 200W, and realized George DeCota lived down that road. He should stop to check on him. Kade had called the night of the attack, and George's wife said he was doing fine, but a personal visit to the tribal policeman wouldn't hurt.

The wind was already busily undoing what the snowplow had done, and small drifts piled on the sides of the road. He found the house and trudged through the snow to the door. When he pounded on the door, he heard George's gruff voice bellow, "Just a minute."

Thumps sounded from inside. The door swung open, and George stood with the aid of crutches in the doorway. "Kade." His brows rose. "Something is wrong?"

"Nope. Just thought I'd check on you."

"It would take more than a broken ankle to keep me down," George said. He stepped away from the door. "Come in."

Kade followed him inside. He sniffed. "Smells like brownies."

"My wife. She thinks food cures pain. Maybe she is right." George grinned and dropped onto the worn sofa. "You find that den?"

"No. I was heading out to look again."

"I was going to call you. My sons say they saw a mother cougar and four kittens yesterday up on Eagle Rock."

Kade had started to sit, but he sprang upright at the news. "Where?"

"The rock wall overlooking the river."

Kade knew it well. "I'll head out there now. Thanks, George!" He headed for the door.

"Call if you find it!"

"I will." Kade ran back to his truck and drove south to the Kitchigami wilderness area. The parking lot was deserted. He parked, grabbed his camera, then started for the summit. The climb wouldn't be nearly as arduous as the last one. His breath fogged out of his mouth, and he trod the path as fast as he dared. The snow crunched under his boots. Fifteen minutes later he stood atop Eagle Rock and stared down at the frozen river.

The rocks hid a small cave mouth along the ledge six feet down. He suspected he might find the den there. His gaze swept the area and latched on to spoor by a pine tree. Big cat prints surrounded it. He touched one with his gloved hand, then rose and trailed the spoor to the edge of the cliff face. Peering over the side, he saw tracks on the ledge below. They disappeared into the cave.

The cougar's lair. He didn't dare jump down and enter. If kittens were inside, the mama cougar would be spitting and snarling. He wasn't sure how to get the pictures he needed. He could settle in and wait, but the cougar would smell him and keep her babies hidden. His gaze raked the area. The tree. His camera took timed shots. He could wedge it in the tree and set it up for periodic

exposures. Tomorrow he might have pictures that would prove
the kittens existed.

～

Only one more day of work this week. Lauri rubbed gritty eyes.
After shutting off her computer, she thrust her arms into her coat,
grabbed her purse, and paused outside Mrs. Saunders's door. She
knocked.

"Come in."

Lauri poked her head inside. "I'm going now, Mrs. Saunders.
Anything I can do for you before I leave?"

The woman's reddened eyes stared back. She bit her lip. "You
want to have dinner with me tonight, Ms. Matthews? My husband is gone, and I . . . I'd rather not be alone. If you've got plans,
that's fine."

"Sure, Mrs. Saunders. I can have dinner." Wes wasn't coming
over tonight. "I need to stop by my home after class and let my
dog out first. Is that okay?"

"Just bring him with you. Here's my address." She slid a card
across the desk to Lauri.

"You mean we're eating at your house?"

"Yes, I didn't make that clear, did I? My cook is excellent."
Mrs. Saunders rose. "About six?"

"Okay." Lauri backed out the door and ran for her car. An
invitation to the boss's house! What a coup. Curiosity gnawed at
her though. The woman's distressed state worsened every day.
Maybe she'd open up tonight.

After her afternoon classes, Lauri ran by her apartment and
grabbed Zorro, who was excited to be getting out. The heater in
her old car didn't work well, and Lauri shuddered with the cold as
she drove along the icy streets of Houghton. When she reached
the Saunders residence, she gasped. Lights spilled from windows

that rose nearly two stories high. The place had to be ten thousand square feet.

She took Zorro up the heated walkway and pressed the doorbell. The shivers she had were from excitement, not the cold. "Be a gentleman," she told her dog.

A woman answered the door. Her glance went to the dog, but she said nothing about Lauri bringing him along. "Mrs. Saunders is expecting you. This way, please."

She led Lauri along a marble hallway. Art lined the walls. Lauri guessed the passage to be ten feet wide. Her boots left wet marks on the pristine floors, but there was nothing she could do about it. As she neared the dining room, the aroma of the food made her mouth water. Some kind of beef, maybe? She hadn't eaten lunch, and her tummy had been complaining for the past two hours.

The woman stopped in front of the arched opening into the dining room. Lauri peeked in at the gleaming dishes and tableware. A huge centerpiece of fresh flowers graced the table. But Mrs. Saunders wasn't in the room.

The housekeeper, or whatever she was, appeared to notice at the same time. "She was here a moment ago. Please be seated, and she'll be right back, I'm sure." The woman walked on down the hall and passed through a door at the end.

Lauri didn't want to make the mistake of taking Mrs. Saunders's seat, so she stood in the doorway feeling awkward. Zorro sat at her feet, then lay down. She glanced around the room, noticing more beautiful art on the walls.

"Stay," she told Zorro. She wandered the room, examining the paintings more closely. Several were Picasso paintings. They appeared to be the real deal, not reprints. Must be a lot of money in accounting. Or maybe it was her husband's money.

Restless when Mrs. Saunders didn't appear after several minutes, Lauri moved back into the hall to look at the paintings there. Each one led her farther away from the dining room. When she decided to go back, she realized she'd taken several turns. Striking off in the direction she thought she'd come, she hurried toward what she thought was the dining room but found a library instead.

She needed Zorro to find her way back. Trying again to retrace her steps, she heard the murmur of voices. Maybe one belonged to Mrs. Saunders, though she had said her husband would be gone, and Lauri distinctly heard a male voice.

She moved in the direction of the sound. The door stood open a crack, and she could see into a living room or sitting room of some kind with sleek leather furniture and glass-topped tables. Very modern and expensive. But the voices, not the room, riveted Lauri's attention.

Mrs. Saunders's voice rose in a wail. "You killed her?"

"Your husband has to know we mean business. He's got two days or Alexa is next. You'd better convince him."

"I've tried." Mrs. Saunders's voice was choked. "Please don't hurt her."

Steps sounded on the floor. Lauri started to back up, but the door swung open before she could react, and she saw the man she'd delivered the briefcase to at the library. Mr. Jones.

"I thought someone was here." Mr. Jones grabbed her arm and jerked her inside the room. He shoved her onto the sofa beside Mrs. Saunders.

"What did you hear?"

"No-nothing," Lauri stammered. "I got turned around when I was looking at the pictures, and I was trying to find the dining room again." The derision on his face told her he didn't buy her excuses.

Mrs. Saunders rose and pulled Lauri to her feet. "Down the hallway and turn left," she said. When the man started to grab Lauri's arm again, her boss stepped between them. "This is between us, not her. You touch her and I'll call the police."

The man rolled his eyes then went toward the door. "She'd better be telling the truth." With the warning, he exited.

Tears welled in Lauri's eyes, but she wasn't sure why. He hadn't hurt her, but he'd scared her. And murder. Mrs. Saunders said he murdered someone. "Who is that guy?" she whispered.

Mrs. Saunders sank back onto the sofa and put her head in her hands. "A very bad man, Lauri. You didn't hear anything, did you?"

"No," she said. The lie didn't sit well on her conscience, but the terror welling in her chest kept her from admitting the truth. "What does he want?"

"Nothing for you to be concerned about. Maybe you'd better go home, Lauri. I'm not very good company."

Who should she tell about this? Kade? Mason? Or should she just keep her mouth shut and hope to fly under that guy's radar? She said her good-byes, grabbed Zorro, and headed straight for Wes's mobile home. Darkness shrouded the yard, but she knew where the tools were and avoided falling over them on her way to the steps to the trailer. The light was still on in the living room, so she knew he was up. Not bothering to knock, she opened the door and stepped inside with Zorro on her heels.

Wes lay stretched out on the sofa. He sat up when Lauri came in. "Hey, what's wrong?" he asked.

Lauri sat on his lap and told him what had happened. "I'm scared," she said. "He murdered someone."

"What's his name?" Wes asked.

Lauri shuddered, and Zorro whined and put his cold nose against her cheek. "Bill Jones, but that's got to be fake."

His jaw jutted. "No one messes with my girl."

"Am I your girl? Did you break it off with Maura?"

"Tomorrow," he promised. "But you know what—we might be able to exploit this thing."

"What do you mean?"

His eyes shone as he leaned forward and grasped her hand. "You heard incriminating evidence, Lauri! He might cough up enough money for me to start my own outfitting business. He's not going to want you to tell what you know."

"He might *kill me* if he knows what I overheard! Or don't you care about that?"

"Kill you. Listen to yourself. You're so melodramatic. He's not going to kill you, especially if he knows I know too. He can't go around killing everyone."

Suddenly cold, Lauri clasped her arms around herself. "You don't know this guy."

"No, but I'm going to find out."

"What do you mean?"

"I mean if I watch your boss long enough, he's bound to show up. And I can get his plate number and track him down."

"Don't do anything," she begged. "I'm scared, Wes. Please listen to me."

But his gaze was distracted and she knew he didn't hear a word she said. She was going to have to talk to Kade.

16

IF SHE HEARD JENNA GIGGLE ONE MORE TIME AT KADE'S jokes, Bree was going to dump this colander of spaghetti on her head. Didn't Jenna realize how inappropriate it was to flirt with a married man? Or maybe she flirted with everyone.

Bree put the food on the table. "Dinner," she called. The least Jenna could do was help around the house. She hadn't lifted a finger since she moved in. She left her bed unmade and dirty towels on the bathroom floor. Maybe she was used to a maid, but Bree wasn't about to pick up after her.

Her gaze went to the window. Darkness fell early this time of year. Was that man out there watching? If only she knew who he was. Her suspicions had to be wrong. She'd seen Rob's remains. Still, who would want to confuse and taunt her—and why?

After dinner, Bree waited until Jenna went to bed to talk to Kade about her. The fire threw shadows around the living room, and the cinnamon scent from the candle soothed her ire.

Kade dropped beside her on the sofa and hugged her. "You were quiet through dinner. Everything okay?"

Bree's first reaction was to stiffen, but she reminded herself Jenna's behavior wasn't his fault. She was the one who had invited Jenna to stay. "It's Jenna," she said. "It's driving me crazy the way she flirts with you. She's been here over a week now."

"I haven't been flirting with her!"

"I didn't say you were, but I'd like to see you discourage her a little."

He pulled her tighter. "I've never seen you jealous."

She struggled against his grip. "I'm not jealous! It's just not appropriate." He laughed, and she wanted to punch him. "It's not funny, Kade."

"Your green eyes are throwing sparks," he said, his voice teasing. "She's just a kid."

"She's only a few years younger than me."

"Well, she acts like a kid. I've just been trying to make her feel at home."

"She's quite enough at home," she muttered. "I want her to leave." She should be ashamed of herself, but there was enough going on without the constant annoyance of Jenna.

"We can't just kick her out," he said, his smile fading.

She rubbed her head. "I know. I keep thinking she'll get tired of small-town life and leave, but she does seem to love her brother. I'm not sure she'll go anywhere until Victor is released."

"You look at the sudokus any more?"

"I've been checking on all nine-digit numbers I can find for any connection to Pia or Florence. I'm about halfway through the list. There are so many. How about your search for the mountain lion?"

His smile vanished. "I'll check my camera tomorrow. Maybe I'll have some shots."

"Why are you so uptight about all this? I've never seen you so desperate."

His lips flattened. "Lots of stuff going on at work. Finding the cougar will . . . will help."

"Help what?"

He shrugged, and she knew he wasn't going to answer that. The doorbell rang. "I'll get it." She rose and went to the door, where she found Lauri on the steps with the snow swirling around her. She pulled her inside, then noticed the younger girl's pallor. "What's wrong?"

"Where's my brother? I need to talk to him. Alone."

"In the living room." Bree stood aside as Lauri brushed past. Her sister-in-law could be almost snippy at times, and Bree didn't understand what set her off. Lauri wasn't telling either.

Bree went to check on her son. He was sleeping with Samson on the foot of the bed. The dog didn't move as she stood watching in the doorway, but if she'd been an intruder, he would have been a mass of bristly hair and teeth. She backed out of the room and stopped by the master bedroom, where she peeked in on Olivia. The baby didn't stir, but she'd be awake in another hour for a feeding.

Bree went down the hall to the office and turned on the computer. She called up the browser and began to search for missing children again. A news article from Minnesota caught her eye. "Adoptive Parents Blow Whistle," it read. She clicked the link and began to skim the article. They'd requested a blue-eyed boy and paid a premium of a hundred thousand dollars. After a diagnosis of autism, they tried to find out more about their son and eventually discovered he'd been stolen from a Native American single mother. The father was Caucasian. The police was investigating the possibility of a baby ring.

All the incidences of missing babies in this area were connected to single moms like Ellie Bristol, Bree realized. And maybe of mixed race. Was someone taking them and selling them? Maybe whoever it was justified their actions based on some self-righteous morality or even bigotry.

She'd have to talk to Mason about it. Rising from the computer, she went down the steps. No voices emerged from the living room, and she found Kade alone. "Lauri gone already?"

"Yeah."

"What did she want?"

He rubbed the top of his head. "She said she overheard some guy threatening her boss. It had to do with blackmail and murder evidently. She wanted to know what to do and I told her to talk to Mason. She wasn't ready to do that yet." He made a face. "I love the girl, but it's always something with her." He pulled Bree down on his lap and nuzzled her neck.

Bree tried to snuggle against him, but a stray thought nearly had her bolting from his embrace. If Rob was alive, what would that mean to her marriage?

⁓

Quinn paced until Rosen's knock came on the cabin door. He threw it open. "Took you long enough."

"What're you so riled about?" Rosen asked. He walked to the living room, where he dropped into a chair.

"I'm tired of this whole thing. I can't trust either of you, and I want it to be over so I can get out of this backwater." He'd finally gotten hold of his partner but the conversation met the usual impasses over Florence's death. At this point, he knew the partnership wouldn't survive much longer, so he didn't spare any regrets over it.

"We've got several, um, problems to wrap up. You were supposed to get rid of the boy days ago. Is that something I'm going to have to do for you?"

"He's a nonissue. So's Victor. Neither one of them is talking."

"You don't know that."

"Jenna is inside the Matthews house. She hears everything. The kid doesn't know what he saw. And Victor won't even talk to her."

Rosen's lips thinned. "If one of them fingers me, we're all on the hook. I'm not walking away and worrying when the cops are going to knock on my door. If you don't handle this, I will."

"You'll do what you're told!" Even as Quinn issued the order, he saw the veiled contempt in the other man's eyes. Rosen thought him too weak to do what had to be done.

"The boss has other plans," Rosen said.

"We're partners. I have just as much control over this situation as he does." But Quinn didn't, and they both knew it.

Quinn tamped down the growing panic in his chest. He couldn't be sure Rosen wouldn't move on his own. The danger surrounding Davy was growing.

Friday morning Lauri stood in an alley doorway out of the wind and stamped her feet to keep them warm. Her car had refused to start this morning, and Wes should be along any minute to run her to work.

She spied his old pickup careening around the corner. Moving out of the shielded cubbyhole, she nearly staggered when the wind struck her back. She hurried toward his vehicle and was about to slide inside when a white Mercedes slid to a stop at the curb. The window ran down without a sound, and Mr. Jones looked her over with an expressionless face.

"Get in," he said.

She heard a click and the door locks sprang up. She stood glancing from Wes's front passenger seat to the back door of the other car. Wes shut off the engine of his truck and leaped out. He joined her beside the Mercedes.

"You okay, Lauri?" he asked.

"It's him," she whispered. "Mr. Jones." She took a step away from the truck. "What do you want?"

"I want to talk to you. Not him, just you." He indicated with a jerk of his thumb that he wanted her in the passenger seat.

Wes put his hands on his hips. "She doesn't go without me," He climbed into the backseat before the man could say anything.

Lauri stood wringing her hands. Getting in that car would be stupid. She didn't trust him.

Her gaze rocketed around the neighborhood, but she saw no one she could call to for help.

"Get in," he said again. "I'm not going to hurt you. I have a business proposition."

His mild tone calmed her fears only a little. She reluctantly opened the passenger door and slid inside. The car's warmth soaked into her chilled skin. She dared a glance at the man and found him studying her. She let him look and infused her own stare with defiance.

"You're younger than I thought," he said, his high voice abrupt.

"I'm nearly twenty," she said with an edge to her tone.

Mr. Jones waved his hand in a dismissive gesture. "Look kid, I know you heard stuff that was none of your business. I followed you when you went running to your brother. What did you tell him?"

"I didn't hear anything," she said, desperate to keep her brother out of it. "I just stopped by to say hello."

"Don't play games, little girl."

Wes leaned forward from the back. "We know everything," he said, tipping up his chin. "How you murdered someone and how you're blackmailing the Saunders family."

Lauri nearly groaned. She so didn't want to be here. This was going to get them in trouble. She just knew it.

The man glanced at her. "You going to let this guy speak for you?"

She shrugged and attempted a smile.

He studied her face, then shrugged. "I'll give you ten grand, and you keep your mouth shut about anything you've heard. None of it's your business."

Wes cleared his throat. "We want twenty thousand."

The guy rolled his eyes. "Go right for the jugular, huh? Fifteen."

"I don't think you want to end up behind bars," Wes said. "We're not taking less than twenty. This is huge."

Lauri wanted to tell Mr. Jones she didn't want his money, but Wes could really use the cash. It might be just what they needed to break free of his family. She choked back the fear bubbling up. The guy studied her face, and she bit her lip but managed to hold his gaze. She kept her expression defiant. At least she hoped that's what he took away from it. A serious threat. When he jerked his chin down in an abrupt nod, she nearly sagged in the seat.

He reached into the back and pulled a black snakeskin briefcase into the front with him. Fiddling with the combination, he cursed until the levers flipped up. He pulled out stacks of twenties, which he began tossing into her lap.

Terror filled her. She swallowed hard. She was so going to regret this.

His lips twisted. "Don't go getting any bright ideas. That's all. No more, it's done. If I find out you've told anyone what you heard, you're dead."

Dead? Lauri gulped and studied the hard glint in his eyes. She stuffed the money into her bag. "I won't say anything to anyone. My brother doesn't know anything." Neither did she, not really. Not even his real name.

"Our lips are sealed," Wes said, his voice full of suppressed excitement. A grin tugged at his lips.

"You'd better not, either one of you." He stared at them. "Though there is one more requirement to the deal."

"Requirement?"

"I want to make sure you have incentive not to talk."

Looking into his glittering eyes, she had plenty of incentive. "What do you want?"

"It's about your brother," he said.

"Don't drag my brother into this."

"He's got a son. A young boy."

Lauri sank against the seat back. "Yes."

"I'd like to have a chat with him."

Lauri shook her head. "He's just a little kid. Why would you want to talk to him?"

"That's my business," he said. "All you have to do is bring the kid to the Raccoon Lake picnic grounds and leave me alone with him for thirty minutes."

"I don't want him hurt," she said.

"I'm not going to hurt him. This could all be over for you. Everyone will be happy. Once it's done, I'll know I can trust you because you won't want anyone to know what you did either."

Lauri wasn't sure she believed his smooth voice. Even as an inner voice urged her to do whatever it took to get out of this mess, she envisioned Davy's earnest green eyes and the smattering of freckles across his nose. It would kill her if this guy hurt him.

She summoned her courage. "I can't do that."

He shrugged. "Deliver the kid or pay the consequences."

"He's just a little boy!" Her throat closed, and her eyes grew hot. "What do you want with him?"

"I need some leverage," he said.

Leverage? "Leave him alone."

"Look, kid, I'm not going to hurt a little boy. I'm just going to talk to him. Talk."

Now that he was being persuasive rather than threatening, she was even more afraid. There was something very big at stake, and she didn't have the foggiest idea what it might be.

She wet her lips. "No, I can't do it."

He glanced at Wes. "I think you will. Eventually. I'll be in touch." His tone dismissed her.

She fumbled for the door handle, but it didn't open and she realized it was locked. She flipped the lock and shoved open the door. Her knees trembled as she leaped from his car to Wes's truck. She locked her door and sat shaking in the passenger seat.

Wes exited the backseat of the Mercedes and flung himself under the steering wheel of his truck. "What a rush!" He jammed the key into the ignition switch.

The engine ground. "Come on, come on," she whispered. "Get us out of here." She wanted never to see that guy again.

The engine caught, and the tires spun on the ice as Wes pulled away from the curb. He grabbed her bag with one hand and opened it. "Twenty grand! We can start a new life, Lauri. You'll see."

"He's going to kill Davy, Wes." The words came out between sobs. She loved her little nephew. What had she done?

"You exaggerate everything," he said, his voice sulky. "Calm down, Lauri. We'll have another chat with him."

"You must not have noticed that there's no talking to this guy!" she screamed. "I'm not turning my nephew over to him."

"You don't have a nephew. Just a stepnephew. And what harm can there be to talk? We can keep the money and have our fresh start."

"I'm not letting Davy get anywhere close to him."

Disgust filled Wes's voice. "Sheesh, you're so melodramatic."

The tears flooding her eyes dried. "Wes, you haven't seen this guy as many times as I have. You have no idea how scary he is."

"Scary," he scoffed. "He's good at scaring women and little kids."

All that bravado could get them both killed. Pain pulsed behind her left eye, and she pressed her fingers against it. "You don't understand."

He leaned closer, and his breath stirred her hair. "I understand that you're paralyzed with fear. You're not seeing how our future together is at risk. We can have it all, baby. You'll see. Get the kid and I'll take him to see the guy."

She didn't know what she was going to do, how she was getting out of this fix.

It was only after she reached the office fifteen minutes later that she realized she'd been breathing shallowly all the way there. Her lungs expanded, and her vision blurred as he pulled against the curb and shut off the engine. She leaned her head against her window and drew in a deep breath. And another, until she could see again.

What had they done?

～⁀⁀

Bree glanced at her watch as she sat in Syl's Country Café outside Ontonagon. The woman was late. She'd left Samson sleeping in the Jeep. In the carrier, Olivia squinted at the bright light. She'd found her thumb and so far hadn't uttered a peep.

A young woman rushed into the café. Her long dark hair and vivid blue eyes attracted the attention of the five men in the dining room. The snug jeans she wore hugged every curve, and she stood by the door and scanned the tables. When her gaze landed on Bree, she smiled and moved forward.

"You must be Bree Matthews," she said, her voice low and breathless. "I'm Inga Beckjord. Thanks for seeing me."

The young woman had called an hour ago after getting Bree's number from Mrs. Bristol "Thanks for calling me." Bree waited until the young woman sat down. "You said you had some information about Ellie's disappearance?"

Inga ordered coffee and a turkey sandwich when the waitress approached. Once they were alone again, she studied Olivia. "She might be Ellie's baby."

"When did you see Ellie last?"

"The day she disappeared. She stopped by my apartment on her way to meet the guy arranging the adoption. She wanted me to go with her."

Bree leaned forward, trying to contain her excitement. "Did you go along?"

The waitress brought Inga's coffee. Once she was gone, Inga nodded. "She wasn't sure she wanted to go through with it. When she mentioned this, he said she'd have to pay back all the money if she backed out. She'd already received half of it, then spent it on college tuition and rooming, which was part of the agreement and why she was getting so much."

"What did the guy look like?"

"Small, slim. Good dresser with expensive shoes."

"Ellie didn't mention a name?"

Inga shook her head. "There were no introductions. We met the guy at a coffee shop."

"How were things when you parted?"

"She cried all the way home. Her mom had already told her she couldn't help her raise the baby."

"So she was planning on going through with it."

Inga hesitated. "That's why I called you. While we were on the way home, she called that guy and told him the deal was off. That she'd find a way to pay him back even if it took awhile. I could hear the guy yelling through the phone. Ellie kind of shrank back against the seat and cried."

Poor girl. "What did she say when she hung up?"

Inga bit her lip. "She said she was afraid of that guy, afraid he might take the baby by force."

"Was she planning to go to the police?"

"No, she was too afraid. She wasn't sure if what she was doing was legal or not." Inga stared down at her coffee cup. "But what if she was right?" she whispered. "Maybe he came and took her somewhere until the baby came and then killed her."

Chills ripped down Bree's back. "If he paid her forty thousand, he must have charged the adoptive parents much more. The baby would be very valuable to him." The nightmare scenario wouldn't stop playing in her head. "Did Ellie buy anything for the baby that might prove Olivia is her child?"

"She bought a pink sleeper that had a rabbit on it. With a hot pink nose."

Bree gulped and reached for the diaper bag. She unzipped it and lifted out a sleeper. "Like this?"

Tears filled Inga's eyes. "Just like that," she whispered, touching the sleeper. "Can't DNA prove Olivia belonged to Ellie?"

"It can, but it could take as much as a few months to get test results back. Is there anything else you can tell me about that baby broker, some detail that would help me track him down?"

Inga bit her lip and her eyes took on a faraway expression. "His voice was kind of high. I don't suppose that helps much."

Bree's cell phone rang, and she dug it out of her purse. She glanced at the caller ID and saw it was Mason.

"Bad news," he said when she answered. "I just heard a woman's body was found in the Porkies. She was shot. The wallet with the body identifies her as Ellie Bristol. We're awaiting positive ID from her mother."

"And the baby?" Bree asked, holding her breath.

"The woman recently delivered. No sign of the infant."

"I think Olivia is Ellie's child," she said. Bree's gaze went to Olivia. Motherless, or so it seemed.

17

Sunday after church and lunch Kade rode his snow-mobile toward Eagle Rock. He prayed he'd find the pictures he needed on the camera. He climbed the trail and retrieved his camera. He was about to start flipping through the pictures when his cell phone rang.

He glanced at the display, saw it was Lauri, and flipped it open. "Hey, kid sister."

"Kade, I'm in trouble." Her voice was thick with tears and hysteria.

"What's wrong?"

"Someone broke into my apartment. Stuff from my drawers is all over the floor. They took my camera and my computer." She was sobbing now.

Kade tucked the camera into its bag. "Are you okay? Were you home?"

"No, I'd gone to get a beef pasty. But it's more than just a break-in, Kade." Her voice lowered to a whisper. "Someone has been following me."

"Following you?" He thought back to what she'd overheard. "That guy threatening your boss?"

"I don't know. Maybe. Can you come now? I'm scared."

He glanced at his watch. "I'm a few hours away. Head for my house and I'll meet you there."

"My car isn't working."

"What happened to it?"

"I don't know. It just won't start."

Could someone have tinkered with it? "Okay, I'll come get you. But it will be several hours."

"Can Bree come?"

"I'll give her a call and see if she's busy." He ended the call, then punched in his wife's number. "Hey, babe," he said. "You busy?"

"Just feeding Olivia." She sounded distracted.

"Is something wrong?"

"Mason called. Ellie Bristol's body was just found. Murdered. I talked to Ellie's best friend, Inga. She told me Ellie was going to back out of the adoption even though she couldn't pay the money back. And Inga identified that bunny sleeper as one like Ellie had bought her baby."

He drew in a gulp of air. "So it looks like Olivia is Ellie's baby."

"And her grandmother wants nothing to do with raising her."

Kade saw where the conversation was heading. "We already talked about this, Bree. Let's not argue about it now. We, uh, we've got a situation with Lauri. Her apartment was broken into, and she's shook up. Could you go get her? I'm over in the Kitchigami Wilderness, and it will take me a couple of hours to get to her."

"Sure, Olivia's just finishing her bottle. I'll run over and get Lauri in five minutes. You want me to call her and let her know?"

"Sure. Thanks. I'll be there as soon as I can." He put his camera away and returned to his truck. He'd have to check the photos later.

He was halfway to Lauri's when his cell phone played "Love Me Tender." Bree's tune. He answered it. "Hey, babe. Did you get Lauri all right?"

"Kade, she's not here." Panic strained the tenor of her voice. "I had a key, but I didn't need it. The door was standing wide open. The place is trashed, and I can't find her. Has she called you?"

"No, I haven't heard from her." Kade tried not to panic, but he caught the sharp edge of his wife's fear. "Did you check with the neighbors? Or the superintendent? Did you try calling her?"

"I called you first. I'll try her now. And the neighbors." The baby wailed in the background, and Bree hushed her. "I'll call you back."

Kade accelerated as fast as he dared on the snow-covered road.

Quinn drove slowly into the campground in Houghton. The mark had finally agreed to all their demands. The announcement would be made in two more days. The baby needed to be returned to her parents. And Davy was about to be reunited with his father.

The campground held only three trucks. Snowmobilers, most likely. He'd picked this place thinking they'd be alone. Quinn heard the noisy machines in the distance. He parked under the bare branches of a birch tree and turned to Jenna.

"You look hot in that getup," she said, pressing her lips against his.

He endured her kiss, realizing their relationship was about over. Since being here, he found himself comparing her to Bree every time he turned around. And found her wanting.

"I'll warm you up," she murmured.

"You're good at that." He whispered the lie against her hair. "But we need to talk."

"Talk, talk," she grumbled. "That's all you ever want to do lately." But she settled back against the seat and glanced up at him.

"I need you to grab the kids in two days."

"Kids? I thought it was just the baby."

"The boy too. Davy."

She shook her head. "I'm not taking him. The Matthewses have been good to me. I'd have to have strong incentive to do that." Her gaze grew cunning and she waggled the ring finger of her left hand at him. "Like wedding bells."

"I'm sick of this marriage talk. You'll do what I say or you can get out of the truck now." He wished she'd take him up on it. He'd find another way without her, and he wouldn't have to put up with her constant yapping about marriage.

Her blue eyes filled with tears. "You don't mean it."

She was a good actress. "I mean every word," he said. "You're in this as deep as me, Jenna, don't forget that." His hand touched the softness of her mink coat. "Our deals bought you this and those five-hundred-dollar boots. You want that all to vanish?"

"No," she said, her mouth going sulky. "You never tell me anything. Like how do you know Kade and Bree? And why do you want David?"

His hand shook, and he laid it on his leg. "I knew Bree a long time ago."

"Were you lovers?" she asked. Her face changed when he didn't answer. "I get it. David is your son, isn't he?"

"Yes." He expected histrionics, but she nodded at his admission.

"The news of this just might rattle Kade's faith in Bree," she said with glee in her voice. "He might need some comfort."

"From you?"

"Maybe. Since you don't want me." Her voice grew insolent.

For just a minute Quinn allowed himself to imagine how it would be to have the family back together. But it would never work. He knew how his wife would react to his new line of work. And he wasn't about to give it up, not even for her.

He glanced at his watch. "I'm going to go get something to eat. You hungry?"

"No. I think I'll go shopping. Drop me off at the Copper Country Mall. Call me when you're ready to go."

He nodded and headed toward the mall.

The fur stood at attention along Samson's back. He stood amid the littered pieces of clothing and items from Lauri's drawers. Watching her dog, Bree's alarm escalated. This was more than normal teenager messiness. She wasn't sure whoever did this was looking for something. It appeared vindictive. Furniture was upended, and the cushions had been tossed onto the floor.

"Lauri?" Bree called again though she had no real hope of getting an answer. The only sound was the growl of an engine down on the street. Kade had said to check with the neighbors or the super, so she grabbed Samson's leash and went into the hall. With the baby carrier looped over one arm, she called Lauri's number and heard it ringing in Lauri's apartment behind her. She shut the phone and put it away.

The odor of cooked cabbage permeated the narrow corridor. She knocked on the door directly next to Lauri's. A woman dressed in a University of Michigan sweatshirt opened the door. A baby rode her hip. The infant's bib was stained with peas.

"Can I help you?" the woman asked.

"Hi, I'm looking for Lauri Matthews." Bree indicated the doorway behind them. "Have you seen her?"

The woman turned and called, "Lauri, someone here to see you."

Relief made Bree lean against the doorjamb when her sister-in-law came toward the door. "Lauri, I was so worried. Your room is trashed."

Lauri thanked the other woman, then closed the door as she stepped into the hall with Bree. "That's why I called. I was too scared to stay there. Can we go now?"

"Let me ring Kade. When I couldn't find you, I called him and he'll be worried."

Lauri shuddered. "Call him from the car! Whoever did this might come back."

Bree nodded. "Get your coat." Her sister-in-law wore only jeans and a cotton blouse.

"I'm not going back in there." Lauri folded her arms over her chest.

"I'll get it." Bree handed the baby carrier to her sister-in-law. She darted just inside the door and grabbed Lauri's red parka from the floor by the closet. While she was at it, she snatched Lauri's cell phone too. Samson stayed right on her heels, his fur still ruffled.

She ran to join Lauri and thrust the coat and phone at her. "Put on your coat. The wind is wicked." She took the baby carrier from Lauri.

"Whatever." Lauri made a face but slipped her arms into the coat. She practically ran down the steps to the faded tile by the entry door. Turning, she stared up the steps at Bree. "You coming? I'm not going out there alone."

Bree loved Lauri, but sometimes she wanted to strangle the girl. At least she was okay. Hurrying down the steps, she glanced up and down the street. Nothing appeared ominous or out of place. She unlocked the Jeep with her key fob, and Lauri leaped into the front seat and punched the lock. Bree attached the car seat to the base in the middle of the backseat, then loaded Samson into the hatch area, where he curled up and closed his eyes. At least his alarm was gone. A good sign for her.

Bree glanced up at the apartment house again, then slid under the wheel when no one stared back from a window. "Tell me what happened," she said, fastening her seat belt.

"Just what I told Kade. I got home and found my apartment like that."

"You have no idea who did it?"

Lauri chewed on her fingernail. "Someone has been following me."

"Who?"

Lauri shrugged. "There's Kade." She threw open her door and scrambled out, then flung herself into her brother's arms and burst into sobs.

Bree rolled her eyes. Glancing in the backseat, she saw Olivia was still sleeping. She got out of the SUV and waited for Lauri's hysterics to end.

When Lauri finally let go of her brother, Bree waved him over. "The place is trashed, just like she said."

"I wouldn't lie," Lauri said, following on Kade's heels. "My car won't start either." She indicated her small car parked at the curb.

Kade went to the car and flipped the lever inside to open the hood. Peering into the inner workings of the vehicle, he poked and prodded for a few minutes before slamming the lid.

Wiping his hands on his pants, he rejoined them. "Someone cut your spark plug wires."

Lauri gaped, and the color drained from her face. Bree gulped. "You mean someone sabotaged it?"

"Yeah." His gaze focused on his sister, who was crying again. "Lauri, you said someone was following you. Who?"

She sniffled and rubbed her moist eyes. "Some guy."

"What guy? Have you seen him before?" Bree put in.

Kade frowned as if to say, *Let me handle this.* Bree hunched her shoulders and stepped back to peer through the window at Olivia. The baby slept with her thumb in her mouth. Bree leaned against the vehicle door and waited for Lauri's answer. If Kade wanted her to butt out, she'd keep her mouth shut.

"It's that guy I told you about," she muttered.

"Did you tell Mason?" Bree couldn't help the question that sprang from her mouth.

"No."

"What aren't you saying, Lauri?" Bree asked, her voice stern. She ignored the warning glance from Kade. "You know more about this than you want to tell us."

Tears sprang to Lauri's blue eyes, and she moved closer to her brother. "I don't know anything. I didn't do anything. Make her leave me alone, Kade."

Kade put his arm around his sister. "I'll take you home. You need me to get anything from the apartment?"

"I didn't get any clothes. Can you grab some jeans and tops? They're all over the floor. Oh, and some underwear."

"You have a few things at our place," Bree said, determined not to let Lauri shut her out.

"Not my good jeans though. The Joe's Jeans," Lauri said. "There are three pair up there somewhere."

Bree's eyes widened. "How'd you get the money for jeans that cost over a hundred and fifty dollars?"

Lauri avoided her gaze. "I told you—I have a job now."

"You couldn't have gotten much from it yet."

"I saved it for the jeans."

Bree didn't believe it, but she bit her tongue. No sense in escalating Lauri's defiance toward her. It was a new attitude. In the past, she and Lauri had gotten along great—better than Kade and Lauri most of the time.

She watched Kade jog up the steps and disappear inside. "Lauri, I know you're not telling us everything. How can we help if you hold back the truth? We only want to keep you safe."

Lauri crossed her arms over her chest. "You want to turn my brother against me."

Bree refrained from shaking her. But just barely. "Lauri, what is happening with you? You seem determined to keep us at arm's length and pit us against one another. Have I ever done anything but try to help you?"

For a minute she thought she was getting through to the young woman, because Lauri's eyes filled with tears and she ducked her head. But when she finally raised it and caught Bree's gaze, her eyes were hard and shiny.

"You've taken everything from me, Bree. You talked me into giving my baby to Hilary. You took my brother. You've got it all and I'm left with nothing."

Bree gaped, then stepped forward and tried to embrace Lauri, but the girl stepped away. Bree's arms dropped to her side. "I never talked you into giving up Zoe. It was your idea. My only contribution was to try to help you find a good family. I thought you wanted me to marry Kade. You said you did. We love you."

Her words fell on deaf ears. The defiant expression on Lauri's face didn't dim, and the girl shook her head and folded her arms across her chest. Bree fought the prick of tears behind her eyes. She didn't know how to get through to someone who was determined to believe a lie.

"If you'd taken Zoe like I asked, she'd still be in the family!" Tears sprang to Lauri's eyes even as the words burst from her mouth. "If you'd cared about me, you would have kept my baby."

A lump formed around Bree's vocal cords, and she swallowed it. She tried to embrace Lauri again, but Lauri shook her head violently and thrust her away.

"Things change, Lauri," Bree said, her voice soft. "I was in a different place then. So was Davy. He needed my full attention. And I wasn't married. I thought your baby deserved two parents. When you see Zoe, can't you tell she's happy? You did the right thing."

"I didn't! You ruined everything." Lauri's chest heaved with sobs, and rage twisted her mouth. "My life will never be the same again because you were too selfish."

"Oh, Lauri." Bree didn't know how to answer.

Had she made the wrong decision for all of them? The lump grew in her throat and she tried to summon up all the reasons why adoption had been impossible at the time. Staring into the young woman's face, a sense of failure swamped Bree. She thought they'd come so far in being a family. Discovering Lauri's deep-seated resentment hurt. Badly.

Before Bree could summon healing words, Lauri's cell phone rang. She glanced at the screen, and her face went white. She bit her lip.

"Aren't you going to answer that?" Bree asked. When Lauri didn't answer, she said, "You've got to tell us the truth if you want us to protect you."

"I don't expect anything from you," Lauri said. "You've made your loyalties clear."

Storm clouds gathered overhead. Bree clasped the top edges of her coat closer to her throat. The cold chill spinning down her back was more from the expression on Lauri's face than anything else. Helpless love mixed with anger choked Bree. Lauri had done something stupid. It was written all over her face.

And it would be up to Bree and Kade to get her out. As always.

"Lauri, what did you do?"

Her sister-in-law glanced to the ground as Kade came from the building carrying her clothes. He opened the back door of Bree's Jeep and tossed them inside. Samson popped his head up from the hatch area, then lay back down when Kade shut the door.

He glanced from Bree's set face to his sister's downcast one. "What's going on?"

"She was about to tell me," Bree said.

Kade put his hand on Lauri's shoulder. "You've got to tell us what this is about, Lauri. Let us help you."

At the kindness in her brother's voice, Lauri broke into noisy sobs. "I-I overheard a few snatches of conversation between that guy and Mrs. Saunders, the incident I told you about. The guy followed me and offered me twenty thousand dollars to stay quiet."

"Oh, Lauri," Kade said, his voice quiet. "You took a bribe?"

"I was just agreeing to keep quiet. But I didn't hear enough to hurt him. Not really."

"Twenty thousand dollars!" Bree burst out. She closed her eyes, then opened them again.

"Where's the money?" Kade asked, his voice thin with strain.

"What's left is in the bank."

Kade's sigh was heavy. "How much?"

Lauri swept her hair behind her ears. "How much is left, or how much did I spend?"

"Lauri!" her brother warned.

Her expression turned sulky. "I've got three thousand left."

Bree gasped. "You've spent seventeen thousand dollars? What did you spend it on?"

"I-I gave it to my fiancé to buy outfitting equipment. He's going to start his own business." Her chin had a defiant jut.

Bree knew it would do no good to chide her. She peeked at her watch.

"You'll have to get the money back from Wes," Kade said evenly.

"He's already bought stuff," Lauri said. "He's going to tell his dad today that he's opening his own business. Besides, what good would it do? This man doesn't care about the money. He offered it to me."

"What does he want if he doesn't care about the money? Why is he following you?" Bree asked. Lauri finally looked at her, and Bree saw the fear lurking in her blue eyes. Lauri swallowed and glanced away without answering. Terror began to creep into Bree's veins. This chain of events was likely more dangerous than Lauri was willing to admit.

"We should tell Mason," Bree said.

"No!" Lauri shot a pleading glance at her brother. "You can't tell the cops or anyone. If you do, he—he'll kill me. I know it."

"Kill you?" Bree asked.

Lauri shuddered. "You haven't seen his eyes."

"So if he's paid you to keep quiet, why did he trash your house? Does he think you've spilled the beans?" Kade asked.

Lauri chewed on her lip, and her eyes filled with tears. "I don't know what he wants. Maybe he wants his money back."

"That makes no sense," Bree said. "There's something you're not telling us. Why did he trash your apartment if you're doing what he wants by keeping quiet?" Samson barked from inside the Jeep, and Bree turned to check on the baby. Still asleep. He was probably reacting to the tense situation. "It's okay, boy," she said, putting her hand on the window where he pressed his head against it.

"I'll go talk to Wes," Lauri said. "Maybe he'll know what to do."

Bree noticed Lauri's avoidance of her question. What was she hiding?

Lauri punched a number into the phone. She turned her back on Kade and Bree and walked a few steps away. Bree heard her say, "My brother made me call." At least she didn't claim she couldn't reach Wes.

"I still think we should call Mason," Bree told Kade. "What do you think this is all about? Maybe mob related?"

Kade's brows drew together. "Here? In the UP? That makes no sense. There's no big money to be made up here."

"The Native American casinos," she reminded him. "Plenty of money there. Try to get her to tell you what's really going on. It's not about the money."

He nodded. Bree glanced in the backseat and saw Olivia's eyes were open. "I'm going to have to feed her before she starts wailing. Call me when you're done with Wes." Bree slipped into the back with the baby, relishing the warmth inside the car. She took out the baby-bottle warmer and plugged it into the cigarette lighter. Olivia's gaze roamed the vehicle. She chewed on her fist but didn't cry.

Now that Bree was fairly certain no one was looking for Olivia, she wanted desperately to adopt the child. But what would Kade say?

She watched him and Lauri get into his truck. She turned her attention back to the baby. After checking the bottle, she unfastened Olivia, changed her diaper, then popped the bottle in her mouth. Cuddling her close, Bree watched as her rosebud mouth drew in the milk. Olivia's eyes were half-closed, and she smelled so sweetly of baby lotion. Bree's heart filled with love for the infant.

Samson woofed in her ear, and she reached over to scratch his ears. "Isn't she beautiful?"

Samson strained toward the window, and she turned to look. A man was coming out of the restaurant next door to the apartment complex. He wore a black parka with the hood up, and she couldn't see his face as he stood on the steps and spoke to someone inside.

Samson whined low in his throat, and his tail began to wag furiously. It was almost as if he recognized the man.

"Who is it, boy?" Bree peered closer, waiting for the man to turn around. When he did, their gazes collided. The breath left her body.

She was staring at her dead husband.

18

A DUSTING OF SNOW FROSTED THE MAN'S DARK HAIR, then kissed his cheeks and left a trail there. Bree stood without her coat on the snowy sidewalk and stared at the father of her son. "Rob?" Though there was a question in her voice, there was none in her mind.

This man had been her husband once. Maybe still was, some dim part of her brain asserted.

A cardinal fluttered to a bush beside him. He pushed back the hood on his coat, revealing the dark hair on the man she'd seen beside the truck. "Hello, Bree," he said.

It was the same deep voice that always held a trace of humor. The blue eyes that were so much like Anu's. When he smiled, she caught a glimpse of the tiny chip in one of his front teeth. The chill in her chest had nothing to do with the temperature.

He shoved his hands in his pockets. "Kind of a surprise to see me here, huh?"

All the oxygen left her lungs. No wonder Samson hadn't barked the other night. He'd been the first to recognize his former master. She glanced back at the Jeep, where Olivia lay in her car seat waving her tiny fists in the air and cooing at the dog. Samson had his nose pressed against the window, and his tail wagged so hard, his bottom moved in time.

Part of her wanted to fling her arms around Rob's neck and kiss him. Part of her wanted to pummel him with her fists for putting her through the trauma of his death. Her whole body vibrated with questions.

Staring at Rob's face, she didn't know where to begin. The most important answer she craved was why he had walked away and left Davy alone in the woods. "Why?" she asked, unable to articulate all her rage and hurt.

"Could we get in the Jeep? It's cold out here."

She nodded stiffly and led the way the few feet to the Jeep. This might be a dream, she reminded herself. Any minute now she'd wake up and find tears on her cheeks. It had happened many times in the past.

But she was married now. Or was she? The horror of the question froze her thoughts.

Inside the vehicle, with the street sounds muffled, the situation seemed even more surreal. Rob climbed into the passenger side and slammed the door. Samson barked and licked Rob's ear.

"Good boy, Sam," he said, rubbing the dog's head. Samson wriggled all over with pleasure. Tiny whining noises came from his throat.

Olivia began to fuss, and Bree leaned into the back and removed her from the car seat. The baby settled immediately in her arms. "He's glad to see you," she said, her throat thickening at the sight of her dog's joy.

Rob's grin faded. "But you're not."

"I don't know what to think, how to feel. You walked off and left our son to die in the forest. You left me to grieve you and search for your body. How could you do that, Rob? How could you destroy our lives and just walk away?"

He hunched his shoulders and didn't look at her. "What good does it do to talk about it now?"

"What good does it do? What good does it do?" Her voice rose with every word. "It might help me understand how a man who professed to love his family could walk away, just like that! It would tell me who the man I married really was inside." She shook with the violence of her anger. "I thought I knew you, Rob."

"Oh, you knew me all right," he said, his tone hard. "You accused me of having an affair. That's how little you knew me."

The anger banked a bit. "And I'm sorry for that. I found out it was all a lie, that the woman who called me had never even met you. I often wished I had a chance to apologize."

"It hurt, Bree, it really hurt. I would never have cheated on you. But you can't say the same, can you? Here you are, remarried already."

"Already? Rob, you've been gone for nearly four years! Dead, I thought. Was I supposed to become a nun?"

He pressed the bridge of his nose. "Maybe. I don't know. I was just disappointed to find out you cared so little."

Was he insane? Bree stared at him. "I'm not the one who walked away. You faked your own death."

"I couldn't bear to come home and tell you Davy was dead," he muttered.

Bree blinked and looked hard at him. "Dead? Davy isn't dead. He's in his room."

"I know that now," he said. "But I didn't know it. Not until I came to town last week."

The air grew thin, threatening to suffocate her. Bree stared at Rob's face. Reality spun in a vortex around her. "What do you mean, you thought he was dead?"

He blinked slowly, never breaking their locked gazes. "I saw it on TV." His words were hoarse, choked.

"You saw it on TV?" she whispered. Her lips had no sensation.

"After the accident. I-I don't remember much. I remember waking up in pain. Blood poured from a gash on my forehead, and I touched it, thinking someone must have attacked me. I knew I needed a hospital."

"Where was the plane?"

"I don't remember seeing it. I staggered to my feet and walked through the woods. I took a guess at the right direction and struck out along a brook. My head hurt and I couldn't see much. I finally came to a dirt path."

"You didn't see Davy in the wreckage?" Bree didn't know whether to believe this story or not.

He shook his head. "I never saw the wreckage. I couldn't remember what had happened to me, then I fell and woke up in the hospital. I heard the beep of a monitor. A nurse asked me my name, and I realized I didn't know. Everything was a fog."

She clenched her fists. "Oh please. Can't you come up with a better lie than that?"

He seemed not to hear her. "I asked her to turn on the TV. There was a news report about searchers looking for a downed plane and I realized I was Rob Nicholls. The reporter said Davy was dead."

The agony in his voice convinced her. He'd always loved his boy. Tears flooded her eyes. "Why didn't you call me? You could have told me where to look. I could have found him sooner."

He dropped his gaze. "I-I couldn't face you. Not when I'd killed him."

"It was an accident. Unless there's more you're not telling me. How were your clothes found on the other man? And who is in your grave? I don't understand anything."

"It's none of your business. Not now when you've put another man in my son's life." He flung open the door and stepped out in the snow.

She grabbed at him. "Don't you walk out on me! Don't you dare walk out again without answering my questions."

He slammed the door. "I'll be in touch," he shouted through the window. He ran to the front of the restaurant and jumped in his car.

Bree sank back against the seat. The anger in his voice when he'd talked about her putting another man in Davy's life terrified her. Did he mean to do something about that?

The white landscape passed in a blur. Kade pulled into the driveway of a small place. The house was a mobile home with dented metal siding and concrete blocks for steps. A ramshackle outbuilding allowed air through the cracks. A rusty white pickup sat in the driveway.

Lauri threw open her door and charged up the blocks past the pickup. Kade was right on her heels. He paused when he saw a busted lock and the door standing open a crack.

He grabbed his sister's arm. "Wait a sec." He pointed to the doorjamb. "Has it always been broken like that?"

She started to struggle out of his grip until she looked at where he pointed. "No," she said, her hand going to her mouth. Jerking her hand from Kade's fingers, she shoved open the door. "Wes?"

"Wait, Lauri. Let me take a look first." Kade brushed past her and blocked her view of the trailer. The two kitchen chairs were upended. Blood smeared the table. He hoped it was animal, not human, but his gut clenched. From where he stood, he saw a boot extending into the kitchen from the bedroom that lay beyond. The boot wasn't empty.

He turned and grabbed Lauri's shoulders, forcing her to the door. "Go call 9-1-1."

"Why?" She jerked around and stared down the length of the trailer. Her cheeks paled when her gaze fell on the shoe. "Wes!" she shrieked.

She sprang toward the bedroom, but Kade blocked her access. "Do what I say! Call an ambulance."

Sobbing, she ran back through the door for Kade's truck, where she'd left her bag.

Kade's tread was heavy on the cracked vinyl floor as he walked to the bedroom. The foot hadn't moved, and from the amount of blood on the floor, he feared what he would find.

His steps slowed. He didn't want to see what was connected to those boots, but he had to. His gaze traveled from the foot up the jean-clad legs to the fancy belt buckle. He winced when he saw the blood-soaked chest and the pale face of the young man who lay there.

The pallor told him the boy was dead, but he knelt and pressed his fingers to Wes's neck. Nothing. Straightening, Kade backed out of the room. He didn't want to contaminate any evidence. This was clearly murder. Someone had aimed the sawed-off shotgun lying on the floor at the kid and pulled the trigger.

A slow burn started in Kade's belly. Poor kid. Poor Lauri. She was going to blame herself.

As well she should. Kade didn't want to admit it, but these kids had brought this on their own heads. He heard his sister calling his name in a desperate voice. "Be right there," he yelled.

Careful to avoid the blood on the floor, he made his way through the kitchen to the door and down the block steps, where he found Lauri sitting on a tree stump clutching herself and rocking. He didn't want to tell her the man she loved was dead, but she probably knew in her heart.

She looked up at his approach. Her blue eyes were wide with disbelief and horror. "He's okay, isn't he? I called an ambulance."

Kade crouched beside her and grabbed her hand. "I'm sorry, honey. He's been shot."

"Shot? His gun went off?"

"I don't think so. Looks like murder to me."

She sprang to her feet. "You mean he's dead?"

He could have kicked himself. Bree was much better at these kinds of things. "I'm sorry, honey."

She threw herself against his chest and nearly toppled both of them into the snow, but he regained his balance and held her tight. Sobs shook her frame, and he wished he could absorb some of her pain.

"Mr. Jones killed him," she sobbed. "I told Wes that he was dangerous."

"What does Jones want?" Kade feared the answer. "Why is he following you? Why would he kill Wes?

Lauri threw herself against his chest again. "He wants Davy," she wailed.

Adrenaline hit Kade's head first, then dispersed to his muscles with a jerk. "Dave? What's he got to do with this?"

She wiped at her eyes. "He says he needs leverage."

The kidnapping attempt. It was connected to this guy? Kade didn't understand anything.

Her sobs began to turn to hysteria. "What can we do?" she got out in gasps.

He'd find a way to talk to Mason in private so his family was protected. Kade knew better than to try to handle this on his own.

He had friends. They would help make sure Kade's family was safe.

The ambulance siren blared in the cold air, and Kade stood, his muscles stiff from his position. The vehicle came screaming down the road and turned in the lane. The light pulsed as the paramedics leaped out and came rushing toward him.

He motioned to the trailer. "Back bedroom. But he's already gone."

The men's pace slowed as they approached the door and entered the home. Lauri buried her face in her hands and sobbed. Kade wished again that Bree were here. He'd call her to come as soon as he talked to Mason.

A squad car's siren shrieked before cutting off as it pulled into the drive. Two policemen hurried toward him.

"I'll be right back." Kade peeled Lauri's arms from around his neck and walked out to meet the police. "It's bad, Officer," he said. "Someone shot Wes Townsend with a sawed-off shotgun."

The officer winced. "Either of you see anything?"

He shook his head. "He was like that when we arrived."

He answered a few more questions, then when the men walked toward the trailer, he called Mason and told him what Lauri had done, about the threats, everything. "Lauri says this man wants to talk to Dave in private—something about leverage. The only thing I can think of is when Dave said he saw a windigo bury a baby. Could that have been real?"

"I think it's time I had Dave show me where he saw this burial," Mason said. "I should have done it sooner, but every day we've been hit with something new."

"Wait, I just thought of something," Kade said before Mason hung up. "Lauri overheard the guy at Mrs. Saunders. She'll know his real name."

"I'll go see her."

Kade longed to go with him, but he couldn't leave Lauri in this state. "Call me after you talk to her." He put his phone away, then jogged back to his sister and led her to the truck. She was shuddering with the cold and with shock. He turned on the engine. It warmed up quickly, and he turned the heat on full blast once the thermometer needle moved off cold.

At least he was doing something. It was easy to fix her shivering, but it wasn't going to be so simple to protect his family.

19

BREE DRESSÉD FOR DINNER AT HILARY AND MASON'S. SHE moved by rote, still shocked to have confirmed that Rob was still alive. She zipped up the dress, then glanced at her gold wristwatch and frowned. Kade should have been home by now with Lauri. If he wasn't here in a few more minutes, she'd try to call him.

She swallowed the lump in her throat that swelled every five minutes. How was she going to tell Kade? What was the status of their marriage? How would this affect Davy? And Olivia? Tears blurred her image in the mirror. She was so scared. How could she hold it all together in front of Rob's family? And Kade?

She forced herself to pick up a brush and run it through her red curls. She checked on Davy and Olivia and found him dressed in clean pants and a Michigan sweatshirt. He was on the floor talking to the baby, who cooed up at him.

She dropped a kiss on his head, then turned toward the door. She stopped and turned back to look at him. He'd recognized his father even after all these years. Even if he did think Rob was a monster. "Have you seen the windigo anymore?"

"No," he said. "It's gone." He hesitated. "Mom?"

She looked back at her son. "Yes?"

"Do you ever miss Daddy?"

She retraced her steps and sat on the edge of his twin bed. Kade had made it to look like a racecar, complete with wheels. A boy's perfect bedroom. Her husband had done so much to let Davy know how much he loved him.

She studied her son's face. The dusting of freckles, the earnest green eyes, the red hair that fell across his forehead. "I think about him." More than her son could possibly know right now.

Davy's brow wrinkled. "Isn't it kind of mean to wish he was still alive? We wouldn't be living with Dad now."

Bree leaned over and pulled him from the chair to her side. She wanted to hold him on her lap, but he often resisted that, now that he was such a big boy. Or so he thought. To her, he'd always be her little boy, even when he was forty.

She smoothed her palms over his cheeks, which were too fast losing their baby chubbiness. "Your daddy will always be part of you, Davy." For once, he didn't tell her not to call him Davy. "You walk like him and have some of his expressions."

"Really? I'm starting to forget him, Mom." Tears appeared on his lashes.

Her tongue began to form the words that would say his father was alive, but she knew she couldn't tell him. Not yet. "He'll always be here with you. Even if you sometimes forget his face."

He leaned against her and wrapped his skinny arms around her neck. "Love you, Mommy."

Mommy. It was a word to treasure because she heard it so seldom. "Love you too, Dave."

"You can call me Davy. Just once in a while," he whispered.

She hugged him tight and brushed a kiss over his forehead. He smelled of little boy and soap, and her heart filled to overflowing with love.

"I'd better do my homework now," he said, pulling away.

"We'll be going as soon as Dad gets home," she told him, rising and heading to the door. The sound of a door closing echoed up the stairs, and she heard Samson's nails click on the floor in the hall. "There they are now. You'll have a few more minutes until Dad changes."

She left her son's room and hurried down the hall. Was Lauri crying? What sounded like sobs rose from the living room. Bree rushed down the steps and found Kade guiding Lauri to the sofa. Black streaks from her mascara made her eyes look bruised.

Kade glanced up and saw Bree. Relief lit his eyes. He was pale too as he held out his hand to her. Bree hurried to join them. "What's happened?" she asked.

"He's dead!" Lauri wailed, collapsing onto the sofa. She flung herself onto the pillow and buried her wet face in it.

Bree's confusion deepened, and she sought Kade's face. "Who?" she mouthed.

Kade took her arm and moved her out of earshot of Lauri. "Wes," he said. The lines around his eyes deepened. "Shot. Lauri swears Mr. Jones shot him, and the death was a warning. Mason's going to go see Mrs. Saunders and try to find out his real name."

"He murdered Wes?" Bree needed to sit down. She couldn't think, couldn't take it in.

"There's more, Bree." He turned her to face him. "He told Lauri she has to bring Dave to talk to him. Alone."

All the blood drained from her head. "Absolutely not."

Kade was shaking his head as she spoke. "Of course not. But we have to protect him, watch him. The guy told Lauri that Dave was going to be leverage. I think that whole windigo-putting-a-baby-in-the-snow thing might have some basis in fact. Mason wants Dave to show him where this happened."

Was Rob capable of something so horrific? Once upon a time she would have said no. "Do we have to do that, Kade?" But she knew they did. They couldn't hide in the house forever.

He dropped his gaze, and his shoulders slumped. "I'm sorry Dave's involved."

Bree had reached out to embrace him when she heard Olivia begin to cry upstairs. "I'll be back," she said. "Don't worry, Kade. We'll get through this."

She wasn't sure she really believed it. An earthquake of change was already shattering their lives.

<hr />

Kade drew in a deep breath and squared his shoulders. Lauri was still crying, so he left her on the sofa and went to the gun cabinet. Unlocking it, he checked the available ammo. There was plenty. He locked the cabinet again and went to the kitchen to throw the dead bolt on the back door. But that lock wouldn't slow down a determined intruder with a gun for long.

His gaze lit on Samson's broad shoulders. An intruder would shoot the dog first, and it would kill Bree and him both if anything happened to their dog. "You stay close by me, Samson, hear?" The dog whined and nosed his hand. Kade petted him again.

"Kade?" Bree stood in the doorway. "I called Hilary to beg off the party. I just can't handle anything more tonight."

"Good idea."

"I'll go talk to Lauri," she said, walking toward the living room.

Good. Bree would help get his sister's grief under control. He never knew what to say, and tears made him want to run.

Glancing at the clock beside the bed, he wondered how long it would take Mason to talk with Mrs. Saunders. He decided to check the pictures in the camera he'd left to track the cougars. He went upstairs to the computer room and booted the machine. Once he plugged in the camera, he watched the pictures come up and began to click through them.

Open field. A rabbit. The rear end of an elk. Nighttime with nothing. Nothing here, he decided when he had about ten pictures left. It had been futile. Wait, what was that? He leaned closer and studied the photo. Just at the edge of the photo. He couldn't quite make it out, but there was some kind of animal there.

He flipped to the next photo, and the image of two spotted kittens sharpened into view. His jaw dropped. Though he'd hoped to find this evidence, now that he had, he couldn't quite believe it.

His gaze drank in the kittens. Maybe four weeks old. Their blue eyes were striking against their spotted fur. A lump formed in his throat. He'd get that grant now. This discovery was going to set DNR on its head.

He printed out some pictures for the grant application, stuffed them into a manila folder, then went downstairs. Bree had her arm around Lauri. His gaze went to the baby in the carrier. Samson lay beside Olivia.

Lauri lifted her head. "I need Anu." She rubbed the back of her hand over her eyes.

"I called her," Bree said. "I told her not to come, but she insisted she'd be right over. She loves you very much."

"Let me wash my face before she gets here." Lauri brushed past Kade on her way to the kitchen.

"I don't know how to help her," he muttered, moving closer to his wife.

Bree's eyes softened. "No one does. But hold her when she needs you to, Kade. Let her know you're hurting for her."

"I'm mad at her too," he admitted. "She's brought danger to our doorstep, Bree."

Her head was down, and her gaze stayed on the baby. "So many problems right now," she murmured. "Victor's problems, Florence's and Pia's deaths, the baby. Now this with Lauri and Davy."

He was going to have to explain the situation to Dave, something he didn't want to do. Living in fear wasn't good for any of them, but until this guy was caught, that was exactly what they'd have to do.

Olivia cried until Bree popped the warmed bottle into her mouth. She struggled to maintain her own composure. She was shell-shocked. Davy was the important thing right now. She had to keep him safe. Safe from danger, safe from emotional harm too.

She turned her head and stared at Kade's strong jawline as he sat on the sofa. Was their marriage even legal now? She'd have to consult a lawyer. It was hard not to blurt out that Rob was alive. That the body they'd brought home to rest in the cemetery was someone else.

Who? Rob had refused to tell her. She sensed he was involved in something bad. Why else be so secretive? If only she could talk to Anu about it—but that was impossible until she talked with Kade. She had to tell her husband first.

Olivia had finally fallen asleep. Bree put the baby in the portable crib. The doorbell rang, then Anu came in through the doorway. She had her hands full of pots and bowls on a tray. Bree took the items from Anu. Davy ran to his grandmother and allowed her to pull him into her lap. The bond they shared only seemed to grow with the years.

"You have grown since I saw you last," Anu said, hugging the boy. She held out her hand to Lauri. "*Kulta*, I am so sorry for your loss today."

Lauri's tears were already flowing, so Bree left Lauri to Anu's ministration and carried the food to the kitchen.

Pain began to pulse behind Bree's temples. This night would be one long nightmare of regrets. If only there had been time to tell Kade about Rob before Anu arrived. She couldn't spring the news on him here in front of Rob's mother.

Bree was certain that Rob had been in touch with his mother, however. It would explain Anu's distress the other day. Anu had to have as many questions as Bree. Where had he been all this time? How was he earning a living? He would have to be using a fake Social Security number. Which led to Bree's next assumption that whatever he was doing wasn't exactly legal. Anu probably knew everything. She and Rob had been so close.

Her gaze fell on her husband as he filed in with the rest for supper. Her heart cramped. Rob was going to change everything. There would be custody issues, even marriage issues, to work out. Davy was going to be torn between two fathers.

The disruption of her life loomed like a nightmare she'd never awaken from. Would Rob's family pressure her to leave Kade and go back to him? Would her own heart do the same?

She couldn't deny his presence had stirred old feelings. Just today she'd told Davy it was okay to love two fathers. But it wasn't okay for her to love two husbands. She'd have to choose between her first love and the man who now shared her life. The more contact she had with Rob, the more likely it would be that the love she felt for him would grow stronger. She'd loved him once with her whole being, and his death had nearly destroyed her.

She didn't know how she was supposed to feel about all this or how to find her way to happiness again.

"Bree, you okay?" Kade carried Olivia in his arms. The baby was awake and sucking on her fingers.

"I-I'm fine." She avoided his gaze and stared into the baby's face. "She shouldn't be hungry since she just ate."

"I don't think she is. I changed her, but she seems to want to look around. Don't you, baby girl?" He jostled the infant and she stared up at him as though memorizing his face.

Watching him with Olivia, Bree hoped he was beginning to love the baby, but maybe Kade was just being Kade. He didn't have a mean bone in his body. Kade reached out to every hurt human or animal he met. Quiet and strong, he had been there for her through every trauma.

How was she going to administer such a killing blow to him? And to herself?

The room seemed impossibly close and hot. Bree fanned her face. "I have to step outside a minute." She escaped the stares and rushed for the back deck. Kade called after her, but she waved her hand. "I'm okay. Just hot. I'll be right back."

When she stepped onto the deck, the air cooled her hot cheeks, and her panic receded. She hadn't even asked God for help, and that should have been the first thing she did. The stars twinkled in the night sky as she prayed for guidance, for strength to face the coming hours and days. Anu said God heard every heart's cry. Bree could only trust he would answer in the best way.

Her gaze fell on a line of shrubs. The security light illuminated a flock of cardinals sleeping in the branches. Cardinals were said to mate for life. Was that what God would want? For her to go back to Rob? Her throat closed at the thought.

Through the big windows, she could see her family talking in the dining room. Kade kept glancing at the door as he watched for her. She should go back in. He'd come looking for her soon if she didn't, and the more upset she seemed, the more he would press her for an answer she wasn't ready to give.

She turned toward the door when she saw a shadow move. "Who's there?" she called in a soft voice. But she knew. It could only be one person. "Rob, is that you?"

The shadow moved again, and his face came into view in the security light. "Yeah, it's me."

Hugging herself for warmth, she moved down the first step. "What are you doing here? Spying on us?"

"I wanted to catch a glimpse of my son. Is that so wrong?"

This was all his choice, not hers. "The son you walked away from without a backward glance?"

He moved closer. "You're bitter, Bree."

The regret in her throat nearly made speech impossible. "I'm not. I'm just trying to understand what you've done. And why." Part of her wanted to leap into his arms and part of her wanted to shake him.

Yet the man she loved was in the kitchen behind her. Wasn't he?

Rob moved closer until he was at the bottom of the three steps. Bree was on the first one and nearly eye level with him. Their gazes met. Before she realized it, she'd reached out and cupped his cheek in her palm. "I can't believe you're alive."

"Are you glad, Bree?" he whispered.

"Yes." The word was the barest breath.

He leaned forward and his lips brushed hers. The smell of his breath was so familiar, yet half forgotten. The rough texture of the stubble on his cheek reminded her of the first time they'd kissed. Eons ago. She closed her eyes and remembered.

She was married to another man. The thought made her step away. "I can't," she whispered.

Rob backed away too. "I still love you, Bree," he said, his voice hoarse. He turned and fled.

She stared at his retreating back. God help her, she still loved him too.

20

ALL THROUGH DINNER KADE KEPT GLANCING AT BREE. There was something different about her tonight. She seemed almost feverish in her attempts to cover it up. He saw the desperation lurking in her eyes. At first he thought it might be the threat from Wes's killer, but he'd never seen his fearless wife back down from anything.

This was different.

Maybe she was beginning to realize she would lose Olivia. He jostled the baby on his knees. Cute little thing. He could learn to love her too, but he sensed they couldn't keep her. Now that the grant was a sure thing, they could probably afford it, but he thought Mason would likely track down the parents.

His gaze lingered on Anu. She'd been uncharacteristically quiet tonight, reflective. Had she and Bree had a falling out? He couldn't imagine that. They were as tight as bark on a tree. When she left tonight, he'd have to find out what was up.

His gaze lingered on his wife's face. She'd be thrilled to hear the news about the cougars. One of the great things about Bree was her empathy.

It was nearly ten by the time Anu left. He carried his sleeping son up to bed while Bree put the baby down. Lauri lagged last up the steps, and he saw tears on her cheeks again. The right words never found their way to his tongue. He could only guess at Lauri's pain by imagining how he'd feel if he ever lost Bree.

After tugging off Dave's shoes, he stripped him of his jeans and left him to sleep in his T-shirt. With the blankets tucked under his chin, Dave slept soundly, and Kade studied him in the moonlight. He and Bree longed for a child they'd made together, but he doubted he could love any other boy or girl more than he loved this son. Dave had quickly become the child of his heart. He looked so much like Bree, but Kade found the boy imitating him in the foods he liked, the way he wanted his hair cut, so many things.

God was good to give him such a wonderful family. He'd lay down his life to preserve it.

Leaving the boy's bedroom, he stopped to check on Lauri and found her already in her pajamas with Zorro curled on the bed beside her. She held a Bible in her hand. Not what he expected to see. She usually kicked at being urged to go to church with them.

"You okay?" he asked.

She glanced up. "I don't know if Wes is in heaven, Kade." Her face crumpled. "I never even talked to him about God."

He stepped into the room and wished Bree were here to answer her questions. Or Anu. "I'm sorry, honey. I'll pray for you to come to terms with all this."

She hugged herself. "I'm scared, Kade. What if that guy comes here and hurts Bree or Davy? I'd never forgive myself."

He sat on the edge of the bed and put his arm around her. "Can you remember anything else that might help us figure out who he is?"

She pillowed her head on his shoulder. "I've thought all evening. There's just nothing beyond what I told you."

"Mason never called. He was supposed to call after he talked to your boss."

"They're being blackmailed or something. I bet she won't say a word."

Maybe the woman could be legally compelled. He patted her hand. "Mason will figure it out. I want us all to be extra careful, but we'll be all right."

"What about the money?" she asked in a small voice. "If we give back the money, maybe he'll go away."

"You know what he wants. Giving you that money was nothing but a setup. The guy is after Dave."

Lauri sniffled and scrubbed at her face like a child. "It's all my fault. I'll try not to be so stupid."

He dropped a kiss on her head. "Love you, kid."

"Love you too."

He let her go, then rose. "Get some sleep. If you need me tonight, just call for me."

Her smile was strained, but the tears had dried. "I will. Thanks, big brother. For everything. I don't know what I would have done today if you hadn't been there. I'd probably be dead right now."

He didn't feel like a white knight, not with a family grieving their son tonight. Closing her door behind him, he went down the hall to the master bedroom. Jenna's door was closed. She'd been missing all evening. Not that she had to answer to them.

He paused in the hall and called Mason at home. The sheriff answered after two rings. "Hey, I'm sorry we missed Zoe's party."

"You had a good excuse."

"Any news from Mrs. Saunders?"

"She claims Bill Jones is his real name. That he's just a client and she knows nothing." Fatigue roughened Mason's voice. "She was nervous though. I thought she was going to cry once or twice."

"Can't you get her to break down and tell the truth?"

"Maybe. I'll have another go at her tomorrow. How's Lauri?"

"Devastated. And subdued. I'll let you get to bed. It's nearly midnight. Let me know what you find out."

He put his phone away and pushed open his bedroom door. Bree rocked and sang softly to Olivia in the chair by the window. Already in her nightgown, she smiled when she saw him, but Kade didn't think she was glad to see him. Shucking his jeans, he pulled on pajama bottoms and a T-shirt, then climbed in bed. Crossing his arms behind his head, he waited for her to get the baby to sleep. He wasn't going to be able to drop off himself until he knew what was bugging her.

"I found pictures of the kittens on my camera," he said.

"Uh-huh," Bree said, gazing into the baby's face.

She hadn't paid any attention to what he said. He thought about repeating it but shut up until she told him what was on her mind. He watched her rise and place Olivia in the bassinet. She brushed a kiss across Olivia's fine hair and stepped away. Was it his imagination or was that reluctance he saw as she turned toward the bed?

He patted the space beside him. "We need to talk. Something is bothering you."

"You shouldn't have to ask with the traumatic day we've had."

"The Bree I know rolls with the punches. We're all hurting for Lauri, but I know you. There's something more than that, Green Eyes."

The corners of her mouth lifted. "You haven't called me Green Eyes in forever."

He needed to do better at letting her know how much he loved her. "I'm sorry, babe. There's been a lot going on."

"A lot you're not sharing."

"Yeah, that too." If he expected her to open up, he needed to come clean himself. "I think I'm going to get a pink slip soon."

Her eyes widened, and her hand went to her mouth. "Oh, Kade."

"It will be okay," he rushed on. "I'm applying for a grant and I think I'll get it. If not, I'll find a job. I don't want our boy to have to change schools."

"There's not much here. Maybe when the new mine opens."

"You know how I feel about that," he said before he could help himself. "The mine would ruin the land."

She squeezed his hand. "I didn't mean I thought you should go to work there. I thought maybe it would bring new business to the area. You'll get unemployment for a while. We'll make out." Her gaze filled with love. "You're a good man, Kade Matthews. You've always taken care of us."

There seemed to be a hidden meaning in her words that he couldn't decipher. "I always will," he said. "Whatever's wrong right now, I want to be there for you. You can tell me, Bree."

Her eyes filled with tears. "It's good and bad at the same time, Kade. I don't know what to think."

"It can't be that bad." He pulled her close. Her breathing was ragged. "Babe, what's wrong?"

She pulled away and searched his eyes. Tears hung on her lashes, and her mouth trembled. "Don't leave me, Kade. No matter what I tell you, don't leave me."

A sliver of fear drove itself into his heart. What could she tell him that would be so earth-shattering? "I'd never leave you, Bree." He tried to pull her tight, but she put her palm against his chest and held herself away.

"I have to tell you now or I'll never get the courage." She swallowed, and her throat convulsed. "You remember that guy in the broken down truck we saw the other day?"

"Yeah. Quinn something." He struggled to remember the man's face, but only recalled the leather doo-rag and jacket.

Her mouth trembled. "He-he came out of the restaurant by Lauri's building today."

Kade frowned. "He's following us?"

She bit her lip. "I-it was Rob."

"Rob who?" He couldn't remember any Robs in their life. Her late husband was the only one who came to mind. In a flash, he recalled Anu's strain, but Bree couldn't be talking about that Rob. He was dead and buried.

Bree rolled away and sat up, staring down into his face. "Rob Nicholls, Kade. My first husband."

He stared into her anguished eyes, the green deepened by a pain beyond words. And something else. A gleam of elation maybe? She'd loved Rob tremendously and had held Kade at arm's length for months at first. Did she love him still? The thought was a butcher knife digging out his heart.

"Babe, you've been under a lot of stress lately. Don't go buying into Dave's fantasies. Rob is dead. You buried him."

Tears spilled over her lashes and rolled down the curve of her cheek. "I thought I did," she said. "Kade, don't you think I know my own husband? The man I was married to for five years?"

Husband. The words shocked him as nothing else could. "You're sure?" He wanted to block his ears and not hear her answer. He didn't have to. The conviction was all over her face. He sat up and reached for her, and she came this time.

"What are we going to do?" she muttered.

Holding her, he tried to make sense of it. How had this happened? Where had Rob been all this time? He couldn't imagine walking away from this woman like Rob had done. And he'd left his son to die in the wilderness. He had to have abandoned Dave after the plane crash. A man like that didn't deserve this family. He didn't deserve to have a mother like Anu.

He gripped her shoulders and pushed her away so he could see her face. If she still loved the scumbag, he'd be able to see it in her face. Their gazes locked, and he saw anguish in her eyes. "Do you still love him?"

She wet her lips but she held his gaze. "Of course I still have feelings for him," she whispered. "He was my husband, Kade."

"I'm your husband!" The hoarse cry broke from his lips.

She blinked rapidly, dispelling some of the tears on her lashes. "Are we still married?"

Were they? He wanted to cry along with her. When he realized something was wrong, he'd never imagined something this bad. "We'll have to talk to Ursula Sawyer." Their lawyer was a friend as well.

"I almost called her tonight." Bree melted against his chest. "I don't know what we're going to do, Kade. Davy will have to know. The family too."

His spot in the family might melt away. There might not be room for him with Rob back in the picture. He would be an outsider again. Maybe in Bree's life too. And their boy. Dave was his son. His arms tightened around her, and her grip grew desperate as well. A tremor of unimaginable magnitude rumbled through them, and he wasn't sure they'd ever be able to pick up the pieces shattered tonight.

The aroma of *pulla* wafted out of Nicholls' Finnish Imports. Bree had a key, but she seldom had to use it because Anu left the door unlocked even if the shop wasn't officially open. Samson followed her inside. She'd left the kids with Lauri. What she had to say to Anu needed to be uninterrupted.

"Anu?" she called when she stepped into the shop.

"Back here, *kulta*." Anu's voice came from the bakery area on the other side of the main shop.

Bree walked past the tables of fine wool sweaters into the hall that led back to the kitchen. The aroma of the fresh bread should have made her hungry, but this morning it only unsettled her stomach. She found Anu sliding loaves of bread into the display case. Coffee dripped into a pot at the self-help coffee bar. Bree poured herself a cup to fortify her nerves.

Anu shot her a quick look and wiped the flour from her hands on the apron. "You are up early, my Bree."

"I needed to talk to you." Bree sat her cup on one of the round café tables and pulled out a chair. "Are you at a good stopping point?"

Anu nodded. "The bread is baked. I was about to have a cup of coffee with a piece of bread. You would like some?"

"No thanks." Bree rested her hand on Samson's head. He pressed against her knee as though to tell her to be strong. She studied Anu's beloved face. Was it Bree's imagination or was Anu a little pale and drawn today?

Anu's gaze connected with Bree's. "You are distressed this morning. How can I help?"

"I-I've got more trouble than I know how to handle, Anu." The understanding in Anu's eyes convinced her the older woman knew more than she had said so far. "You know, don't you? About Rob?"

Anu's blue eyes closed, then opened again. The anguish on her face deepened. "I know," she whispered. "I saw him."

The lump in Bree's throat grew to boulder size. "Why didn't you tell me?" she said.

"He made me promise not to say anything yet. I believe he might be involved in something dangerous." Anu's voice broke.

Anu had lived her faith in front of Bree, and it was her and Naomi's witness that had finally led Bree to God. Knowing her son had stepped over the line into criminal activity must hurt Anu deeply. It hurt Bree as well. The Rob she once knew was a straight shooter, a God-fearing man. Or so she'd always thought.

Bree swallowed down the pain. "I saw him yesterday, Anu." The words echoed in her heart as much as in the room. She still couldn't quite believe it.

Anu held Bree's gaze. "How did he seem to you?"

"Older. Jaded. Secretive." So many things she didn't understand. "Dangerous." She said the word reluctantly.

"How could he do this?" Anu whispered. "He walked away from his family. From me, from his sister. Most importantly from you and Davy. He left his son to die in the woods."

That issue Bree could clear up. "He told me he was confused after the impact. When he recovered from the shock, he heard on TV that the search had been called off and everyone was presumed dead. He thought Davy was dead and he couldn't face me." Reciting the facts convinced her again of how lame his excuses were.

The skepticism on Anu's face mirrored Bree's heart. "He should have been a man and come to comfort you and me. Did he tell you who is buried in his place?"

It was a detail that troubled Bree. "No. He said it was a long story."

Tears stood in Anu's eyes. "I do not want to believe my son would harm someone, but this man I do not know. He is not my Rob. Not the boy I raised."

"Have you talked to Mason?"

Anu shook her head. "I could not. Nor Hilary. I know she will be very upset."

Bree didn't want to think about how Hilary would feel. She and Rob were close. Or at least they used to be. Rob's disappearance was evidence that he hadn't been as close to anyone as they'd thought.

She wet her lips. "I think we should ask Mason to look for any other missing persons around the time the plane went down. From here down to Iron River. Or somewhere else in the state. Even Wisconsin."

"The body was wearing Rob's jacket," Anu said. "How did that happen?"

Neither of them wanted to admit his disappearance looked planned. Neither could bear to think he'd murdered someone, then walked away from his own boy. But the facts spoke for themselves. Something had gone terribly wrong that day four years ago. If Rob wasn't guilty of something terrible, wouldn't he have come home?

When Bree didn't answer, Anu seemed to age before her eyes. "We must talk to Mason," she said, her voice heavy. "I will have to tell Hilary."

"Maybe we should let Mason tell her."

Anu shook her head. "No, I must do it. She is my daughter. Rob is her brother. She would be very hurt if I kept this from her." She fumbled in the pocket of her apron and withdrew her cell phone. After punching in the number, she simply said, "Hil, I need to talk to you. Right away, please. Bring Mason." She replaced the phone, and her blue eyes were hooded when she glanced back to Bree. "She will be right here. I would like you to stay."

Bree couldn't resist that pleading gaze. Not when Anu had done so much for her. There was another matter she needed to handle before Hilary got here though. "Lauri is in trouble, Anu. She blackmailed a killer out of some money."

Anu put her hand to her mouth. "Blackmail?" she whispered.

"I'm not sure what you call it. Blackmail, extortion. The man killed Wes, and he's demanding access to Davy." Her voice broke.

Anu cupped Bree's face in her cardamom-scented hands. "God will protect our boy."

The tears Bree had been holding back filled her eyes. "You're my real mother, Anu."

"Someday you must make peace with your own mother, *kulta*. But I'll do until then."

Bree leaned forward and buried her face against Anu's shoulder. "What am I going to do?" she whispered. "Who is my real husband?"

Anu's arms tightened around her. "I do not know, my Bree. It will be a hard situation for you to sort out. I will pray for you. For all of us."

How could God let something like this happen? The question hovered on her lips, but she clamped her teeth against what felt like heresy. Since she'd turned her life over to God, she'd never questioned his workings. This was different. This shook her underpinnings and made her question everything.

Anu seemed to understand the unspoken questions. She smoothed Bree's curls and whispered again, "I will pray, Bree. He is there when the answers are not easy. I know you are wandering in the dark right now, but he will answer in his time."

Rebellion stirred in her heart. She didn't have time. An answer right now would be appreciated. The tinkle of the bell on the front door saved her from the hot words that hovered on her tongue.

Hilary's voice called out, then her high heels clicked along the floor. Mason's heavy tread followed. Samson got up and stretched, then went to greet them. Hilary made a moue of distaste and stepped away from the dog. "Go see your mother, Samson." Her anxious gaze went from Bree to Anu. "What's wrong, Mother? You sounded—not yourself."

"Come sit down, Hilary. You too, Mason," Anu said, pulling out the chairs beside Bree. "Perhaps some coffee?"

"Sure." Mason accepted the cup she offered, then settled into the chair and crossed his legs.

"I had my coffee already." Hilary's gaze pinned Bree in place. "What's this all about?"

Bree wasn't sure if she should tell her or let Anu spring the news. Glancing at Anu, she saw the older woman give a slight shake of her head. Bree took her cue and folded her hands in her lap. "I'll let your mother tell you." She was so thankful Mason was here. He'd be able to calm Hilary if necessary.

Anu's hand holding her coffee shook, and a few droplets fell to the floor, where Samson licked them up. She put down the cup. "Something . . . unbelievable has happened." Her lips trembled, and she pressed them together. She put her hands on Hilary's shoulders. "Hilary, you must not speak until I am done. Listen to what I'm about to say. You too, Mason."

Hilary's face lost its color. "Whatever is it, Mother? You're scaring me."

"Sh. Listen, daughter. It's about your brother. Rob is alive. He is here in town." She leaned forward and put her hand over Hilary's open mouth. "Say nothing yet. Let me talk. I saw him with my own eyes, *kulta*. We have spoken. That isn't his body we buried in the cemetery."

Hilary's eyes fluttered and began to roll back in her head. Bree jumped up and grabbed her, pushing her head between her knees.

Mason leaped up at the same time. "Hil?" He put his hand on the back of her neck.

"Okay, I'm okay." Hilary drew in a deep breath. She slowly raised her head. Moistening her lips with the tip of her tongue, she stared from Bree to Anu. "It's true?"

"It's true," Bree said. "I've seen him, talked to him." She launched into an explanation of all that she knew. When she finished, her gaze went to Mason. "Can you check for anyone who went missing just before or after the plane crash? And we might need to exhume the body."

"Can't Rob tell you all you need to know about this? Where is he? I want to see him." Hilary's eyes began to shine.

"You are not listening, Hilary," Anu said, her voice tired. "He is not the same man. The Rob we knew would never leave his son's broken body in that plane."

Hilary blanched. "What's happened to him?" she whispered.

Bree was desperate to know the answer herself. She glanced at Mason. "And who's buried in that grave?"

21

KADE PICKED UP DAVE AFTER SCHOOL MONDAY AFTERNOON on the snowmobile. He drove at a slow pace to make sure his boy didn't fall off the back. *His boy.* Maybe not for long. He hadn't slept last night, and neither had Bree. Sooner or later he was going to have to meet the other husband, see how Bree reacted in his presence. The thought terrified him.

Dave tapped his shoulder and shouted above the roar of the engine. He pointed to a line of rosebushes covered with snow. Several cardinals perched there, their plumage bright against the white. Kade slowed the machine, then stopped it. He shut off the engine.

"It was there," the boy said, pointing to the drifts of snow. "Right behind the bushes." He hopped off the back of the snow-mobile and thrashed through the drifts on his snowshoes.

Glancing around to ensure they were alone, Kade grabbed the shovel he'd brought and followed. Mason wasn't here yet, so he wouldn't dig, but he wanted to be prepared. He didn't expect to find anything without digging. At least a foot of snow had fallen since the day Dave thought he saw a baby buried here.

Dave crouched by the shrubs and peered at the birds. "Look at the cardinals, Dad. There are hundreds of them."

"Well maybe not hundreds. But at least fifteen or twenty." It had been a good year for the songbirds. Bree had gone through three or four bags of birdseed so far this winter.

He heard the growl of Mason's snowmobile and turned to see the sheriff and Deputy Montgomery approaching on their machines. The men dismounted and approached Kade and Dave.

"Hey, big guy," Mason said, touching the boy's head. "You doing okay?"

Dave hung on to his uncle. "It was right here I saw the windigo, Uncle Mason." He pointed just behind the rosebushes. "He buried the baby here. Dad brought a shovel so we could dig."

"Good man," Mason said. His gaze drifted around the clearing. "Tell me where you were, Dave. And Victor. Miss Florence too."

Dave walked to the pond, about twenty feet from the roses. "Me and Victor were here fishing. I think the windigo didn't see us because we were sitting in front of these bushes. Victor heard something and got up to look. I did too. The windigo had his back to us. He was digging a hole."

"In the snow?" Mason asked.

Kade walked toward the bushes where Dave had pointed. "Right about here?" he asked.

Dave nodded. "He dug down in the snow, then picked up the baby and put it in the hole. It had black hair."

Mason and Kade locked glances. "One of the Native American babies?" Kade murmured too softly for Dave to hear.

Mason's nod was quick and subtle. "Did he cover the baby with snow?" he asked.

Dave nodded and left his spot by the water. "Are you going to dig now?" He craned his head and stared at the snowdrift he'd pointed out.

"Not just yet," Mason said. "But you've been a big help. Tell me again what Miss Florence did."

"She yelled at the windigo and told him to go away. Victor grabbed my hand and we ran away then."

"So the windigo had a shovel?" Mason exchanged another glance with Kade.

Florence had been killed with a shovel. The blood drained from Kade's face when he remembered why Dave called the killer a windigo. The man had looked like Rob.

"We'd better go," Kade said, taking Dave's small hand. "I need to stop by the office and take care of a few things."

"Thanks, Dave," Mason said. "You've been a big help."

Kade started the snowmobile and drove away with Dave clinging to his waist. When they reached his office, he retrieved a voice mail from Mason. He'd found a perfectly preserved baby boy right where Dave said it would be.

He said nothing to the boy though. He opened the folder containing the grant application. Studying it, he saw Landorf had inflated the numbers well beyond what Kade had suggested, then signed it. Kade started to attach the pictures to the application. His gaze went to his son. What kind of example was a man who did what was expedient rather than what was right?

Slowly, he tore the application in two.

"What are you doing?" Landorf stood in the doorway.

"I found the kittens." Kade held out the pictures.

Landorf took them and began to leaf through. "You'll get that grant for sure," he said, smiling.

"But I'm going to do it the right way." Kade held his boss's gaze. "We only need half that money for a proper study. I can't inflate the figures."

Landorf's mouth tightened, then he shrugged. "You're a good man, Kade." His tone held grudging admiration. "Redo the application, and I'll sign it. You're right. It's not honest." He touched Dave's red curls. "You've got a good dad, kid."

"He's the best," Dave said, tracing the picture of the kittens on a piece of paper.

But would Kade even be allowed to raise the boy he loved?

Fighting tears, Lauri got behind the wheel of the car Kade had repaired and started the engine. She longed to go see Wes's parents. Should she risk it? She'd just pulled out onto the main road when her cell phone rang. Dread congealed in her stomach when *unknown* flashed across the screen.

She didn't dare not answer it. Holding her breath, she flipped it open and waited. On the other end of the line she heard noise like from a bar or a coffee shop. People laughing, ice in glasses tinkling.

"Little girl," a man's soft voice said. "No games."

"I'm here."

"I want the kid tomorrow night. Leave the back door unlocked. Keep the dog in your room. No one will ever know you helped me. And you're home free. Nothing else ever said about the money. It's all yours."

"You can't have him."

"Would you rather see your brother shot? I could arrange that, just like I arranged for the boyfriend to die."

"You said you just wanted to talk to Davy. Now you want to take him? That wasn't the arrangement."

"I'm going to talk to him, then bring him back. No one will even know he was away."

The false note in the man's voice told her differently. "I can't do that," she whispered.

"Then you can bury your brother."

"No!" Lauri chewed on her lip. What could she do? Talk to Mason?

"If you're thinking about calling in the cops, don't. I'll know if you do. The sheriff will come to the lighthouse to find you all dead."

She believed him. He'd already killed Wes. If only she'd never overheard the conversation with Mrs. Saunders. She and Wes would still be planning a future.

She closed the phone without answering, then shut it off when it rang again almost immediately. Chewing on a ragged thumbnail, she drove on north. Maybe she could get Mrs. Saunders to tell her something. Kade said Mason hadn't been able to get anything out of her.

She accelerated along the snow-covered road, slowing only when she fishtailed in the curves. The office was only twelve miles away. Pasting a neutral expression on her face, she went past the receptionist and down the hall.

Mrs. Saunders's shut door presented a do-not-enter message, but Lauri knocked on it anyway. The woman didn't answer at first. "Mrs. Saunders. It's Lauri. I have to talk to you."

"Come in." The woman's voice held no warmth.

When Lauri stepped into the office, she expected to see the woman still upset and red-eyed, but Mrs. Saunders sat composed behind her desk. "You never came in Friday. I buzzed you three times."

"I'm sorry, Mrs. Saunders, but I have a personal crisis happening right now. I thought maybe you could help me."

The woman arched a brow. "I've been working through a personal crisis of my own, and I expect you to do the same."

"I-I think our problems are connected," Lauri stammered. "That man I saw at your house and here in your office—he's trying to force me to give him access to my nephew. A-and he killed my fiancé."

Mrs. Saunders frowned. "I don't understand. The sheriff said a man named Wes Townsend had been shot. Was he your fiancé? What does all this have to do with me?"

Lauri sighed. She was going to have to tell her boss how she got involved. Lauri would almost certainly lose her job. Launching into the story, she watched Mrs. Saunders's face.

The woman pressed together lips that had gone colorless. She rubbed the back of her neck. "You were incredibly stupid to have gotten involved in this."

"I know. My fiancé is dead because of it. And now my brother's family is in jeopardy. What is it all about? Why is he blackmailing your husband?"

"Like I said, I can't help you." She rose. "Take your things from your office and don't come back."

Lauri's eyes filled with tears. "Please, Mrs. Saunders! Davy isn't even eight yet. His life is in jeopardy. I have to help him." She dug out a picture of Davy with his gap-toothed smile. "This is my nephew."

Mrs. Saunders barely glanced at the picture. Her eyes flashed. "Don't probe any more. Don't you think you've already done enough? If your meddling causes them to harm her . . ."

"Harm who?"

"Get out of here. I don't want to see you again in this office."

"Please, Mrs. Saunders! Don't you care at all about a little boy?"

Mrs. Saunders paused, and Lauri could have sworn there were tears in her eyes before the woman shook her head, went to the door, and held it open for Lauri to exit.

Lauri pressed the picture in Mrs. Saunders's hand. "Think about it."

22

HE WALKED A DANGEROUS TIGHTROPE. QUINN LET HIM-self into the cabin. The temperature couldn't be more than fifty inside. He tossed kindling and logs in the woodstove and lit it, but it would be awhile before the fire pushed back the chill, so he kept his coat on.

He realized the window was open. No wonder it was so cold. When he went to close it, he heard Rosen outside talking to someone on the phone. Making arrangements to take Davy and the baby. And eliminate Quinn himself.

Anger tightened his neck. He'd suspected it would come to this.

He waited until Rosen ended the call, then rapped on the window. "What are you doing out there?"

"Waiting for you to get home." Rosen's smile was feral. He went around the side of the cabin and entered. "You get the baby?"

Quinn still mulled over what he'd discovered. Half a mil, and he hadn't seen a penny of it. His best bet was to confront his partner. Rosen tended to be a pawn.

"I've made arrangements to pick her up tomorrow, now that our demands have been met. Jenna is on the inside. It will be a piece of cake." He'd have to make sure he moved before Rosen did.

"What about the witness?" Rosen asked. "The Matthews boy."

The Nicholls boy. The adoption wasn't final and, if Quinn had anything to do with it, never would be. So far he'd said nothing about his relationship to Davy, and he was unsure how much to reveal now. "I'll handle that. It's not your job."

"The boss says it is."

"And I say it isn't." Quinn lowered his voice to a menacing growl. "I'll handle it."

Rosen shrugged. "Then take it up with the boss. Until he says differently, I'll move ahead."

He couldn't let on that he knew of their plans, so he said nothing. He waited until Rosen left, then moved to the bedroom. He noticed through the window that Jenna's car was parked by the Dumpster, so she had to be here. He found her curled in the bed with the covers practically over her head.

He shook her. "Jenna, how long have you been here?"

Her eyelids fluttered open. "Quinn? Are you finally here?" She sat up and yawned. "That baby has been keeping us all up at night. What time is it? You're late."

"Sorry. I hope you had a nice nap. Did you meet Rosen when he stopped by?"

"Someone was here? I didn't hear them knock. You know how hard I sleep."

He never knew when to believe her. She'd likely overheard, but it didn't matter. "I got you some kiwi, sleepyhead. Want one to wake you up?"

"That sounds great." She staggered a bit when she got out of bed to follow him. "What did Rosen want?"

"Just checking in." He handed her a kiwi. "Got a new wrinkle in the situation and you could really help me, hon." The unfamiliar endearment nearly gagged him.

She stopped cutting the kiwi. "I'll do anything I can. You know that."

"Tell me more about the Matthews family."

Her eyes narrowed. "Why the questions? You left them behind years ago. Do you still love Bree?"

"No, of course not."

"Then stop with the questions. Once we get little Olivia, we'll never have to see them again. I want to take Vic to civilization with us."

"I might not be able to hang around until he's out of jail. *If* he gets out of jail."

Her lips tightened. "I've given up everything for you, Quinn. He'll be out of jail soon and I'm not leaving him behind."

He shrugged. "Whatever you say." He would leave her behind if necessary.

She yawned and took a bite of kiwi. "I'm so ready to get out of here. There isn't even a decent mall within ten miles."

"What about Bree's husband? Kade's a park ranger, right? Is he gone a lot?" At her suspicious glance, he rushed to explain. "I'm trying to figure out some logistics."

"Just normal hours, though he's been working some overtime. He's quiet. I think he's worried about something. Really nice guy though. The kind you could trust with your life."

He raised an eyebrow. "You sound like you admire him."

"He's a total hottie. He and Bree make a perfect pair. He's the kind who'd lay down his life for his family."

The perfect new husband. He wanted to make a face, but he kept his expression impassive. He got a beer from the fridge and faced her again. "Do you think you could ask about taking Davy out cross-country skiing? I could meet up with you."

"What are you up to?"

He pulled her tight against his chest so she couldn't see his expression. "I'm going to take my son with me."

Her eyes narrowed to a hard slit. "I won't do this for nothing,

Quinn. I'm taking a risk here. I need to know it will pay off." She
wiggled her ring finger at him.

He wanted to refuse again, but from the inflexible line of her
lips, he knew he had to cave or she wouldn't cooperate. "I've got
the ring all picked out. Two carats."

Her smile came. "When do you want to do this?"

"Tomorrow afternoon."

"Okay. Bree won't mind, I'm sure."

"Thank you, Jenna. You're my lifeline in everything." Lies, all
lies. He'd figure out how to get rid of her when she brought him
his son.

Breakfast was a silent affair. Bree had tried to call her attorney,
Ursula Sawyer, yesterday, but she'd been in court all day. Until she
knew the legal issues she and Kade faced, she didn't want to talk
to Davy about Rob. While her son was bound to be thrilled to
learn his father was alive, he would soon enough wonder why Rob
walked away and left him in the plane wreckage. Bree's heart
broke at the thought of the rejection Davy would feel.

Samson came down the stairs and plopped down at Bree's
feet. Bree looked up at Kade and broke the silence "I called
Ursula and told her about the situation. We're discussing it this
afternoon." She closed her eyes and grimaced at the thought of
what lay ahead. "Can you pick Davy up after school?"

He winced. "I've got a meeting. I don't think I can get out
of it."

"What's happened?" Lauri asked, looking up from her cereal.
Zorro lay at her feet. "You're not getting a divorce, are you?"

"Of course not," Kade said. He and Bree locked glances. He
shrugged. "She's got to hear it sooner or later."

Lauri straightened. "What's wrong?" Her gaze went wide. "Is someone else dead?"

Bree bit her lip. "Just the opposite," she said. "Someone we thought was dead is alive."

Lauri's brow furrowed. "I don't get it."

"Bree's first husband, Rob, isn't dead. He's back in town." A muscle in Kade's jaw twitched and he glanced down at his half-eaten omelet.

Lauri's jaw dropped. "Holy cow," she said softly. "So where does that leave you, big brother? Without a wife?"

Kade flinched. "Nice jab, Lauri. You know where to stick the knife."

"Sorry," she muttered. "But it looks like Bree has two husbands. Aren't you worried about which one she'll pick?"

Kade's head stayed down. Bree hardly knew what to say either. They had no idea what the legalities of this situation were. While a part of her loved the man Rob had once been, the reality of what he'd done sank deeper every hour. And cut more painfully. Kade would never walk away like that. Never.

Kade cleared his throat when Bree said nothing. She realized she should have reassured him, but the moment had passed. And really, what was there to say? Finding their way through this maze was going to take time.

Lauri was biting her lip so hard it was a wonder she didn't draw blood. "You okay?" Bree asked. Olivia began to fuss in the carrier on the table, and she lifted the baby into her arms and jiggled her.

Lauri's eyes turned glassy as she stared at Olivia. "It's been a hard week," she mumbled finally. She pushed back from the table and rose. "I'm going to go shower," she said.

When Lauri left the room, Kade leaned across the table. The

back of his hand brushed Bree's jaw, and he gazed into her eyes with loving intent. "We'll make it through this, Green Eyes," he said.

She caught his hand and pressed it against her cheek. "Yes, we will, Kade. We'll get it sorted out. I love you."

"That's all I needed to hear. That you're not sorry you married me." His Adam's apple bobbed in his throat.

"Of course I'm not!" She clung to his hand for support. Though she was befuddled by all that had happened, she didn't doubt her love for him.

Jenna entered the room before he said any more. Bree let go of his hand and leaned back in her chair. "Anything new with Victor?" she asked.

Jenna poured milk over her cereal and shook her head. "Just more of the puzzles. He's still not talking. Mason is calling in a psychiatrist to see if he can get through to Vic, especially now that he found the dead baby." She carried her bowl to the table. "I thought I might take Davy cross-country skiing after school if it's okay." She directed a brilliant smile at Kade.

Jenna's offer evaporated Bree's continuing irritation with her houseguest. "That's so sweet of you, but I need to keep him close to home. A situation has come up." She broke off, unwilling to explain it all to Jenna.

"It would solve our problem this afternoon," Kade said.

Bree frowned. "I can probably get Anu or Hilary to pick him up," she said.

"Look, I know you think I'm a complete airhead, but I can take care of him just fine. I already mentioned it to him, and he's all excited," Jenna said. "We'll take the path along the lake with lots of people. I don't know what's worrying you, but he'll have fun."

Bree exchanged a long look with Kade. "I think it's probably okay, babe, but it's your call," he said.

Bree bit her lip. "Take Samson with you, okay?" The dog would protect Davy no matter what.

Jenna shrugged. "Whatever you say."

"You'd better get to work," Bree said to Kade. "I'll get Davy." She called her son down for school, then kissed Kade and Davy good-bye. She spent the day surfing the Web for information about dead husbands returning when the smart thing to do would be to wait and see what Ursula had to say.

At two, she loaded Olivia in the carrier and drove to Ursula's office. She left Samson at the house so he could go skiing with Davy. The receptionist took her back right away. "What did you find out?" she asked the minute Ursula entered the room.

An attractive brunette of about fifty, Ursula inspired trust in everyone she met. "It's not bad," Ursula said, sitting at her desk.

Her friend's brisk, confident manner put Bree at ease. She set Olivia's carrier on the floor and pulled back the quilted cover. The baby was awake and sucking on her thumb. "So what's the scoop?"

Ursula adjusted her reading glasses and opened a file on her desk. "A death certificate was filed with Rob's insurance. All legalities were met. So your marriage to Kade is legal. As far as the law is concerned, Rob was dead and you were free to remarry."

Bree breathed a prayer of thanks. "Kade will be so relieved too."

"That's not to say there aren't issues to work on. Rob will want to see Davy. We'll need to reach a custody agreement and ask him for child support payments."

Bree's gut clenched. "Kade is in the process of adopting Davy. It's not final yet."

Ursula pursed her lips. "Now that the biological father is back in the picture, that might be difficult. Unless you get Rob to agree."

"He abandoned his son to die! Don't we have a legal recourse?"

"The circumstances might carry some weight with the judge. If you want to take it that far." Ursula sat back in her chair. "Have you thought this through, Bree? What it's going to do to your son to have all this come out?"

Bree tugged on a curl by her ear. "I've been able to think of little else. Davy idolized Rob. When he realizes what his father did, how he left him . . ." She choked up. "I don't want to tell him."

"Maybe Rob will just disappear again. It might be the kinder thing if you can talk him into it."

Bree bit her lip. "He wants to see Davy."

"Talk to him about it," Ursula advised.

"I will if I can find him." Bree rose and grabbed Olivia's carrier. "Thanks for working me in, Ursula. I won't take up any more of your time."

"If you need anything, just call." She embraced Bree. "Hang in there, Bree. It could have been worse."

Bree managed a smile. Right now she couldn't see how. Their family was about to be ripped to shreds.

She pulled the cover back around Olivia and went to the Jeep. A hint of moisture hung in the air. More snow was coming. "Let's stop and see Mason," she told the baby once Olivia was fastened in.

She wanted to tell Kade the news, but he was probably still in his meeting. She decided to call anyway and leave it on his voice mail. She smiled as she left the message. "It's okay. Our marriage is valid."

She hurried with the baby through the cold air. The deputy out front buzzed her back to Mason's office. Bree lifted a fussy Olivia from the carrier and pulled a bottle from her bag while she waited for Mason.

"Bree, you okay?" Mason asked, closing the door behind him.

"As okay as I can be with this. How's Hil?"

"She hasn't slept much. I didn't know there were that many tears in the world. She jumps between mad and glad. She's desperate to see him, but he's nowhere I've looked." He went around his desk and sat down in his worn leather chair. "Did you find out anything from Ursula?"

Bree nodded. "She says my marriage to Kade is valid. That's one good thing. But the adoption is up in the air unless Rob doesn't contest it."

Mason rolled his eyes. "Who knows what he's going to do." He jiggled his mouse and leaned toward his computer. "I found out some interesting stuff. I lifted some prints from the doorknob on your back door after you said he'd been out there. They match a Quinn Matilla. He's been implicated in some small-time smuggling, some bigger racketeering, and a suspected bank robbery. But the interesting thing is that he's suspected of dabbling in black-market babies too." He nodded toward Olivia. "I suspect we're going to find she's part of that too."

Her arms tightened around the baby. "You think Ellie Bristol sold her?"

Mason shrugged. "It looks that way to me."

"And Pia's death?" Bree whispered. "Surely Rob didn't kill her."

"I hope not. It would hurt Hil and Anu too much." Mason's face was grim. He glanced up, his eyes shadowed. "The coroner suspects the baby we found buried in the snow died of tetanus. Could have had it from birth if the umbilical cord was cut with a knife. It wasn't murder."

Bree's vision swam and she closed her eyes, then reopened them. "I don't want to think about that," she whispered. "How could he steal babies?"

"This stuff might be the least of what he's done."

Nausea churned its way up her esophagus. "How do we find out more?"

"I need to talk to Rob. Did he give you any hint at all where he's staying?"

"No."

"If he contacts you again, try to get word to me. Text me or something while you keep him there."

"Maybe he'll agree to come in and talk to you. You're family."

Mason snorted. "Not likely, Bree. He's not the Rob we knew."

The knowledge of how much her former husband had changed kept slapping her when she least expected it. "What about missing persons around the time the plane went down?"

"Several actually. I'm still checking them out. The one I have my eye on is a young state cop by the name of Henry Boxer. Lived in Houghton. He told his wife he was going fishing and never came home." He rose. "I want us to talk to Victor." He glanced down at Olivia, whose eyes had drifted shut. "Maybe seeing the baby will break through to him. Stay here and I'll go get him. It's a little unorthodox to bring him in here, but I don't think he's dangerous. I'm going to release him today in light of the new evidence."

"What about him buying baby stuff? And Ellie's mother said he'd been in contact with her."

"I thought you believed in his innocence."

"I do. But I thought maybe you could explain what he was doing."

Mason shook his head. "Not that. But whatever Victor's done, it's not murder. I suspect he's been used by Florence."

Bree nodded. "I'd like to talk to Palmer Chambers." She'd been thinking about it ever since she realized Rob was alive. Palmer had been convicted of Rob's murder by tampering with the plane. "He should know who was in the plane when it left."

"I'll put in a request for an interview. He has the right to turn you down though."

"I don't think he will." She and Rob had been best friends with the Chambers family once upon a time.

Mason left the room. Olivia spit the nipple out, and a dribble of formula trickled from her rosebud mouth. A wave of love swept over Bree. She didn't understand how the baby's mother had been willing to sell her. There were so many tentacles in this situation, and she had no idea how they all connected.

She burped Olivia and laid her back down in her lap, inhaling the baby's milky aroma. The baby's delicate blue-tinted eyelids fluttered, then opened. Her lips lifted, and Bree realized she was smiling.

"Oh, such a sweet girl," she cooed. The baby's head turned at the sound of her voice, and Bree was rewarded with a smile focused in her direction.

Tears flooded her eyes. Was she going to have to give up this precious little one? She brushed her lips across Olivia's soft head and cuddled her close. She and Kade hadn't talked about it since discovering Rob was alive.

The door opened and Victor shuffled into the room with his wrists and ankles in cuffs. "Does he have to wear those?" she asked Mason.

He shrugged. "I'll take them off. I started the release proceedings." He unfastened the cuffs. "I'm going to release you, Victor. You can go home in a little while."

Bree stood and approached Victor, who stood with his gaze focused on the ground. "Victor, it's Bree. Look, I brought the baby to see you." Victor still didn't raise his gaze. She exchanged a helpless glance with Mason. "Did you see a man bury a baby?" she asked softly. "Did Florence see it too?"

Victor rubbed his wrists. He glanced at the baby, then ducked his head. "Miss Florence was sad when the baby died," he croaked. "The man took it away."

Bree exchanged a glance with Mason. "What baby, Victor?"

Victor rocked back and forth and began to sing in a rusty voice, "Hush little baby, don't say a word, Papa's going to buy you a mockingbird, and if that mockingbird don't sing, Papa's gonna buy you a diamond ring."

No matter how much she tried to get him to say more, he continued to sing the same stanza over and over. Bree sighed and let Mason lead him away before she hurried to the Jeep.

Bree got back in the Jeep and drove toward home. As she passed Naomi's house, Bree noticed Sheila MacDonald's blue Escort in the drive. The older woman was Naomi's mother's best friend and had her fingers in every pie. If there had been any rumors going around about Rob, Sheila would know, though she wouldn't have told anyone since it affected Naomi's best friend. Bree parked behind the small car and retrieved Olivia. Charley barked from inside the house as they approached. She rapped on the door, then walked in. Charley's tail drooped when he saw no sign of Samson.

"Naomi, got a cup of coffee for me?" she called. She unsnapped the baby's carrier cover and lifted Olivia out. The baby looked around with wide eyes as Bree walked to the kitchen.

"Hey, girlfriend, glad you could stop by," Naomi said. She held out her hands. "Come see Auntie Naomi, sweetheart," she cooed. She lifted the baby from Bree's arms and tucked her into the crook of her arm.

Bree poured herself a cup of coffee and joined Sheila at the table. "Sheila, I stopped when I saw you were here."

The older woman raised her brows. "You were looking for me?"

There was no way she was going to find out what she wanted without revealing the truth. What possible reason could she have for asking questions about Rob four years after his disappearance?

Bree glanced at Naomi. "Something has happened. I need you both to promise not to repeat it."

"You don't even have to ask," Naomi said, her tone a reproof.

"If you ask me not to speak of it, rest assured I won't, Bree," Sheila said.

Bree's pulse hammered in her throat. It was still so hard to talk about, to even believe. "Rob isn't dead," she said.

Naomi gasped, and the baby gave a start, her face puckering. Naomi jiggled her. "I don't think I heard you right."

"Rob didn't die in the plane crash. He walked away and left town. I thought I saw someone who reminded me of him the weekend of the winter festival and a few other times. Then I actually talked to him. It's Rob, no doubt about it." She turned to Sheila. "Something made him walk away that night. He says he thought Davy was dead, but if that were the truth, I believe he would have come home to comfort me. It's more than that, and I have to know the reason. Did you hear any rumors about Rob before he disappeared or right afterward?"

Sheila reached over and took Bree's hand. "You sure you want to hear this? I never wanted you to know. I never even told Martha."

Bree gripped Sheila's warm fingers. "I have to know."

Sheila held her gaze. "His secretary was my cousin. She turned him in when she discovered he was embezzling money from the city. He was about to be brought in by the state police and questioned."

Bree shook her head, unable to take it in. "If that's true, why wouldn't Mason have known about it—and told me?"

"Maybe the state cops didn't tell Mason," Naomi suggested, jiggling Olivia.

"I don't think they did," Sheila said. "I've never heard a mention of it from anyone but my cousin. It all ended with the plane crash."

"Embezzlement," Bree said. The word sounded foreign on her

lips. It didn't fit the Rob she knew. "We were having some financial problems, but I can't see him resorting to that to fix them."

"I watched a show on TV a few months ago," Sheila said. "I thought of Rob when I saw it. According to the show, most people caught up in embezzlement have every intention of paying the money back—they think of it as a temporary loan. Then it gets out of hand and they're in too far before they know it."

"This will kill Anu," Naomi said softly.

Bree nodded. "Hilary too." She rubbed her forehead. "I'm going to have to tell them." It wasn't a conversation she was looking forward to.

She'd just finished her second carrot muffin when her cell phone rang, and she saw Mason's name on the caller ID. "Hey, what's up?" she asked.

"Palmer has agreed to talk to you. Since he's so far away, I've arranged for a phone conversation. Hang on, and I'll patch you through."

Bree held up a finger to Naomi, then moved to the living room where it was quiet, leaving Olivia in the kitchen with the women. She heard a click, then distant voices. "Hello? Palmer?"

"Hang on," a gruff voice said.

The next moment Palmer was on the other end. "That you, Bree?"

It had been two years since she'd seen him or heard his voice. The last time had been at his trial. How did she talk to an old friend who'd tried to kill her and her son? "Yes, I'm here. I-I have something I need to ask you."

"Ask away. You got me out of a nasty work detail." He laughed and his voice held a forced cheerfulness.

"Rob isn't dead, Palmer. He walked away from the plane and never came back." She told him what Rob had told her.

"You mean I'm sitting in this stinking prison and he's not even dead?" Palmer's voice rose.

"You killed Faye Asters," she reminded him. "You tried to kill me and Davy."

"All to cover up Rob's death." He sounded like he was gritting his teeth.

"Look, I need to know who else was on the plane when it took off. Someone else died in that crash. Whoever it was wore Rob's jacket, and that's how he was misidentified."

"I wondered where that other body went," Palmer muttered. "I figured animals got it."

"Did you kill him too? Who was it?" she demanded.

"No, I didn't kill him, at least not on purpose. Rob agreed to let him catch a ride home at the last minute."

"Who?"

"Cop by the name of Henry Boxer. He showed up to talk to Rob but fell in the river on the way there. Looked like a drowned rat. Rob loaned him his jacket. I guess that's how he came to be wearing it."

Bree closed her eyes. She didn't know Henry, but his family would be able to get closure. She knew well the agony of wondering what happened to a loved one. Sometimes it wasn't what you thought.

LOW-HANGING CLOUDS ACCUMULATED IN THE WEST, AND the breeze freshened where Quinn stood in the drift-covered meadow. A snowstorm was coming. Maybe it would help him. He'd pray if he thought it would do any good, but he'd long ago turned his back on what little faith his mother had instilled in him.

He glanced at his watch. Nearly three. Jenna should be here with Davy any minute. How would he tell the boy who he was? In his heart of hearts, the man who used to be Rob Nicholls hoped his son would recognize him. That a sliver of love still existed.

A bark drifted toward him. It sounded like Samson. Surely Jenna hadn't brought the dog. The bark came again, then Samson bounded into the meadow. The snow came to his chest and he was relishing the contact. His destination seemed to be Quinn's side. Dogs never forgot and still loved after many years. Especially one with a heart as big as Sam's.

"Here, boy," Quinn said, whistling. He could properly greet the dog, something he hadn't been able to do the other times they'd come in contact with one another.

Samson leaped through the snow with his tail swishing furiously. He reached Quinn and leaped up, putting his paws on Quinn's chest. His excited barking was a shot of adrenaline. At least someone was glad to see him. He seized Samson's head in his hands and roughed it up in their long-ago pattern of greeting. Bending down, he let the dog lick his cheek.

He heard the sound of voices and glanced up to see Jenna and a young boy skiing toward him. His heart squeezed at the realization he was about to come face-to-face with the son he'd thought was dead. With the earflaps down on his hat, and the collar of his coat pulled high, not much of his face was exposed to the cutting wind. Would Davy recognize the little he could see?

The last time Quinn had seen him, Davy was three. This young boy resembled the toddler he remembered, but he was taller, stronger. The shape of his face was more boyish and less babyish. But the eager grin was still all Davy.

The child stopped in front of him. Jenna remained a few feet away. Her eyes held a sharp gleam, and a smug smile pulled at her mouth. He wished she weren't watching. Things were going to hard enough without her butting in.

"Hello," he said, smiling down at his son. The boy was his, not Kade Matthews's.

"Hi," Davy said. "Sam acts like he knows you." His gaze traveled back to Quinn's face, and his eyes held a question.

Should he tell Davy now? Or wait until he had him to safety? Quinn glanced at the clouds that were dragging lower. The snow would begin any time. There wasn't time to get into a long discussion.

"You're Davy Nicholls," he said. "I . . . I know your mother."

"It's Dave Matthews," the boy corrected with his chin tipped up. "Davy is a baby name. You can call me Dave if you want though."

Quinn wanted to laugh at the solemn assertion. It stung a little that Dave was so adamant about his last name now. He could tell from the way the boy studied his face that there was a memory trying to surface. Better not let it just yet.

He held out his hand. "Come with me, Dave. We're going to go on a little trip."

His son drew back. "I'm not allowed to go with strangers."

At the sound of the edge in his voice, Samson's tail stopped wagging. The dog sidled closer to the boy and planted his front paws as if to block access to Dave.

Maybe he'd have to reveal everything to avoid a struggle. Quinn didn't want to have to fight Dave and Sam too.

"Son," he said. "I'm not a stranger." He squatted to put himself at eye level with Dave. Ripping the hat from his head, he asked, "Do you remember where you've seen me before?"

Dave chewed on his lip. "You look a little bit like pictures of my first dad. He died in a plane crash though. Are you related to him?"

Maybe that was the easiest explanation. "Kind of related, yes," he said.

"Why haven't I seen you at Grammy's then?" the boy went on, his voice doubtful.

"Look at me, Dav—Dave," he said, catching himself before the old nickname could slip out. "You know who I am if you let yourself."

"You're a windigo," Davy whispered. "You've taken over my daddy's body. That's it, isn't it?" His voice grew louder, more fearful.

The fur on Samson's back raised, and a rumble started in his chest. Recognition or no, the dog would protect the boy against anyone. "Easy, Sam," he said.

"You call him Sam," Davy said. "No one calls him Sam but me and my daddy. You *are* a windigo!" He backed up a step. The dog kept pace with him and kept his body between Quinn and the boy.

"There's no such thing as a windigo," Quinn said. "I am your dad, son."

"No, he's dead!" Davy backed up several more feet. His lips moved, and the words *God* and *help* came through in whispered gasps.

"Davy, it's all right. I'm really your dad. I didn't die in the plane crash."

Davy's brow furrowed, and his gaze locked with Quinn's. "What's my favorite book? The one you used to read me?"

"*Green Eggs and Ham*," Quinn said without hesitation. "You liked it because of Sam."

Davy's eyes grew wider, and panic flared in them. "Only a windigo could know that."

"Or your real dad," Quinn said. "Your mom knows I'm alive. I saw her too. And Grammy."

Davy shook his head. "They would have told me."

"I'm sure they were going to."

The boy chewed on his lip as the first fat snowflakes began to fall. "What song is Mom's favorite?"

"'Hound Dog,'" Quinn said. "She's a big Elvis fan. And she loves pistachios. You like peanut butter and thimbleberry jam. Your aunt Hilary is my sister and she cans jelly every year and saves some just for you. Your Grammy makes the best *pulla* in the world, and she still sings you '*Suomalainen kehtolaulu*' just like she did me when I was growing up." He hadn't thought of some of these memories in years.

All this reminiscence was making him crazy. The old life was no more. He could never go back. But he could go forward with what belonged to him—his boy.

Dave took a step nearer. "You really are my daddy?"

"Yes. I really am."

The boy moved past Samson until he was close enough to reach up and touch Quinn's face with gloved hands. "You left me," he said.

"I thought you died in the crash," Quinn said. "I was wrong."

Doubt still darkened the boy's eyes. He dropped his hand. "I want to see my mom."

How would he tell Davy that he'd never see his mother again? It would be best not to go there. "Let's go. I have so much to tell you and show you." He held out his hand to his son. After a brief hesitation, Davy took it with no more questions.

Quinn glanced over to see Jenna staring at him. He held out his other hand to her. He needed to make sure she didn't desert him now. If she ran off and told Bree, his plans would come crashing down. "Come with us?"

She frowned but took his hand. He squeezed her fingers. They turned back toward the road where he'd parked his truck. This storm would sweep in fast and furious. And hopefully cover their tracks.

"Where are we going?" Jenna asked when they reached the truck and Davy and the dog had gotten inside. She stood by the hood as he slammed the back door and came toward her.

"They want to kill him," he said.

"Who is they?" she asked.

"It's better if you don't know. We've got to disappear. Besides, a boy belongs with his father." He forced a coaxing smile. "I want you with me, Jenna. We can be married and raise Davy." He thought that would placate her worry, but the doubt remained in her eyes.

"Won't they find us?"

"Not if they think we're dead." The daring plan he had in mind was dangerous. And he still had to figure out how to get his share of the money.

"What about Vic? I can't leave him behind."

"We'll send for him," he lied. He guided her toward the truck. She got in on the driver's side and slid across to the passenger seat.

Davy leaned forward. "It was you, wasn't it?"

Quinn twisted around to stare at the boy. "When?"

"The man I saw putting the baby in the snow. Did you kill it?" The accusation in Davy's eyes matched his voice.

Quinn winced. He'd hoped the boy hadn't seen anything. The danger to Davy just escalated. "No. It wasn't me."

"Was she your baby?"

There was no way to explain he'd stolen the baby from a poor Native American woman so he could sell her, and then something had gone terribly wrong.

"It wasn't me," he said again, the lie slipping easily off his tongue.

"What about Miss Florence? Did you hurt her? She yelled at you."

Quinn set his jaw. "No more questions. We've got to get out of here before we can't get through the drifts." He started the truck and pulled out onto the road.

The clock on the mantel moved much too slowly. Bree kept glancing at it, then at her watch. Where could they be? The storm had come in faster than predicted, and she'd expected Jenna and Davy over an hour ago. It was nearly six, and darkness hovered on the horizon. Dinner had congealed in the pans on the stove, but that was the least of her worries.

The TV momentarily snagged her attention. A perky reporter smiled into the camera. "Michael Saunders, CEO of the Kitchigami Mining Corporation, announced today that the company has scrapped plans for a new mine near the Ottawa National Forest. When asked what caused the about-face, Saunders said that after reviewing financial forecasts, the board decided the cost of the new mine would be too great."

The camera zoomed to the park headquarters. "For reaction to this story, we interviewed Gary Landorf, Forest Supervisor."

Gary's smiling face came into focus. "Here at the park service, we're delighted by this news. As you know, we were concerned the mine would affect our wildlife and resources. I applaud the mining corporation for their wise decision."

Kade was going to be happy to hear this news. Bree turned off the television. She tried Jenna's cell phone again but hung up when she got her voice mail. She'd already left three messages. Glancing through the front window, she saw Kade pull up. He'd know what to do.

Her gut told her to go out and find them. Jenna had said they were taking the upper trail along the lake. But Bree couldn't take Olivia out in this weather. And without Samson, she would be deaf and blind in the storm.

She met Kade at the door. "Jenna isn't back with Davy yet."

His brows drew together, and he glanced at his watch. "It's getting bad out there already."

Just as she'd feared. "We need to find them, but I don't have Samson."

"Call Naomi. Get her over here with Charley. I'll get Zorro."

"He does better with Lauri."

"Lauri will want to come. Is she here?"

Bree shook her head. "She went to town for coffee."

"I'll call her." Kade drew out his cell phone.

While he called his sister, Bree used the house phone and called Naomi, who promised to come immediately. She also called two other members of the Kitchigami Search and Rescue team but didn't reach either of them. Her urgency kicked up a notch now that she'd decided something was definitely wrong.

Maybe one of them had fallen. Or the storm had disoriented them and they were lost. But no, they had Samson. He'd lead them home, blizzard or not. Olivia was wailing for her dinner, and Bree stood, torn, in the middle of the floor. She needed to call Anu to come care for the baby. She placed the call quickly, then saw Mason approaching the front of house with his head down against the driving snow. Had he heard about her missing boy already?

Kade snapped her out of her thoughts. "Lauri said she saw Jenna and Davy heading this way in a truck. She's on her way too."

Bree closed her eyes in relief, then opened them. "Maybe Jenna's cell phone is dead."

Lauri's car pulled up behind the sheriff's SUV, and she hurried through the snow to join him on the porch as Bree opened the door. Both came in stomping snow from their boots and brushing it from their coats.

Mason glanced from Lauri to Bree. "What's going on?"

"Davy didn't come home from a ski trip with Jenna. Isn't that why you're here?" Bree asked. "It's okay though. Lauri said she saw them heading this way."

He shook his head. "I asked the Houghton police to bring Mrs. Saunders in for questioning. We managed to get the truth out of her. It seems the adopted daughter of Mike Saunders, CEO of Kitchigami Mining, was kidnapped. It's all hitting the papers now. The baby was taken to force him to pull out of his new mining project near the forest. Plus he was paying kickbacks to state officials to get the mining approval through. His wife spilled it all early this afternoon."

"I saw on the news about the mining project being withdrawn," Bree said. Her lungs froze. "Are you saying you suspect Olivia is that kidnapped baby?"

Mason nodded and pulled a picture from his pocket. "Here's a picture of the child."

Bree's fingers closed on the picture and she stared at it. Olivia, as she'd looked the first time Bree saw her, stared into the camera. "I-I see," she managed.

Mason pulled at his chin. "Mr. and Mrs. Saunders are coming to get Olivia tomorrow, once the roads are clear."

The baby continued to cry in the portable crib in the living room. Bree went to get her and held her close. The infant settled with her fist in her mouth. Mason and Lauri had followed her, and Kade joined them with Zorro, who was already in his search vest.

"Does she have any proof that Olivia is her daughter?" Bree asked Mason. "More than just a picture?"

"The adoption papers. She faxed them over to me. They look legitimate. Ellie Bristol signed her daughter over to the Saunderses, who agreed to pay medical costs plus living expenses for four years while she was in college."

Bree batted back the tears in her eyes, but they dropped onto Olivia's face anyway. It would rip out her heart to turn over this baby.

Kade came to stand behind her. He put his big hands on her shoulders in unspoken comfort. "Where did you see Jenna and Davy, Lauri? I thought they'd be here by now."

Lauri frowned. "I did too. She was in a black truck. A guy was driving. Davy and Samson were in the back. I thought they were heading here. I saw them before I stopped at the coffee shop."

A big black truck. Just like the one that belonged to the man who had tried to take Davy from Naomi's. Rob. "Jenna and Davy are with Rob," she said. She stared up at Kade.

Had Rob told Davy the truth? Bree couldn't bear the pain her son would feel when he began to question what had happened. Bree gestured at the falling snow illuminated by the porch light. "It's dark and the weather is atrocious. What kind of person would keep a child out in this without calling? Jenna is in on this with Rob." Her voice trembled and she told herself to hold it together somehow. She'd get him back.

She heard the front door open, then Anu's light steps down the hall. "We're in here," Bree called. When Anu appeared, Bree told her what had happened. "Has Rob been in contact with you?" Her throat kept clogging with tears.

Anu shook her head. Sobs heaved her shoulders, and she clung to Bree. "I am so sorry, my Bree, that my son would bring this sorrow on our heads."

Bree hugged her close. "It's not your fault, Anu." Tears burned her eyes. She wanted her boy back. Now.

If only she had Rob's cell phone number. Would he just take Davy and disappear without a word? She couldn't fathom the man she once knew being so cruel.

Anu pulled away. "I will care for Olivia. Go. Find my grandson."

Mason was putting his phone away. "I don't think anyone is traveling far on these roads. We've already gotten six inches with another foot predicted. High winds too. My crew tells me it's nearly impassable outside town."

Bree paced. "We've got to find Davy! Can we get out the snowmobiles?"

Mason put his hand on her shoulder. "Sure. But the wind chill is fifty below. Rob must be holed up somewhere. He's not going any farther than we are. When the snow stops, I can get choppers in the air and have every trooper in the UP watching for him. He's not getting far."

Bree knew what Mason said was true, but she wanted to do something. She couldn't just sit here in the house and not look for her son. She sent a silent plea to her husband.

Kade nodded. "I'll get the snowmobiles out," he said. "We've got warm clothing, Mason. In the direction Lauri saw them headed, they had to be going east on 38. They couldn't have gotten much farther than Baraga, not in this weather."

"That's forty miles of open road," Mason pointed out. "You'll have hypothermia by the time you get there."

"We've got heated gear," Kade said. "Heated socks, the whole nine yards. It won't be comfortable but we'll be okay."

As if to punctuate his words, the wind shrieked around the windows and howled down the chimney, scattering cold ashes onto the floor. Was her son out in this? The thought made Bree shudder.

"I'm going to try Jenna one more time," she said.

Conscious of their gazes, she picked up the cordless phone. Before she punched in the number, she had a thought. What if Jenna had called Rob from this phone? Bree cycled through the redial numbers. Anu's number, Hilary's, Naomi's, Mason's, Lauri's, two more of Anu's numbers.

Then there it was. A number she didn't recognize. Not local. The area code was farther east, over by the Soo.

She pressed the button to dial it and prayed. *Please, please, Lord, let this be Rob's.* Let him listen to me. The dial tone rang in her ear. One ring. Two, three, four. Her fingers tightened on the phone. He wasn't going to answer, and she waited to be dumped into voice mail.

Then his voice spoke in her ear. "Bree?"

"Rob!" She nearly sobbed with relief. "Is Davy all right?"

"He's fine. Sleeping. I debated about answering, but I knew you needed to know. Don't try to find us, Bree. You'll put Davy in danger. I'm saving his life."

Her angry tears dried. "What are you talking about?" she whispered.

"Some very powerful men want him . . . silenced. His only hope is to disappear with me."

"He saw you bury a baby, didn't he?"

"I'll take good care of him, Bree. I'll let him call once in a while."

Bree spoke at the same time as the phone went dead in her ear. "Rob!" Nothing. She tried to call again, but this time he didn't pick up. She burst into tears and told Kade what he'd said.

Kade took her hand and glanced at his sister. "Where exactly did you see them?"

"Heading this way on Houghton Street."

"They could have turned off on Kitchigami, then hit the highway," Mason said.

Hysteria numbed Bree's thoughts. "I need Samson," she said, her voice breaking. "I've got to find Davy." Bree listened to Mason call the jail. He told the deputy to put out a lookout on the truck. He also called for help from the state police.

"Victor is mixed up in this somehow," Mason said, putting his phone away. "Victor and Davy saw Rob bury a baby. It's all got to be connected. Victor is the key. Plus he's Jenna's brother. She knows more than she's told us. Get me those puzzle copies you have."

Bree forced herself to focus. Anything to help find her son. She handed the baby to Lauri, then pulled out the file of sudokus, then added a pad of paper to the stack. "That nine-digit number is always the same. But I can't seem to find out what it means." She spread the puzzles out on the coffee table so the men could look.

She wanted to jump in the snowmobile and search for her son, but he was in a vehicle. He'd be untraceable by the dogs. Plus, she was severely handicapped with Samson missing too. She had to figure this out another way if she could think past the panic numbing her brain.

Kade picked up two sheets. "We've been focusing on that number across the top, but have you checked the numbers in the following rows?"

Bree peered at the puzzles he held, then down at the one in her hand. She grabbed the pad of paper and jotted down the number from the second row: 325714698. She scanned the number across the top: 896417523. "They're the reverse of one another," she said. "On all the puzzles."

"So which one is our clue?" Kade asked.

Mason joined them and glanced at the numbers too. "Let me run them through the department and see if anything pops up." He pulled out his cell phone and called in the request.

"Could we talk to Victor again?" Kade asked.

Mason shrugged. "Sure, but I don't see that he's going to help us. He's lost in another world. I released him, by the way. I left a message on Jenna's voice mail. A man showed up to get him. Short, kind of mashed-in face and a high voice."

Lauri gasped. "That sounds like the guy who's been threatening me."

24

THEY WERE WELL AND TRULY STUCK. QUINN HIT THE STEER-
ing wheel with both hands. He hadn't counted on this, and there
was no easy way out. His gaze went to the rearview mirror and his
sleeping son in the backseat. Had he taken the boy only to watch
him freeze to death in a blizzard?

Jenna roused from sleep and tossed her hair out of her eyes.
"Are we there?"

"No." He let the silence bring her around to staring out the
windshield at the white death waiting to swallow them. *Think,
think.*

He used to know the area around this little side road well. It
was dotted with caves. He had survival gear in the back. Shelter
would be all they needed to ride it out in relative comfort. They
were off the beaten path, so no one was likely to stumble on the
truck. Tomorrow when the storm passed, they could hike out.
Maybe law enforcement would assume they'd perished in the blizzard. They could start a new life the easy way.

"Are we stuck?" Jenna asked.

He gritted his teeth at the stupid question. "Good guess,
Sherlock." He ignored the way she flinched and felt relieved to
spout off some of his anger.

"What are we going to do?"

"Find a cave, make a fire, and ride it out." He shoved his door

251

open against the wind and went around the bed of the truck, where he peeled back the tarp and removed it. He rolled it up to take with them, then grabbed his backpack of gear and the two bedrolls. Jenna got out with him and he tossed her the backpack, then shouldered the rest of the stuff.

"Get Davy!" he shouted above the wind.

She nodded, then went around to the back door and roused the boy. Davy rolled out into the wind sleepily with his jacket still unzipped and no hat.

"Get your hat and gloves!" Quinn shouted.

Davy blinked sleepily but reached in and got his belongings. He pulled his ski mask and hat over his head and grabbed his skis. "Should I put my skis on?" he asked, the wind snatching away some of his words.

Quinn nodded and grabbed his own. They'd make better time on skis. Only Samson would have to brave the drifts. The dog would wear out fast, and Davy wouldn't go anywhere without the dog, so they needed to find shelter quickly. He led them toward a rocky crag rising from the snow.

Carrying so much stuff was awkward on skis, and the half-mile trek took so long he couldn't feel his face by the time they reached the cliff formation. He shined the halogen flashlight on the cliff face but saw only high drifts of snow. There had to be caves around here. The darkness of the night and the heavy snow hampered his view.

Tossing his burdens to the ground, he grabbed the backpack from Jenna and unzipped it, then took out the collapsible shovel. He extended the telescoped handle, then used it to prod the snow along the rock face. When the tool plunged in up to his shoulder, he knew he'd found a cave. He tossed the shovel down and began to scoop out armfuls of snow until the entrance loomed as an even darker space than the night.

The cave was clear of animals, but he was surprised to find the interior covered in ice. Huge ice formations hung from the ceiling. Still it was big enough for them all, with room for a fire too. He motioned for the rest of them to come in.

Jenna held back until Davy and Samson entered, then ducked in herself. "It's good to be out of the wind!" She blew on her gloved hands. "Can we have a fire?"

"If I can gather enough sticks." He tossed the sleeping bags to the ground. "See what you can do about spreading these out and getting you and Davy warm. I'll be back with the wood."

He left one of the flashlights with her, then stepped back out into the blizzard, where he grabbed his quickly vanishing shovel and glanced around for trees. It was too dark to see, and even his flashlight didn't pick out any likely trees. He went up the hillside to the right of the cave and found an armful of wood.

By the time he returned to the relative warmth of the cave, his breath pumped in and out of his lungs in spurts. Jenna had spread out the sleeping bags and Mylar blankets. "Looks cozy." He dropped the wood and built a fire near the cave mouth, leaving access if someone needed to go outside.

He shaved off bits of wood and blew on them as he coaxed the fire into being. A nearly forgotten skill. Davy crouched beside him, and Quinn was conscious of the boy's stare.

"Who is in the cemetery?" Davy whispered once the fire crackled. "Me and Mom go every month to visit. Who were we visiting?"

Quinn had known the question was coming. "We'll talk about it another time," he said in a voice that warned Davy to give up the interrogation.

"What about the baby? Did you kill it?" Davy's tone suggested he'd already made up his mind on that one, even though Quinn had initially denied it. The kid was smart.

He pressed his lips together, and his gaze met Jenna's. "No.

The baby went into convulsions and turned blue. A doctor told us he had tetanus, probably from cutting the cord with dirty scissors. By the time we found out something was wrong, we couldn't help him."

The boy threw his arm around Samson's neck. "Why did you throw him away? You could have taken him back to her mommy."

Quinn sighed. "Look, Davy, let's not get into all this. It was a business, that's all." He motioned for the boy to climb under the covers.

Davy's lip came out. "I want my mom," he whispered. Samson whined and licked the boy's face.

"Well, you can't have her," Quinn snapped. "Get some sleep." He crawled under the covers himself and curled up spoon-fashion with Jenna. The dog would keep Davy warm.

Once he was sure his son was under the covers, Quinn allowed his eyes to shut. He roused when he heard a sound and glanced at his watch. He'd been asleep about an hour. He sat up to see what had alerted him. The fire was almost out, but it still cast a dim glow in the cave.

Where were Sam and Davy? He kicked out of the sleeping bag and stood with his pulse jumping in his throat. He leaped the fire and went to the mouth of the cave, where he saw Davy and the dog running back toward the truck. "Davy, come back here!" He floundered through the snow, but he was still faster then the boy and managed to tackle him.

"Run, Sam!" Davy screamed. "Go find Mom. Bree, get Bree!"

Davy squirmed in Quinn's arms, but his efforts were puny. The dog danced around them both, barking. Quinn made a grab for Sam's collar, but he jerked away.

"Go, Sam!" Davy yelled again. "Get Bree!"

The dog turned and raced away, disappearing into the driving white storm.

The wind howled through the trees and Kade thought of the windigo. One had appeared all right. And it was about to devour his family. But he wasn't going to let it. The wind drove cold spikes into his flesh as he uncovered the snowmobiles, gassed them up, then drove each one to the front of the house. There would be four of them including Mason and Naomi.

The wind snickered at his attempt for warmth in spite of his heated gear and the heavy wool sock hat on his head. He'd need more layers. So would Bree. He trudged through the driving snow and drifts to the house, where he met her in the hall.

He glanced at her clothing. "Put on three or four layers. It's brutal. Full blizzard conditions. I'm going to add another two layers of long underwear. How many do you have?"

"One plus the heated." She turned and followed him upstairs. "Hurry!"

They quickly added more layers of underwear, plus two more sweaters. They both had a Pillsbury Doughboy appearance as they waddled downstairs, but their preparations might make the difference between freezing to death and finding their boy. Kade took a moment to call his boss and request assistance from other rangers. Though the reception came in and out, Landorf promised to try to find some help.

Naomi had arrived with Charley by the time Kade and Bree got to the door. "Any word?" she asked.

"No." Bree quickly filled her in on what they knew. "Mason suspects they might have been forced to stop in Baraga, so that's where we're headed."

Charley whined, and Naomi calmed him with a hand on his head. "Can't Mason call ahead and ask law enforcement there to check out the motels in the area? Go door-to-door?"

"He already did, but they're all out searching for a bunch of stranded hunters who got caught by the storm. They'll get to it when they can, but it might be tomorrow. And Rob could be gone with Davy by then." Bree's voice trembled.

Kade eyed Naomi. "How many layers?"

"Four counting the heated gear. Donovan insisted." She glanced at her dog. "There's no way to take Charley on the snowmobile, is there?"

Kade shook his head. "Not in these conditions. I wish we could. He might help us."

Mason stepped out of the living room and joined them. He had enough layers to mimic a bear. "Ready?"

Kade nodded. "Yeah, I was about to go get you." He raised his voice. "Lauri, Anu, we're going now."

Both women appeared in the doorway. "I will be praying," Anu said.

"We need it more than anything else." Kade held no optimism for their journey tonight. Too many things were stacked against them. "If you hear anything, call my cell. I've got it on vibrate and it's next to my chest."

They nodded, and he saw the fear in their eyes. "We'll be all right." He hugged his sister, and she burst into tears. He released her and opened the door to the howling wind. They stepped out into blinding conditions. The security light did nothing to illuminate the path, and Kade found the snowmobiles more by instinct than anything.

"It's going to be hard to stay on the road!" Mason shouted above the shriek of the storm.

"I've got GPS on the snowmobiles," Kade yelled back. "They'll help guide us." He mounted his sled and fired up the engine. He could barely hear it above the wind. His gloved hands were clumsy, and he had trouble turning on the GPS unit. The backlit display glowed, then the trails came up. He switched it to show the highways. They'd stay as close to the road as possible in case they found Rob's truck stuck in a drift, though Kade didn't think they'd be that lucky.

Once his sled was ready, he glanced back to make sure the rest were lined up to pull out. Their headlamps were on, but the lights barely penetrated the thickly falling snow. He waved his arm to show he was starting, then guided his machine up the driveway. The drifts were piling up fast.

The wind cut through his ski mask the worst, but when they made the curve onto the main road, the wind was at their backs, and that helped some. He was only able to go fifteen miles per hour. They passed through Rock Harbor. Most businesses had shut down early, and house lights barely penetrated the driving snow.

Kade led them out of the city limits and onto Highway 36 east to Baraga. Without the break from the buildings, the conditions immediately worsened. Their sleds barely crawled up the huge drifts, and the only way he managed to stay halfway on track was by watching the GPS mounted on the front of his machine.

Not another vehicle passed them. Their four sleds moved in a line through a deadly white world.

He no longer felt his face, and he prayed that Bree and Naomi were doing okay. The few times he'd tried to look behind, he saw only their silhouettes. A sheltered area would be a good place to take a break, and he watched for one. There, just past a patch of trees.

He guided his sled into the small area, which had drifts on all sides but one so the wind didn't blow here quite so fiercely. He waited until the others joined him, then left his machine running and dismounted. He leaned into Naomi's ear. "How are you doing?"

"Okay," she yelled. "Frozen, but I'll live."

He walked back to the next bike and found Mason. Wait, there were only three sleds. He tore off his ski mask so he could see better and looked wildly around for his wife. There was no sign of her sled. No lights, no hulking machine in the snow.

He grabbed Mason's arm and pointed. "Where's Bree?"

Mason twisted on his sled. "She was right behind me a few minutes ago!"

"Stay here!"

Kade ran to his sled and mounted, then veered back the way he'd come. He drove a mile but saw no sign of his wife. Just a few feet away and the wind had already covered their tracks.

"Bree!" he screamed into the wind, knowing it was futile. His words were snatched away almost before they left his lips. He needed help.

⌇

Stupid cell phone. Bree's snowmobile had stuttered to a halt, and she tried to call Kade, but she had no bars. She wanted to throw the phone in the nearest snowbank but she didn't dare. By the time she got it going again, darkness surrounded her, and she was alone with the snow swirling in eddies and blinding her to any familiar landscape. She wasn't sure which way they'd gone.

She should stay put. Kade would notice she was missing and come back for her. She huddled in her parka, but her limbs were blocks of ice, even with her heated gear turned up all the way. If she had to, she could pull out her Blizzard Survival Bag and Mylar foil blanket and ride this out, but she was sure her husband would notice her missing very quickly. She prayed they'd find Davy in Baraga. The thought of him out in this storm terrified her.

She dismounted and ran around the sled a few times to warm up. It didn't help much. She flapped her unfeeling hands against her sides. Frostbite maybe. The brutal weather was taking its toll already. They'd seen no vehicles moving on the impassible road, which led her to fear Rob was stranded along with her son.

She decided to mount the biggest snowdrift she could find and try to call Kade. The compass would serve to guide her back. She trudged up a drift and pulled out her phone. One bar. She tried Kade's number but got only silent air. She moved around onto the top of the drift to see if she could get a better signal, but it was useless. Slipping and sliding, she went back to the sled.

The low growl of an engine caught her attention. She stilled and listened. It sounded like a snowmobile. She glanced in all directions. There, coming from the east along one of the snowmobile trails. The sled had nearly reached her before its lights penetrated the wild flurry of snow.

The driver cut the engine when he caught sight of her about five feet off the highway. A dim, bulky figure climbed from the sled and approached her. With every inch of exposed flesh covered, just as hers was, she didn't recognize the person. Bree tore off her hat and ski mask to reveal her identity.

The other person did the same, and she stared into the face of Gary Landorf, Kade's boss. "Gary, I'm so glad to see you," she gasped. "Have you seen Kade and Mason? I got separated from them."

"Yeah, they're back there a ways looking for you." He jerked a gloved hand behind him, then replaced his hat and mask.

The wind drove needles of snow into her flesh, so Bree quickly did the same. She shuddered with cold. Or maybe it was reaction to being separated from the others. "Could you take me to them?" she asked, raising her voice above the wind.

He nodded, then walked back to his sled and mounted. Machine and rider moved ahead of her and paused until she got back on her seat and followed. He veered to the snowmobile trail. To her surprise, she found the trail a little easier than the road. It was better protected by shrubs and trees and fewer huge drifts. They were able to pick up their speed a bit.

She rode through the narrow trail with snow-covered pines on either side. Surely they'd find Kade and the others soon. They seemed to have gone a long way before realizing she was missing. But the visibility was low, she reminded herself. They'd been focused on finding Davy.

The sled ahead of her veered, and she followed. When the other snowmobile braked, she did too. What was that outline? She peered through the snow. Was it a cabin? Dim light pierced the falling snow, and the flicker meant a fire inside. Had Kade found her boy? She dismounted and slogged through the thigh-high snow toward the front door.

The door wasn't locked, and she burst into the warm cabin with an eager smile. And came face-to-face with Victor.

Her elation seeped away. "Victor? How'd you get here?" He stared from her back to the open door as Landorf's bulk filled it.

The park ranger supervisor entered and shut the door behind him, then locked it. He removed his hat and ski mask. Victor shrank away when the ranger's face popped into view. He sat on a small wooden chair and began to rock back and forth. He wore his coat and insulated pants.

Landorf still hadn't spoken. He began to peel the layers of clothing away until he got down to his park service uniform.

"Where're Kade and the others?" Bree demanded. Victor began to thrash his arms around. She touched him to try to calm him. "It's okay, Vic," she said.

"Probably looking for you." Landorf went to the coffeepot and poured himself a cup. "Coffee?" he asked.

She badly wanted something hot, but not while her husband and two others were out battling this storm. "You said you were taking me to them."

"I thought I'd let you warm up first."

"They'll be worried." She pulled out her cell phone and checked it. Still no bars.

He held out a cup of coffee, and she stripped off her gloves, then took it. Being cold herself wasn't going to help Kade, Naomi, or Mason. "You have a thermos? We could take them some hot coffee."

"Sure. We'll go out in just a minute. They're not far."

She glanced around. "Where is this place?"

He took a sip of his coffee. "Just off the reservation, not far from Baraga. I've owned it a few years. I come here to get away from the stress of the job." He gestured to her coat. "You might as well get out of that until we're ready to go out again."

There was something about his manner or his smile that raised the skin on her spine. "I'm ready now. I need to let them know I'm okay."

Victor began flapping his arms again. He stood and went to the door, where he tugged at the handle. Bree put down her coffee and went to slip her arm around him. "Come sit down, Victor."

He glanced up and met her eyes, then glanced away, but not before she saw the anguish in them. She glanced at Landorf and realized he wore an eagle bird band as a ring on his index finger. Her gaze fell on the number. The number she'd seen over and over again on Victor's sudokus.

25

THE REST OF THE TEAM JOINED KADE IN TURNING AROUND to search for Bree. Kade wished desperately for Samson or Charley. Either dog could have found her trail because snow or rain intensified the scent. She couldn't be far, but she knew better than to veer off the road.

Unless she'd seen Davy?

Nothing would have stopped her if she'd caught sight of her son. Checking his cell phone, he found no messages. And no signal. He stopped his sled, dismounted, and went back to talk to Naomi and Mason.

Naomi's teeth chattered audibly. She reached into her pack and got out gel-filled hand warmers. "No sign?" she asked.

"Nothing. She knows better than to leave the path where we'd look for her," Mason put in, dismounting and grabbing a warmer for himself.

Mason's words ramped up Kade's fear. Could she have had an accident? What if they'd missed her and her sled was covered with snow in a ditch? "When did you see her last?"

Mason consulted his watch and his GPS. "We'd just passed the road to Seven Mile Lookout. I glanced back and saw her still on my tail."

"Two miles from where we turned around to look for her."

The realization that she had to be within these two miles encouraged him. "You and Naomi take the south side of the road. I'll take the north. Comb every inch of the ditches. She can't have just vanished."

"I'll comb it on foot," Mason said.

Mason and Naomi rode off on their sleds, back the way they'd come. Their lights disappeared in the dark and blinding snow. Kade walked along the ditch on his side of the road about twenty feet before driving his sled a bit farther. He was on his third pass that way when he saw a drift that looked like sleds might have passed over it before being covered with more snow.

Not certain it was anything, he checked the GPS. A snowmobile trail did cross the ditch here. He followed his GPS to the trail and found the wind not so biting. He saw sled tracks not yet covered by snow. Pausing his sled, he checked his cell phone. Still no bars. He'd have to go back for Naomi and Mason. Chafing at the delay, he got his machine turned around and moved along the road until he saw the lights of the other searchers.

Mason and Naomi were both on foot now. Their shadows wavered in the glow of headlamps. They walked back to Kade's sled.

"I found tracks along a snowmobile trail!" He told them where they were.

"Why would she leave the road?" Mason asked.

"It looks like there might have been more than one sled. Maybe she found them. Come on!" He turned his machine and headed back the way he'd come.

The onslaught of snow began to taper just a bit. He could make out the trees lining the highway, see the road signs. He guided the sled slowly on the trail, watching the marks left by whomever went before. *Please, God, let this be Bree.*

Was this punishment for how close he'd come to lying on that grant application? No, he didn't believe that. God promised a way out of temptation, and he'd given Kade the strength to say no. Even now, he knew God was in control of this situation.

The sled tracks veered from the trail at a break in the trees. They angled across an open field. He could barely make out the glow of light from a tiny cabin. His first instinct was to accelerate his engine and head for the cabin, then reason kicked in. If Bree had followed Rob, it was possible the noise of his engine would endanger her.

He turned off the snowmobile and dismounted as the others came up behind him. Motioning for them to do the same, he waited until they joined him under the branches of a large oak tree.

"Let's go in on foot," Kade said. "See if she's in that cabin. Maybe Rob and Davy are there too." Some sixth sense warned of a problem.

The three of them trudged through the snow. The white stuff muffled their steps, and the wind also helped to whirl away any sound they made. He crept to the window and peered in to see his wife sitting beside Victor.

Their hands were tied. Bree still had her snowmobile suit on, but her hat was off, as was her ski mask. She was straining at her bonds, twisting and pulling at her wrists. Victor sat still.

Kade saw Mason unzip his snowmobile suit and reach inside to pull out his gun. Before the sheriff's hand cleared the fabric of his layers, a hard, sharp object prodded Kade's back. He froze, recognizing the poke of a rifle. From the corner of his eye, he saw a figure in a ski mask move closer.

The man plucked the revolver from Mason's hand. He gestured with the gun toward the door. Mason, Naomi, and Kade shuffled to the cabin entrance and went inside. The warmth rushed to greet them, but Kade still felt the cold edge of fear when he saw his wife's panicked eyes.

He stepped quickly to her and put his hand on her shoulder. "You okay, babe?"

She nodded, but her lips trembled. "I figured it out," she whispered. "All of it."

"Shut up," the man said.

Kade knew that voice. His head came up, and he stared at the figure reaching up to remove his hat and ski mask. Landorf?

Bree nearly moaned when her husband shuffled inside with Mason and Naomi. She'd hoped they wouldn't get caught in this trap.

"Surprised?" Landorf smiled at Kade and tossed his gloves and hat on the table. "Have a seat. All of you." He grabbed the coil of yellow nylon rope on the table. The gun stayed in his hand. "Take off your coats."

Naomi removed her hat and ski mask, then tugged her snowmobile suit off. She pulled a chair up beside Bree. The women exchanged fearful glances. Mason and Kade locked gazes. Neither man had a choice with the gun bearing down on them. They took off their outerwear, then pulled wooden chairs out from the table.

Kade sat on the edge of his chair. His smile to Bree was encouraging, but she couldn't take heart from it. Landorf held all the cards right now.

Landorf tied him up. When Mason and Naomi were bound as well, he stepped back with a smirk. "Confused, aren't you?"

"I'm not," Bree said. "Not once I saw the band."

Landorf frowned. "What band?"

Her gaze went to the bird band on his finger. "That one. The number is the same as on Victor's sudokus. He's been trying to warn us."

"Smart lady. At least at figuring out the number."

Bree pulled at her bonds. "You *used* Victor."

Landorf stared at the band, and his fingers traced the engraving. "Florence used Victor to help her with the babies occasionally. He enjoyed being useful, and he loved the babies."

"Di-did you kill Florence?" Bree had to know the truth.

"Quinn did, and he's going to pay for it." Landorf's face darkened. "I was going to marry her. He's planning to double-cross me. He didn't spare Florence when she got cold feet, but he had no call to change the plans. He's going to be eliminated, but that's not your concern right now."

Bree stared at the cruel face of the man. "How do you know Rob took Davy?"

"I told him," Kade whispered. "When I called for some of the rangers to help search."

"My son knows nothing," Bree said, her voice careful. Her bonds had loosened a bit. Maybe she'd get free yet. But what could she do against Landorf's gun? If only she had Samson.

He shrugged. "Even if it's true, it's irrelevant now."

Her loops loosened again. "You arranged for Olivia to be kidnapped to force her father into pulling the mining project out of here."

His gun came higher. "I always knew you were smart, Bree." Landorf waved his hand. "My former partner and I have our fingers in much bigger pies. The casinos, politics. My job is the perfect cover for all that."

"But the mine would have brought too much attention to the area," Mason put in.

Landorf's attention swung to the sheriff. "I feared I might lose my job myself. I couldn't let that happen."

A frenzied barking came at the door. Samson! The dog's barking turned to snarling, and Bree could hear him pawing at the door. Moments later his head was at the window, but he couldn't break the glass. His barking distracted Landorf for a moment. She tugged at the ropes again and they slid free, allowing her to twist them off.

She sprang to her feet but found Landorf's gun trained on her. Her dog was going crazy outside the cabin. Bree itched to let him in, but she didn't dare move.

"Perfect," Landorf said. "Wherever the dog is, the boy can't be far behind, can he? And where the boy is, the father who took him will be found. Let's go, shall we?" He gestured to her hat and ski mask. "You might want them. I'm not sure how far we'll have to travel."

He walked to the stove and scattered the remaining logs, then opened the flue. "Happy freezing, friends. When you're dead, I'll stop back and remove the ropes. Everyone will think you froze with no wood." He grabbed Bree's arm and dragged her to the door. "Control the dog or I'll have to shoot him. Understand?"

She nodded. Her gaze went back to her husband. In this wind, the cabin would cool quickly. He strained at his bonds, but Landorf had tied him with four or five loops, and his hands were nearly purple from the tight bonds. He'd never get free. Victor wasn't even trying. Mason was bound just as securely. Only Naomi seemed to have a chance.

Landorf opened the door, and eighty pounds of furious dog came leaping into the cabin.

"Samson, heel!" Bree said. She snagged him by the collar as he was about to leap at Landorf's gun. She could nearly smell the cordite and powder from the barrel when his finger twitched.

The dog settled, though he still bared his teeth at Landorf. "You'd like to eat me, wouldn't you, dog?" Landorf chuckled "Tell him to take us to Davy."

Bree took her dog's muzzle in her palms and stared into his eyes. "Find Davy, boy. Take me to Davy. Samson whined, and his tail came up. "Search, Samson. Find Davy."

Samson dashed into the snow and she followed, conscious of

ndorf's gun still trained on her back. Landorf left the cabin door
open, and the last sight she had of her husband and the others she
loved was them sitting at the table with the wind blowing snow in
swirls toward them. They'd freeze with no covering and no heat.
Very quickly.

"Let's take the sleds!" Landorf yelled above the wind. He shoved
her toward her snowmobile, then hopped on his.

She prayed as she drove behind the dog into the howling storm.
The tears nearly froze in her eyes, and she tried to cling to a small
seed of hope, though it was impossible to see how they were going
to live through this night.

26

QUINN HAD NEVER BEEN SO COLD. WITHOUT THE FIRE going, the cave grew frigid even out of the wind, and black as the deepest sea at night. Davy's warm body curled on one side of Jenna, and Quinn lay on Davy's other side so the boy was cocooned by their bodies. At least he was probably comfortable.

The boy slept, his breathing calm and even. Quinn tried to see through the gloom but nothing penetrated their hidey hole. Not a sliver of light glimmered anywhere. He sat up, then wished he hadn't when a blast of cold air hit his face.

"What's wrong?" Jenna murmured in the darkness.

"I'm cold." He lay back down. "It will be morning soon and we can try to get out of here." He pulled the sleeping bag back around him.

"What are we going to do, Quinn? Who are you really? How did we get to this place?"

"One step at a time, Jenna. Just like everyone does." He reined in his impatience with her. "I got into a spot of financial difficulty. I was the controller here in Rock Harbor and thought I'd just borrow five hundred dollars from the city. I could pay it back the very next month, I was sure. The next month came and I was a little shorter. Just a little more, I thought. Before I knew it, I'd embezzled fifty thousand dollars."

"What about the plane crash?" she asked.

He didn't like to think of that time. "I was about to be arrested for embezzlement. The cop was a friend, someone I'd played cards with, gone fishing with. He showed up at the camp just before we flew home. He wanted to warn me what was coming down, that he'd be showing up with a warrant when he got back."

"It's his body they buried?" she asked.

"It has to be, though I don't remember much beyond coming to and wandering until I found a road. Someone picked me up and took me to the hospital. When I realized who I was and what had happened, I thought Davy was dead. What good would it have done to go back home? Bree and my family would have been disgraced when I was arrested. It was better to just fade away, to take on a new identity."

His excuses sounded lame to his ears, but he'd made his choice. "Once you start down a road like that, it's pretty hard to go back. Smuggling was good money, then I met Landorf and we expanded our operation. Casinos, providing babies for adoption, drug running." He laughed. "A lot more exciting than this backwater."

Her fingers trailed down his arm. "Power makes a man sexy."

He pressed his lips to her temple, relishing her warmth. "I can't wait to get a decent hotel with a pillow-top bed."

"And a Jacuzzi."

"And room service." The sooner he shook the snow of this place off his boots, the better.

"Did you really bury that baby in the snow?"

"She died of tetanus. I hated it, but it was the practical thing to do."

She shivered. "It's so cold. How are we going to get out of this?"

His plan seemed juvenile in the cold. "I don't know," he said finally. "Landorf wants Davy eliminated. I can't do that."

The wind drove needles of snow into her eyes. Bree lost track of time, of distance. She couldn't feel her face, hands, or feet. All she could do was numbly guide the snowmobile up and down the drifts of snow in the black night that was as cold as death. The glow from the GPS on her bike caught her attention. They were over blue—water. She was too cold and disoriented to figure out which lake, but it didn't matter. Whatever it was, it had frozen over long ago.

Her gaze went back to her dog. He was tiring as he led them on through the drifts. She prayed for Samson, prayed that her husband would find the strength to free himself and the others, prayed that her son would be alive when she found him.

At a mammoth hill, Samson stopped. He began to bark and paw at the hillside. Bree blinked nearly frozen eyes, then dismounted. A hint of pink showed in the east, and she prayed the sun would bring an end to this bitter storm. She dismounted and approached Samson.

So did Landorf. "What's he doing?"

"He acts like Davy is here." She trained her flashlight on the monolith looming in front of her. Something seemed "off" with the landscape. She swept the beam around the immediate area.

And out to where open water rolled a mere fifty feet away.

"We're on Superior," she gulped. "The storm surge is starting to break up the ice. The waves are tearing apart the ice volcanoes too."

Landorf turned with a jerk and his gaze followed the light. He turned back to the structure in front of them. "Why would they be in there?" he asked.

"I think it's an ice cave," she said. She joined her dog in digging at the outcropping of ice.

The lake was unpredictable. Solid ice could break apart with no warning when an under-ice wave knocked it apart.

She pounded at the icy wall she believed separated her from her son. "Davy!" The cry burst from her heart.

Landorf shoved her and she fell. "Shut up!"

From her back on the ice, she stared up at him. She heard a sound and craned her neck to see the ice breaking up where the surf stuck it. The water was five feet closer than it had been.

"We've got to get them out!" She crawled to the snow and ice and began clawing at the ice again. Samson had never stopped.

"Sam! Mom!"

The distant cry came from inside and was quickly hushed. He *was* in there! With renewed determination, she dug at the cold stuff barring her from her boy. Sitting on her backside, she kicked at the snow and ice. Again and again. Pain flared in her thighs and shins, in her arches, but she kept striking at where Samson indicated the opening should be.

Just when she was beginning to think it was futile, her right foot went all the way through and up to her knee. She kicked again, and the whole face began to crumble away until the hole was big enough for someone to crawl through.

She scrambled for her flashlight and shined it into the opening. "Davy!" she called.

"Mom, is that you?" His cry rose to a frantic wail. "Let go of me. I want my mommy!"

At the sound of Davy's voice, Samson dove into the hole. Bree was right behind him. The darkness inside was broken by a flashlight that radiated dim light. The ice cave rose twenty feet in the air. Icicles hung from the ceiling.

Rob held on to her boy, who kicked and screamed to be allowed to come to his mother. Samson began to bark and lunge at Rob's arm. It was clear the dog didn't want to bite him, but Samson wanted him to release Davy.

"Attack, Samson!" Bree said, pointing at Rob.

It was all the direction the dog needed. He launched at Rob's chest, driving his arm away from the boy. Davy was sobbing as he stumbled into his mother's arms. Bree engulfed him in a hug and held him to her chest. His cheeks were cold, but he was okay.

Samson's front paws pinned Rob to the ground. Rob thrashed around, trying to get up, but the dog held him in place. She backed away toward the opening. And ran into a hard chest. Landorf.

"What a cozy reunion," he said, his voice expressionless. "Call off the dog or I'll shoot him."

"Samson, release," she said. "Come here, boy." She patted her thigh. The dog stepped off Rob and ran to her side. She edged to the sea cave wall to allow Landorf to step closer to Rob. If he moved away from the door, maybe she and Davy could escape.

Her mouth went dry just thinking about the icy water about to engulf them. Very little time remained.

Rob struggled into a seated position, then stood to face the man with the gun. From somewhere, he'd drawn a pistol as well. "Stalemate," he said. "You've double-crossed me for the last time, Landorf."

The ice beneath their feet shuddered, and Davy looked up at Bree with wide eyes. "We've got to out of here," she said to him. "We're on Superior and the ice is breaking apart with the storm surge."

─────

The wind howled through the open door and up the chimney, creating a wind tunnel that quickly cooled the cabin. Kade shuddered with cold, and he knew the others were nearly goners too. Naomi was only half-conscious, and Mason's color had seeped away. No one knew where they were.

They would die if he didn't get free. He glanced at Victor, the only one of them who still wore a warm coat. The autistic man seemed to be faring a little better, but he hadn't even tried to free himself.

"Victor, can you hear me? You've got to get yourself free." Kade's voice was hoarse from his past efforts to persuade Victor to help them. "Do you want Jenna to die? She's out there in the storm. We've got to go find her."

He'd tried to tell Victor that Jenna was in trouble and the bad man would shoot her. Maybe the storm would be something Victor could relate to better. "The snow is deep. It's cold and she needs a coat," he said. "I think you can get your hands loose if you'll just try. Then we can find Jenna and help her."

Victor still didn't look at Kade, but he began to twist his wrists ever so slightly. He grimaced as though it hurt, and Kade knew the long hours of being tied up had caused the blood to pool in his hands.

"It's okay, keep trying," he coaxed. "For Jenna. And Davy. They're both cold. We have to help them."

Naomi lifted her head. She licked her lips. "Victor," she said. "Please help us. We'll all die if you don't."

Victor worried his bonds harder. Then they dropped off his wrists. "You did it, Vic!" Kade said. "Now untie one of us. Naomi first. She's right beside you, and she wants to go help Davy and Jenna."

Keeping his head down, Victor flexed his fingers, then slowly stood. Stamping his feet in place, he made no move in Naomi's direction.

"Help me, Victor," Naomi whimpered. "I'm so cold. And I have to go to the bathroom."

Victor's head came up. "Bathroom," he repeated.

"You have to go too? Untie me and I'll take you," Naomi said.

Victor stooped over her and began to work the ropes on her hands. Kade glanced around. A knife would be faster, but he saw nothing that would cut their bonds. He had a knife in his pocket, though he doubted Victor could be talked into getting it out.

The autistic man grunted and labored over the rope, but it was several minutes before he had Naomi free. She quickly untied her feet, then ran to the door and slammed it. The cold wind stopped its rampage through the cabin.

"Bathroom," Victor said, grabbing at her hand.

She glanced around. "There," she said, pointing to a closed door.

"I've got a knife in my pocket," Kade said. "The right one." She knelt by his side and fished it out, then opened it. She sawed at his bonds as Victor shuffled to the door.

He returned nearly immediately. He had a tape recorder in his hand. "Bathroom," he said again, putting the recorder on the table.

"Must have been the bedroom," she said, still working the knife over the rope. It popped loose and she handed the knife to Kade. "Free Mason while I find the bathroom." She grabbed Victor's hand and led him to the other door. "Bingo," she said. She pushed Victor inside and shut the door.

Hugging herself, she stomped her feet. "I'm so cold."

Kade had Mason's hands free in seconds, then knelt to cut the bonds on his ankles. Kade's teeth were chattering and so were Mason's. Kade glanced at his watch. "They've been gone over half an hour," he said. "We're lucky we're not icicles by now."

Victor came from the bathroom and Naomi ran in. Kade began to pull on his layers of clothing. "Let's get out of here and go find my wife," he said. "Naomi, you get the fire going. I'm going to find Bree and bring her back here. She'll need a place that's warm."

Naomi opened the door and stepped back out. "I want to go with you."

"No, I need you here with Victor. Keep the fire going. Mason and I will find them."

"Find them," Victor echoed. He toyed with the recorder then clicked it on. An eerie scream filled the room.

Kade and Naomi exchanged a long glance. "The windigo," Kade said. "He played it to scare the Natives."

"Sick," she said.

"You stay with Naomi," Kade said, yanking his ski mask over his head. "We'll be back soon."

Mason had his layers on as well, and both men rushed for the door as Naomi began to work with the fire. Kade mounted his sled, then turned on his GPS unit. How would they find her? The sun was beginning to come up, so at least they had a little light. Maybe the wind had spared enough of the trail to follow.

"There!" Mason yelled, pointing to the ground.

Kade saw the faint impressions of sled tracks. "Go slow," he said. "Make sure we don't miss any turns."

Mason nodded and led the way. The tracks turned toward the big lake, and the men followed on their machines. At the edge of the water, Mason stopped his sled. "The ice doesn't look safe," he said. "It's breaking up out there. I can hear it."

Kade heard it too, the groaning and crackling of Gitche Gumee claiming her own. "The tracks clearly go out there," he said, pointing. "I don't see Bree anywhere though."

Mason stared hard. "Maybe they circled back toward the shore. There's a trail along the lake. Let's take that. Maybe we'll run into them."

"I'm afraid to leave the trail. We might never find it again," Kade said. "You go that way and I'll follow this. When you find service, call for help."

Mason nodded. "You have any bars?"

Kade checked. "Nope, not yet."

"Should be something around the bend," Mason said. "Call me when you have a signal. Let me know you're okay."

Kade nodded, then revved his engine and rode out onto the lake. The ice shuddered under him, and he wasn't sure he'd see the other side.

The ice bucked again. Black water yawned at the back of the cave. A wave swept over the top of the ice and nearly touched Bree's boots. She gripped Davy's hand. They had to escape.

Her gaze on the hole, Jenna sprang to her feet. "Let me out!" she wailed.

Landorf swerved his gun toward her. "The water might kill you, but I sure will if you move again. Step over by your boyfriend. Drop your gun, Quinn."

Quinn had the gun aimed at Landorf's head. "No, you drop yours."

"I'll shoot her."

Quinn shrugged. "Go ahead. You'll save me money."

Jenna's mouth gaped. "You swine!"

His gaze flickered to the mouth of the cave, and Bree nodded. Tightening her grip on Davy's hand, she inched toward the opening. The ice crackled and moaned. Was it her imagination or did it rise under her feet? Davy's eyes widened and he stared up at her. She put her finger to her lips and gave him a reassuring smile.

One more foot and they'd be able to dive for safety.

Landorf's gun came her way. "I know you don't want the boy to die. Drop the gun or he's dead, Quinn. I can shoot him before you drop me. You willing to take the chance?"

Bree held her breath. She saw murder in Landorf's eyes.

Rob lowered the gun.

"Drop it," Landorf said. The gun slipped from Rob's fingers, and Landorf smiled. "Get over by your husband," he said.

"He's not my husband," she said. "I'm married to Kade." And she knew she belonged to him. Not to this stranger with the cynical eyes, the one who'd broken her heart and walked away. She could only pray the man she loved still lived. Rob had good in him. She'd seen it. But he'd chosen a crooked path, and she wasn't going to follow it.

She heard a sound and turned to see Kade's head poking into the cave. Her involuntary movement attracted Landorf's attention.

Landorf's eyes widened, but as he brought the gun around toward Kade with clear intent, Rob shoved Jenna toward the opening, then launched himself at Landorf. The two men fell to the ice and rolled over and over, first one, then the other on top.

Rob managed to wrench the gun from Landorf. "Get my son out of here!" he yelled.

His words broke the spell over Bree. She felt the ice lurch again, then it began to break apart under her feet. She thrust Davy into Kade's arms, and her husband pulled the boy to safety. Jenna went next, then Bree ordered Samson to follow.

"Bree!" Kade called, his voice frantic.

She turned for one last look at the men locked in grim battle on the only sliver of ice left. Landorf lurched away from Rob and grabbed the gun. Rob fought for possession of it and someone pulled the trigger. The bullet struck by Rob's feet and spit ice into the air. As Bree dove for the opening, the ice began to break apart. The men fell into the icy water together.

Tears clogged her throat, but there was no time for mourning. All around them, the ice shattered. The cracks and moans announced doomsday. A huge fissure separated the ice they stood on from the shoreline.

"We're going to have to jump!" Kade said. He swept up Davy in his arms. "Jump, Samson!"

The dog leaped two feet over open water for the only solid ice.

Jenna wasted no time in following suit. Bree didn't think she had th strength to make it. Kade jumped across with Davy in his arms.

He set the boy down. "Jump, Bree, I'll catch you."

She slumped to her knees as the gap widened to three feet. "I don't think I can make it," she sobbed. The crackling ice disoriented her.

"I'll come get you." Kade coiled his knees and prepared to jump back across.

"No, stay there! I'm coming." She had to try or he'd fall and she'd never be able to pull him to safety. She looked at the dark waves. Another second and it would be much too far for her to reach.

Whispering a prayer, she leaped, then she was sailing, sailing through the air with her gaze locked with Kade's blue eyes. She thought she was actually going to make it, then her feet touched nothing but water and the shock of cold stole her breath. Icy waves closed over her head, and she saw nothing but blackness.

Her clothing was soaked in an instant and the heavy drag pulled her down, down. Superior held her close in its unshakable embrace. Until a hard hand yanked on her collar. She sailed up toward the gray sky. Her head broke the surface, and she drew in the sweetest breath of her life.

Kade's harsh breath rasped in her ear as he struggled to pull her to safety. He lay on his stomach on the ice and dragged her toward him. "Hang on, Green Eyes. Don't let go. Don't you leave me." His gaze bored into hers, and she drew strength from that lifeline.

Then she lay gasping like a dying fish on the ice while a wave crashed over them all and threatened to sweep her away.

"We've got to get to shore," Kade panted. He crabbed backward, dragging her farther from the black water that hadn't given up on her yet.

Bree struggled weakly to help him, then darkness claimed her.

27

BIRDSONG FILTERED THROUGH BREE'S CONSCIOUSNESS.
She blinked and opened her eyes. Warmth flooded her muscles,
and she stretched drowsily.

Davy!

She bolted upright and realized she was home, in her own bed.
Her gaze took in her husband on top of the covers, still in his
clothes. Davy lay between them, snuggled down in the covers with
his face turned toward her.

They were all still alive.

Tears sprang to her eyes. Thank God, thank God.

She must have made an involuntary sound, because Kade's
eyes flew open. He sat up. "Bree? You okay?" He bolted from the
bed and rounded it to sit on the edge of the mattress by her.

She clutched his hands. "Fine, I'm fine," she said, sobbing the
words. "Just so thankful to see you and Davy are safe. What happened?" She dimly remembered him hauling her from a certain
cold and watery grave.

"You passed out. I carried you to shore. Mason called in a chopper and got us all back to town. Doc stopped by to check on you
and said you're suffering from exposure and fatigue and to let you
sleep. I'm supposed to call him."

Her throat thickened. "Rob?"

Kade's tender smile slipped away. He shook his head. "I'm

sorry, Bree. He and Landorf didn't make it. Mason said we may never find their bodies. Superior keeps its own."

She knew that well. It had tried to keep her too. Her gaze touched her sleeping son. "It's going to be hard on him."

Kade nodded. "He knows about his dad. He cried some and clung to me for a while, but he's going to be okay. He's thought of Rob as dead for so long."

Thank God for Kade. Her husband was one in a million. She struggled to make sense of what she knew—and didn't know.

"Where's Jenna?"

"Telling Mason everything she knows."

There was a note in his voice that made her look up. "Is she in trouble?"

"Probably. She did help him take Davy."

Bree was suddenly aware there was no crying baby. Her lungs squeezed. "Where's Olivia?"

"Sleeping." He glanced at his watch. "But her parents will be here in a few minutes, I think."

Bree threw off the covers and got up. Her throat tightened, and she blinked at the moisture in her eyes. "So soon?"

"They've been looking for days," Kade reminded her.

"Is the adoption even legal?" Bree asked, hope stirring.

"Mason says all the documents are in order. Any illegalities were well-covered. Ellie's mother could question the adoption, but she isn't interested." He tipped his head to one side. "I think I hear a car."

She heard it then. Samson stretched and padded to the door, then looked back at her. Pulling on a robe, she went to the bassinet and lifted Olivia in her arms. She kissed the baby's soft head one last time. Her throat thickened with the memory of the baby's first smile. She prayed Olivia would have a happy life.

The doorbell rang. Her gaze met Kade's, and she forced down

the lump in her throat. He picked up Olivia's diaper bag and followed her down the stairs.

"Go to the living room and I'll get the door," he said.

Holding Olivia close, Bree went to the chair by the fireplace and sat. Her gaze went to a picture of her son. God had allowed them to come through last night, but she'd so hoped he would answer her heart's cry for this child. Giving up Olivia would tear out her heart. Her vision blurred and she pressed her lips to the infant's sweet-smelling skin.

She heard a woman's voice, full of stress, then footsteps as Kade led the couple to the living room. Bree's arms tightened around Olivia. If only she had the right to refuse to turn over the baby, but she had no authority.

A woman stepped into the room. Blonde, professional. Except for the tears raining down her cheeks. A distinguished man followed. She took a timid step forward. "I'm Karen Saunders. I think you found our daughter. Can I see her?"

Bree pulled the blanket back from the baby's face. Karen's tears dried, and a smile lifted her lips. "Alexa," she breathed.

"Her name is Alexa?"

Karen nodded. "Alexa Grace." She went to her knees in front of Bree and held out her arms. Bree had no choice but to slip the baby girl into them, even though she wanted to hang on tight. Mike Saunders looked on with a watery smile.

Karen nuzzled the baby and hugged her to her chest. "Oh, Allie," she said, her voice choked. "I've missed you so much." She pulled back and stared into the baby's face. "I prayed and cried every night for her safe return. I thought maybe God wasn't listening."

"God always hears the cries of his children," Bree whispered, echoing what Anu had told her. Though her own heart was about to explode with grief, she knew this was right. Olivia belonged with this woman who had mourned and prayed for her through the long nights. The woman who had finally stood up to evil and told the truth.

Mr. Saunders put his hands in his pockets. "Thank you for caring for her, for loving her. The sheriff told us you loved her very much."

"I do," Bree managed to choke out. "I'll miss her so much."

"Come see us sometime," Karen said, rising from her knees. She dug a card from her purse and handed it to Bree. "Here's my contact information. You can call and check on her any time."

"I will. Thank you."

The two women, united in their love for the baby, stood with gazes locked for a long moment. Bree's heart was filled to overflowing. "Take good care of her," she whispered.

"You know I will." Karen carried the baby to the door. Her husband picked up the diaper bag and followed.

Bree heard the door open and close, and she let the tears she'd been holding back fall. Her arms were empty. No, not empty. She had Kade and Davy. Those blessings could so easily have been taken from her.

Kade stood in the doorway. "You okay, babe?"

"I will be," she said, crossing the few steps that separated them.

He put his arm around her and they walked upstairs to the bedroom. Davy still slept.

Bree took off her robe, suddenly exhausted. She climbed into the bed. "What about Pia?" she asked, remembering the other death.

"They picked up Rosen for kidnapping the baby. He agreed to turn state's evidence against Landorf's operations in return for a lighter sentence. He told Mason he shoved Pia, trying to make her tell where the baby was, and she fell on that pointed branch."

Pain engulfed her. She knew the pain of losing a child, had experienced that long dark year when she thought Davy was dead. At least Olivia's mother loved her.

She stared into Kade's eyes. "Rob killed people, Kade. I can't wrap my mind around it. How could I have been so deceived?"

Kade's held her gaze, and the compassion anchored her. "He had good in him, Bree," he said. "He saved us all. But the downward road is a slippery one. You take one small step and slide down a yard. The conscience gets hardened, little by little." His grip on her hands tightened. "I can see how it happened. It almost happened to me. Landorf wanted me to skew some figures and some data on the grant application. I went along with it until I asked God for strength to fight it."

"Rob was always self-sufficient," she said. "He never liked to admit a weakness." *Rob*, her Rob, had done so much evil. Swindled people. Sold babies. Smuggled. And embezzled money. "Does Anu know all he did?"

Kade nodded. "She's a strong lady, but it knocked the props out from under her. She didn't go into the shop today. She's coming over to check on you later this morning."

Closing her eyes, she let the tears slip out. Tears for who Rob might have been, for Anu's pain, for Hilary's. And for her own. She'd loved him once. Maybe a tiny part of her still did.

She opened her eyes and stared into her husband's face. The love she'd had for Rob was an immature love of a young girl. This man was her soul mate. The other part of her heart.

"I love you," she whispered.

His blue eyes crinkled with his smile. "I love you too, Green Eyes. We have a lot to get through, but we'll make it as long as we're together."

Paulie sang outside her window, a pure tune full of hope and joy. Kade was his own self through and through. There was no pretense with him, no mask. Just like Paulie had raised a cowbird deposited in the nest last spring, Kade raised a chick that wasn't his own.

She pulled him down, and his lips covered hers. "Why don't you move Davy to his bed?" she whispered. She loved his smile, the warmth of his eyes, his integrity.

"Don't go away," he said. "I'll be right back."

"I'll be here," she said. "Forever."

Acknowledgments

Dear Reader,

I wish Rock Harbor were a real place! But to me it is, and it was so fun to go back in this novel to the glorious Upper Peninsula of God's Country—Michigan, where the natives show you their hands and point out where they're from on "the mitten." *Cry in the Night* was a true labor of love for my readers who have asked for more in the Rock Harbor series.

My unending love and gratitude goes out to my Thomas Nelson family: publisher Allen Arnold, who asked me to write another Rock Harbor book for you; senior acquisitions editor Ami McConnell, my friend and cheerleader, who has amazing insight into story; editor extraordinaire Natalie Hanemann, who puts up with my numerous requests for help with a smile and a hug; marketing manager Jennifer Deshler, who brings both friendship and fabulous marketing ideas to the table; publicist Katie Schroder, who helps me plan the right strategies and is always willing to listen to my harebrained ideas; fabulous cover guru Mark Ross (you SO rock!), who works hard to create the perfect cover—and does it; fellow Hoosier Lisa Young, who lends a shoulder to cry on when needed; editor Amanda Bostic, who is still my friend even though she doesn't work on my books anymore; Becky Monds and Jocelyn Bailey, who contribute with more help than I even know. I love you all more than I can say.

My agent, Karen Solem, is my biggest cheerleader, and that includes kicking an idea to the curb when necessary. I wouldn't be anywhere without her. Thanks, Karen, you're the best!

Erin Healy is the best freelance editor in the business—bar none. I was so afraid of losing her when I found out she was writing her own stories, but she's hanging in there with me. Check out the book she's written with Ted Dekker called *Kiss*. Thanks, Erin! I couldn't do it without you.

Writing can be a lonely business, but God has blessed me with great writing friends and critique partners. Kristin Billerbeck, Diann Hunt, and Denise Hunter make up the Girls Write Out squad (www.GirlsWriteOut.blogspot.com). I couldn't make it through a day without my peeps! And another one of those is Robin Miller, president of ACFW (www.acfw.com), who spots inconsistencies in a suspense plot with an eagle eye. Thanks to all of you for the work you do on my behalf, and for your friendship.

Thanks to my husband, Dave, who carts me around from city to city, washes towels, and chases down dinner without complaint. Thanks, honey! I couldn't do anything without you. My kids— Dave, Kara, (and now Donna) Coble—and my new grandsons, James and Jorden Packer, love and support me in every way possible. Love you guys! Donna and Dave are bringing a new baby girl into the family, and she will have arrived by the time you read this. I've been waiting for Alexa Grace for a long time!

Most importantly, I give my thanks to God, who has opened such amazing doors for me and makes the journey a golden one.

I love to hear from readers! Drop me an e-mail at colleen@ colleencoble.com and check out my Web site at www.colleen-coble.com. There's a forum to chat about books, and I try to stop in, since books are my favorite things in the world. Thank you all for giving up your most precious commodity—*time*—to spend it with me and my stories.

Reading Group Guide

1. Pia found herself deep into something she regretted. How does someone slide in a wrong direction?

2. Kade was asked to lie on a grant application. Saying no to a boss's order can be hard. Have you ever been faced with a similar situation? What did you do?

3. Was Kade right to withhold his worries from Bree? Why or why not?

4. Jenna and Quinn both liked things and didn't care what they had to do to get what they wanted. How do you think people become that self-centered?

5. Lauri's weakness through the series has been that she doesn't have good sense about men. Have you ever known someone like that? What do you think drives them to choose the wrong kind of man?

6. Mrs. Bristol didn't have any interest in helping her daughter raise a grandchild. Was this an attitude you could identify with or not?

7. Scents can be one of the most powerful ways to recall a person or memory. What scent has the ability to take you to another time and place?

8. Have you ever wondered if God hears your prayers? What helps you remember that he does?

9. A few weeks after my beloved grandmother died, I saw a woman in a drugstore who looked so much like her it was scary. I stared and stared, but I knew it couldn't be her. What would it take to convince you that someone you were sure was dead really lived?

10. Rob took one step in the wrong direction, then another then another. At what point could he have turned back?

11. Kade ultimately made the right decision about his grant application. What do you think gave him the strength to do the right thing?

12. Has there ever been something you asked God for that he didn't give you and you later realized he couldn't answer yes to your prayer and someone else's too?

An excerpt from

⟨ LONESTAR SECRETS ⟩

1

MILES OF EMPTY ROAD STRETCHED AHEAD OF HER. SHANNON ASTOR HAD
babied the old Jeep along I-10 west from San Antonio until the traffic
ran out. She watched a million stars in the sky through the windshield
as the hill country gave way to desert and the sun began to peek above
the dark horizon in her rearview mirror. The Big Bend area was only
an hour away now. She smelled smoke from the wildfires in southwest
Texas and hoped the flames didn't get any closer.

Shannon glanced in the rearview mirror, and her heart melted with
tenderness. Her daughter Kylie slept peacefully in her booster seat,
her head resting against the back of the seat. The glimmers of sunrise
gilded her pale blond hair. Shannon would do anything for her, even go
back to the place she'd sworn never to set foot in again.

She was doing the right thing. She could never get ahead with the
cost of living in San Antonio, and facing her demons back in Bluebird

Crossing was worth getting her daughter out of the slum apartment. This job was her lifeline to something better for Kylie.

Her cell phone rang and she grabbed it off the seat beside her before the chimes to "The Last Unicorn" could awaken Kylie. Who would be calling at six in the morning? Her friend Mary Beth's name flashed across the screen. Shannon flipped her phone open. "Mary Beth, what are you doing up?" Only silence greeted her at first. "Mary Beth?"

"I . . . I shouldn't have called," Mary Beth gasped out. Music blared out of a radio in the background.

"What's wrong?" Shannon struggled to make sense of the sounds flooding into her ear: road noises, music, labored breathing.

"Listen, I don't have much time. I . . . I'm going to be away for a while." Mary Beth ended the statement with a sob.

Shannon pulled to the side of the interstate and stopped the Jeep. "Mary Beth, have you been drinking?" Her friend had been known to tie one on every now and then.

The short bark of laughter on the other end of the line sounded all too sober. "I wish it were that simple."

Shannon heard the sound of screeching tires and the road noises. Mary Beth's gasps were louder. "Mary Beth? What's happening?"

"I was trying to help you. I had no idea it would come to this."

"Help me? What are you talking about?"

The phone went dead in Shannon's ear. Was Mary Beth in trouble? Or was Shannon reading too much into the strange call? She tried to call Mary Beth back but was dumped into her voice mail. Shannon punched in Horton's home number. He'd be up having his morning tea by now.

His proper British voice answered on the second ring. "Horton here. Shannon, have you broken down already?"

Hearing his voice made her long for the safety of her little apartment in San Antonio, even if it was a hole in the wall. "Horton, have you heard from Mary Beth? I think she might be in some kind of trouble."

"What's happened?"

Shannon told him about Mary Beth's call. "Do you think something's wrong?"

He cleared his throat. "Maybe she had an argument with a boyfriend. Who is she dating right now?"

Shannon rubbed her arm again. "I don't know. I think probably a married man. That seems to be her normal mode."

"What can I do to help?"

She glanced at her sleeping daughter. It would do no good to overreact. "Nothing. I'm sure I'll hear from her soon. If she calls you, let me know."

"Will do, my dear. Are you sure you don't want to come back? Your position hasn't been filled."

"I can't let this opportunity slip through my fingers. The clinic will be my own, the pay is good, and Kylie will get a chance to grow up in wide-open spaces."

"Be careful, my dear. I'll let you know if I hear anything about Mary Beth."

"I'm sure everything will be fine," Shannon said, more to reassure herself. She was beginning to regret she'd called Horton over something so silly. Driving through the night must have set her nerves on edge. "I'll call when I get to town and see if you've heard anything more." She disconnected the call and drove on into the dawn.

TALL AND IMPOSING, THE OLD HOUSE DOMINATED THE TEXAS LANDSCAPE and loomed over the weathered barn and outbuildings. Chickens still scratched in the thin dirt, and the buildings were even more dilapidated than she remembered. The Chihuahuan Desert wind moaned through the eaves of the old house, and the familiar sound made Shannon realize she was really home. Even though it wasn't much, it was theirs.

Her work here was cut out for her. At least it was better than the trailer she'd lived in for so many years, and she'd hoped to show the town right off that she was a landowner now, not the quiet kid they'd been only too happy to ridicule. There was nothing to be gained by sitting here looking at it. She dropped her Jeep back into drive and accelerated toward the ranch.

"This isn't it, is it, Mommy?" Kylie looked up from her coloring book and peered over the edge of the door out the window. A dilapidated windmill creaked painfully around its axis. "It's scary."

With her uncle gone, it wouldn't echo with his disapproval any longer. "It just needs some work, sweetie. Uncle Earl lived here fifty years, and I don't think he painted a board. We'll get it shipshape in no time." Well, it would maybe take a while. It would be several weeks before she had any money coming in.

She pointed to the side yard. "Look, we have a barn. We'll get a pony, and you can have a dog. In fact, Moses might still be here." She whistled for the old stock dog. "Here, Moses. Here, boy." Only the wind answered her. If Moses was still around, maybe he was roaming the desert.

Every bone in her body ached from driving all night, and her nerves were shot after Mary Beth's mysterious call. She parked the vehicle in front of the hitching post by the porch, then sat listening to the groaning windmill. The sounds had echoed her own pain when her parents died.

"Are we going to get out?" Kylie asked, fidgeting.

"Sure, baby." Shannon opened her door and moved around to unbuckle her daughter's car seat.

Kylie hopped out and took her hand. "Do we have to go in? Maybe there's ghosts."

"No ghosts. It's just a little dirty and rundown, but I'll give it a good cleaning," Shannon promised. "Our old apartment was way worse. Here you'll have your own room and a playroom too." She took Kylie's hand and they stepped past straggly creosote bushes that scented the air. The porch steps sagged as though to swallow them whole. She and her daughter mounted the porch and approached the door. The key in her hand needed to be jiggled in the lock before it would open.

Stale air that stank of mouse droppings rushed to meet them. Kylie wrinkled her nose and pulled back on her mother's hand. "I don't want to go in. It smells nasty."

"I'll soon have it smelling like Pine-Sol and lemon," Shannon promised. But after letting her gaze sweep the foyer lit with dim morning light, her courage faltered. She was too exhausted to face the monumental task. They should have stopped for the night so it didn't seem so overwhelming.

Kylie tugged on Shannon's hand. "Can I sit out here until it's better?"

Shannon hesitated. Her gaze swept the barren landscape. There was nothing to see but the unbroken panorama of yucca and prickly pear cactus, the crags and peaks of the hills until the desert met the Chisos Mountains in the distance. She'd once loved this devil's playground even when it was as hot as his home, but today it felt lonely and dangerous.

She rested her hand on the top of her daughter's hair, and the contact filled her with determination. "I need your help, honey." She took her daughter's hand again and led her into the foyer.

The flowered wallpaper was peeling and faded. A layer of grime dimmed the olive green paint on the woodwork. Shannon sneezed at the odor of decay. She could see their footprints in the dust on the scarred wooden floors. It seemed the moment her uncle died three months ago, the desert stepped through the doors and windows to reclaim the house.

She heard a squeak when they entered the kitchen, and a mouse ran for cover along the counter before disappearing from view.

"Ew, a mouse," Kylie said. "We're not staying here, are we, Mommy?"

Shannon grabbed a broom from the corner and shook the cobwebs from it, but the rodent didn't reappear. "You'll love it after I get it fixed up. I've got some mousetraps in the car." She stepped to the utility room on the other side of the kitchen and lit the propane gas water heater. It began to rumble and chatter. "We'll leave our stuff in the car until we get it clean."

The last thing she wanted to do was clean, but she had to have this place in better shape before she'd allow Kylie to sleep here. Nightfall wouldn't make its appearance for another twelve hours. Plenty of time to at least get the main rooms clean and the beds ready. Everything would have to be washed, every stitch of bedding, every towel, every kitchen utensil.

A monumental task when she was tired to the bone. But it was nothing new. Many nights she'd had to rush to the vet hospital and would have to work all day on little or no sleep.

She looked under the sink and found cleaning supplies. She wiped off the table and the counter, then dived back under the sink for cleansing powder. While she was on her hands and knees, she thought she heard tires crunching on gravel outside. She sprang to her feet to peer out the window. Nothing there. She sure was skittish.

"Are there any horses in the barn?" Kylie asked. "I can go pet them with my sister."

Kylie's invisible playmate. Shannon never had the heart to tell Kylie of the real sister who died at birth, but somehow the little girl had never let go of her unknown sibling. "I don't think so." But now that she thought about it, Shannon realized Felipe Mendoza, her uncle's old ranch hand, hadn't come to greet them. He was always around the house. And where was Moses, the ranch dog?

"Tell you what, Kylie, you can play on the porch for a little while with your toys. I've got to get some things out of the car." And make a quick stop in the barn. Shannon took her daughter's hand and led her to the porch. After digging out a tub of toys and depositing them on the porch with Kylie, she made the made the little girl promise not to leave the porch.

Shannon went to the side yard where the big old barn stood. She glanced behind her to make sure she could see Kylie, then walked toward the building. The door yawned open, an unusual state. The hair on the back of her head stirred. She told herself it was her exhaustion, but her senses tried to sample everything around her as she walked across the flat sand toward the outbuildings.

The barn needed a coat of paint and boards replaced. The desert claimed everything left uninhabited. She hurried to the barn and peered inside. "Hello? Felipe?"

She heard a dog whine, then begin to bark, an agitated sound that made alarm bells go off in Shannon's head. Her cell phone was inside the house in her purse. She could call the sheriff, but it would take him a while to get here. What if Felipe had fallen and was lying injured? Moses would never leave him.

She ducked into the barn. The aroma of dust, hay, and manure struck her. Funny how after five years in the city the normal smells of a ranch overpowered her when she didn't used to even notice them. She glanced through the open tack room door. Only bridles and saddles there.

Dust motes danced in the air, and she sneezed. "Felipe?" she called again.

Moses broke into another frenzied round of barks, and she followed the sound. She passed several stalls, unused now. No livestock lowed or rustled in its hay. "Moses, where are you, boy?"

The dog whined and barked again. Shannon climbed over a gate when she couldn't open it and then over the railing at the back of the stall. There she saw Moses, a border collie, standing over what she took to be a pile of clothing. A second later she registered that it was Felipe lying in a mound of hay.

"Felipe!" She dropped to his side and rolled him over. He was quite dead. She scrabbled back on her haunches and fought the shriek building in her throat. Kylie would be frightened if she heard her mother scream.

"Stay calm, stay calm," she muttered. She called the dog to her, and Moses came reluctantly with his tail between his legs. "Good dog," she crooned, burying her face in his fur. The dog's musky scent and rough coat soothed her nerves. He whined and licked her face.

She had to get hold of herself. Her legs trembled when she released the dog and stood. Moses made a move as if to go back to his watch at Felipe's side, but she grabbed his collar and dragged him from the barn with her. The barn door screeched when she shut it.

Even though Felipe had likely died of natural causes, the fact there was a dead man in her barn made her race to the house to get to her daughter. Kylie was still on the porch with her stuffed unicorn, and the tightness in Shannon's chest eased.

Her daughter saw her and jumped up with her gaze on Moses. "We have a dog?"

"His name is Moses. We'll take him inside with us to the living room, and you can pet him."

Moses looked up at the sound of his name, and Shannon called him to her. She ran her hands over him. No broken bones or abrasions, though his coat was rough and dull. She made a mental note to get him on better food.

A vehicle rumbled up the drive, and she squinted at the vaguely familiar male figure in a shiny black pickup. Rick Bailey, from the adjacent Bluebird Ranch, climbed out of the truck. A pretty woman with black curls was with him, and a little girl hopped out of the backseat. A border collie leaped from the truck bed. Shannon struggled to remember the dog's name—Jem.

She broke into a run. Rick would know what to do.